VISION: THE PATH TO DANGER

Vision: The Path To Danger

Jacqué Stoddard

To Donna,
Enjoy!
Jacqué Stoddard

iUniverse, Inc.

New York Lincoln Shanghai

Vision: The Path To Danger

iUniverse books may be ordered through booksellers or by contacting:

iUniverse
2021 Pine Lake Road, Suite 100
Lincoln, NE 68512
www.iuniverse.com
1-800-Authors (1-800-288-4677)

ISBN-13: 978-0-595-36256-1 (pbk)
ISBN-13: 978-0-595-80701-7 (ebk)
ISBN-10: 0-595-36256-7 (pbk)
ISBN-10: 0-595-80701-1 (ebk)

Printed in the United States of America

To the Big Guy who has enriched my life in so many ways.

To my mother, my family and friends for all of their love and support.

You've all helped to make this dream a reality.

CHAPTER 1

▼

Helen walked into her aunt's mystic salon wishing she'd never made the call.

"Oh, dear, I have been waiting for this for months." Madeline said as she rushed to greet her, her multi-colored skirt swirling around her thick legs. "What is it? Something new? Come on back here and talk to me for a while. It is something new. Dear, I've been feeling your trouble all day."

Helen cringed at the sight of all of the symbolic bullshit adorning the walls as she followed her aunt into her parlor. The woman had only two things in common with Helen's mother, green eyes and a clairvoyant gift. Other than that the sisters were opposites. Helen much preferred her mother's quiet ways to Madeline's flamboyance.

"You're going to make a fortune with your gifts. What did they pay you the last time? Oh, I wish I had your intensity. Please sit, my dear."

Helen sat on the satin wrapped chair and stared into Madeline's dark green eyes. "I want to know why this is coming to me."

"I knew it was another case." Madeline smiled. "You're going to be famous."

"I don't want to be famous, Madeline, I want it to stop."

For days visions of murders had been torturing Helen. The women were defenseless against the slashing blades. It had been hard on Helen when she'd worked with the police to find a kidnapped boy but the visions of murder coming to her now were much more intense. When the bloody images invaded her mind her whole being went cold.

Madeline sat down on the stool by the red desk and smiled. "You can't force this either way. You know that dear." She crossed her arms over her ample breasts and studied Helen for a long moment. "You're so much like your mother. She could have gone far with her intuition but she wanted no part of it, only enough to make ends meet after your father died. She never experimented with her potential and neither have you."

"I don't need you to tell me how you feel about my gifts or my mother's. I want you to tell me why this is happening."

As her aunt spoke the image of a horrified young woman flashed into her mind. The blond was screaming and bleeding from her face and arms as she scrambled backward. She stumbled over the coffee table as the knife thrust into her chest.

Helen covered her face and tried to force the gory pictures from her mind.

"Look at me." Madeline reached for the newspaper clutching it as she spoke "Don't analyze the questions." She took a deep breath and slowly let it out. "What are you seeing?"

"Murders. And…" Helen looked up at the large silver half moon on the wall behind her aunt as tears pooled in her eyes. "Horror."

"When did you meet Detective Hamlin?"

"Three months ago."

Madeline nodded. "It's him."

"What?"

"You asked why it's happening and I believe it's because of him."

"How?"

"You connected with him. How soon after you met, did you start thinking about the kidnapping?"

"That night."

"When did he get the case?"

"That night."

Madeline smiled. "You worked with him for weeks. The connection is even stronger now."

"I don't want it, Auntie." Helen turned to face her. "The sense I would get when I was reading for someone who had bad in their life…I talked to you about it…I could turn it away. I could force it out of my mind. This is different. The feelings are so sharp, so clear. My so called intuition has changed dramatically." Helen wiped the tears from her face. "When I was trying to find that boy, the feelings of panic and despair were so intense it made me sick."

"I remember."

"This is much worse than that…these are decent people being murdered in their own home…I can't handle it. I really believed that what happened with that boy was a fluke. I thought it would all end once we found him and it did for a while…but now this."

"I know it's trying. I believe your mother had this too…she would be so unhappy for days at a time. She knew things." Madeline shook her head. "You need to put your personal feelings aside and accept this. You need to think about the good you can do with your gift. You helped find that little boy…there's a reason for you to help again."

Madeline opened the newspaper and pointed to the headline. "Second campus murder."

Helen took the paper and immediately spotted Detective Hamlin's name. She jumped to her feet, tossing the newspaper onto the chair.

"It's not a gift it's a burden. Damn it. I don't want to be involved with this. If I can block you, why can't I block this? It's making me crazy, Auntie." Helen spun around to face her, her green eyes wild. "You don't know what I'm feeling, what I'm seeing…I can't think." The stark images haunted her from the moment they'd begun to assault her mind.

"I've given this a lot of thought, my dear. You need to help him and resolve whatever it is that you need to with the man. I must caution you, I don't feel this is a temporary connection rather something quite the contrary. I feel a plan here. Fate." Madeline shook her head. "I don't envy you your task. If I could take it from you, I would."

Helen reacted to her aunt's softening tone. "I know you would. We may not always agree but I do love you Madeline." Helen smiled at her. "I'm not sure why or how but coming here has helped me. Thank you."

The women embraced and Helen started for the door.

"Do you want the paper, dear?"

"No." Helen glanced back at her. "I'll call you."

Helen walked out to her car as the rain slowed to cold drizzle.

Helen drove to the police station thinking about the last time she'd spoken to Detective Martin Hamlin. He'd scared her away with an all too tempting kiss. Helen thought she'd never see him again. Now the visions were bringing her back.

She wondered how uncomfortable their meeting would be as she walked up the old wood stairs of the police department.

Helen walked over to the young officer seated at the desk in the center of the room. "Is Detective Hamlin in?"

"How are you Miss Staples?" The young man smiled.

"I'm fine. Is he busy?"

"He's in his office. I'm sure he'll be glad to see you." The officer's smile widened.

Helen walked up the steps and as she started down the hall she heard the familiar thump of the darts hitting the board. Helen knew it was a signal that he was stumped or upset. She took a deep breath, smoothed her hands over her auburn hair and tapped on the door.

"Come in."

Helen opened the door and stared at the long legged detective as his brown eyes widened. Her throat tightened at the sight of the handsome man. Detective Martin Hamlin was a man she'd thought of often over the months since they'd worked together.

"Well, this is a surprise." Martin said as he set the steel-tipped darts on the edge of his cluttered desk. "Have a seat." He pulled out a chair for her. "So what brings you down here?"

Tears welled in her eyes. "Your case."

"Which case?" Martin sat in the large leather chair, staring at her with big brown eyes as if drinking in her presence.

"The college murders. He's going to do it again." Helen trembled as the latest vision replayed in her mind.

"Are you sure it's the same man that murdered both women?"

"Yes. He's already stalking his next victim. It's going to happen soon."

Martin slammed his fist on the desk then leaned back and took a deep breath. "That consulting job's still open. You should probably take it since it appears you'll be doing the job anyway."

"I don't want the job."

Martin narrowed his eyes at her. "You're one hard nut. You could've made thousands on the last case Helen. It really doesn't make sense."

"A lot in my life makes no sense." Helen shrugged. There were no words to explain what she was feeling and seeing. It was shocking, upsetting and clear. "I didn't come here to talk about myself." She stood and walked to the map on the wall. "You need to get extra security out to this area." She said as she ran her hand over a two-block area. "Do you have a pencil?"

Martin joined her at the map. "That's off-campus housing."

"This is where he's going to strike again." Helen marked the four corners and returned to the chair.

"What can we do to stop him?"

"Maybe visible security will scare him away."

"Until we leave."

Helen nodded. "I'm afraid so. This guy isn't going to stop until he's caught. He enjoys it too much."

"Can you describe him?"

"I've been trying to block the whole thing." Helen avoided his dark eyes as she spoke. "I didn't want to go through this again but this guy is worse than the last. I had to come to you with it."

"You look thin." Martin sat on the corner of the desk and touched her shoulder. "I know the kidnapping case took a lot out of you. Are you sure you're up to this?"

"No. But I don't have a choice." Helen couldn't ignore the evil any longer no matter how upsetting it was.

"Did you read about the case?"

"No."

Martin nodded. "Two college students from different states, they were both in off-campus housing, both pretty, both good students. They were attacked in their apartments just two days apart. They were raped, tortured and murdered. No prints. No DNA. He used protection or used something other than his-."

"He used a curling iron on the last victim." Helen said, tears streaming down her face.

"We're testing it." Martin's tone softened. "OK, now, there are one hundred apartments in this complex. Can you narrow it down for me?"

"Not from here. Let's take a ride over there, maybe I can feel where he's been." Helen picked up her purse off of the chair as Chief Howe walked through the door.

"Is this business or pleasure?" The chief smiled as he extended his hand to her.

"Unfortunately it's business." Helen managed a smile for the tall, husky man.

"You've accepted the job?"

"No." Helen wished she could run from her thoughts. She wasn't about to sign on for some long-term participation in solving crimes.

"Not yet." Martin said as he approached the door. "I'm going to keep working on her though."

"It's a large retainer and I'll include back pay for the last case if you accept."

"I'll keep that in mind." Helen nodded.

"So for now, you're volunteering your time?"

"Yes."

"Thank you. Hamlin, give her whatever she needs."

"Yes, sir. She sees trouble in the Scholar's Studios area. We're heading over there now."

"Welcome back."

Helen was quiet on the ride over to the apartment complex, her senses were being deluged with one flash after another. She scanned the area as they pulled into the parking lot.

"Go to the end. Okay, this is fine." Helen got out of the sedan and walked toward the fence that surrounded the pool. When she touched the gate she could feel the killer's energy. Helen looked back at Martin, nodding. "He's been here." She walked around the pool and pointed to the buildings closest to it. "It's one of these. He comes here often."

Martin followed her as she walked back to the gate.

"He might be a cop." Helen said, touching the gate again. "Or he was at one time. Something to do with law enforcement." Helen shook her head and walked back toward the car. "I've had enough for now."

"A cop?"

"Hey I don't know where it comes from but that's what I'm picking up. He's been here watching her for weeks."

"Before the first murder?"

"Yes. He's watching several women. He's been at this for a long time." Helen said as she got into the car.

"Can you come back to my office and look over what I have? Maybe something will strike you."

Helen nodded and rolled down the window. She was in on it now. She had no choice but to see it through to the end.

His cell phone rang. "Sure...okay...yes. Fine, chief...I'll let her know. Thanks." Martin hung up and put the phone in his pocket. "He's put you in for the job. He said it makes you look more credible being on the payroll. You can quit anytime you want but he took flack having a civilian working on the last case, so, well, it would make his life easier if you just take it."

Helen rolled her green eyes. Getting compensated would make up for the canceled appointments but it didn't thrill her to be taking money from the police department. It wasn't even clear to Helen why she so mistrusted the police in general, it was a bit out of character but it was there. Maybe it was because she'd read for so many of their spouses and what she saw didn't impress her. Even so she wasn't in the habit of categorizing people.

Helen looked out the window, thinking about what Madeline had said about her mother. She wondered if her mother ever had the same type of experiences. She remembered times when her mother would watch the news or read the paper and cry as if she'd lost a dear friend. Her mother wasn't comfortable discussing their gifts, as she called it. It was an undeniable part of their lives, which in her mother's view meant it wasn't necessary to talk about except on rare occasions when the situation warranted it.

Helen remembered how her mother had behaved the first time she told Helen to take an appointment. She was just seventeen at the time.

"Mrs. Philips will be here in fifteen minutes. You do her reading and tell her up front that it's free today. I'm not up to dealing with her."

"I haven't done it, what if I'm mistaken."

"You won't be, dear. I'll be down at three." She turned and disappeared up the stairs to their apartment.

Helen swallowed hard when the door closed behind her. She didn't want to do it. She didn't want the so-called gifts that caused her mother to be talked about. The women would come in once a month, but if they didn't like the answers her mother gave they would make fun of her. Even if they did like what she told them, they would say she was strange and wonder aloud if she was a witch.

Helen couldn't refuse. Her mother had been ill for months and was declining quickly. Another thing her mother didn't wish to discuss was her health and that frustrated Helen as she watched her mother fading away.

She was in a panic when Mrs. Phillips arrived. She greeted Helen's announcement with enthusiasm and followed her into the sitting room. Within fifteen minutes Helen had answered her questions. A week later Mrs. Phillips requested another reading with Helen. From that point on she worked with her mother doubling the business in a year's time.

When they pulled up in front of the police station Helen was ready for a break from the negative energy. "Listen, I'm not feeling very well. I haven't eaten all day and I think I need some time before I hear what you have to tell me."

His chocolate eyes softened as he held up his hands. "You don't have a schedule."

"Fine then." Helen reached for the handle. "I'll see you in a couple of hours. Should I call first?"

"Let me take you. You do look pale."

"I want to keep this professional."

"I understand. I wasn't asking to take you home for a nightcap, just out for a thick steak. Cops get hungry too." Martin smiled.

"I'd rather be alone, thank you." The last thing Helen needed was someone to lean on. It would only served to weaken her further. She got out of the car and lit a cigarette before walking down the street to the restaurant.

Helen could feel his annoyance with her but it was something they were both going to have to adjust to if they were going to be working together.

CHAPTER 2

▼

After a long dinner alone Helen returned to the police station feeling stronger. Martin's door was open.

"Come in." He said keeping his eyes on the papers spread over his desk. "I've got everything here for you. I have men staked out at the apartments. Before you look at this, I'd like you to study the map, see if you get anything else. You said he's been watching more than one…I'd like to figure out where she is so we don't scare him to her."

"I'd like to figure that out too but I don't have all the answers." She said looking at the map's markings and photos. "It's all coming from this area."

Helen turned to find him standing by the desk staring at her.

Martin pointed to the paperwork on his desk. "I've got this set up in four sections including a file on a few unsolved rapes and murders that go back about ten years. You won't be able to get through this tonight but you can use my office to get started. I have some other business to take care of. I'll be back in two hours. Any questions." Martin said picking up a blank legal pad. "Write it down and we'll discuss it then."

Helen was relieved when he walked out. She sat at the desk and as she picked up the first report, the horrifying image of a woman being slashed slammed into her mind.

The girl screamed for help as her arms were sliced again and again. Helen covered her face attempting to block out the terror the young woman felt. It was someone else, a voice she hadn't heard before. Though the fear and the sounds were clear the vision wasn't. She could see the woman's arms being cut with some sort of hunting knife. She could feel the panic and confusion. She heard the pleas for help as the attacker continued slicing at her as she tried to get away from him.

Helen was possessed by the vision when Martin walked back into the office.

"I forgot my notebook." Martin stopped, studying her. "What is it? Did you notice something already?"

"No. I…he's done it again."

"What?"

"He's just killed another girl…another blond…with a knife."

"A knife?"

"Where?"

"I'm not sure. Could I have a drink of water, please?" Helen wrung her hands as her heart raced and her body turned cold.

Martin went out to the hall and returned with the water, sitting opposite her. "What else can you tell me, Helen?"

"Just that he's killed again." She looked up at him, preferring his image to the horrific sights flashing in her brain. "It's the same man." It played out in her mind as she spoke. "She was young, innocent, and blond like the others. She was smiling when she let him in. He attacked her right away." Cold sweat streamed down her back as she spoke.

"Did she know him?"

"No. He made her think she was in no danger. He has a badge."

"You're pale as a ghost, Helen."

"Damn it, Martin, you have to stop this animal." Helen took another drink and set down the glass. "I can't tell you anymore right now. They'll be calling. The neighbors had to hear her screams…she screamed until she died."

The woman's horror echoed in Helen's mind as she sat staring at Martin.

"When you can I'd like you to write what you saw."

"You write it. Damn it." Helen cried. "Why is this happening to me?" She took a deep breath as he picked up the pad and pen staring at her. Helen explained the vision in as much detail as she could while he took notes.

The phone on his desk rang. He answered, listened for a few minutes and hung up his eyes wide. "I wish I knew how you do it."

"It's a curse."

Martin leaned closer as she looked up at him. "No, Helen, it's a gift."

"You're wrong. It's a burden."

"You have the ability to stop him from killing. I call that a gift."

"You wouldn't if you experienced it."

"I have to go. Are you up to coming out there with me? I know its asking a lot."

Helen nodded. She'd already seen it. It could be no worse than what had invaded her mind. The woman was at peace now. "Her name is Sue."

"Yes. Susan Tillis."

*   *   *   *

They arrived at the Hillsdale apartment complex, which was just a mile from the one they'd visited earlier that day. Concerned and curious neighbors lined the way, brought out first by the screams, then by the police cars and ambulance.

"Hey, Hamlin." A young officer approached them as they got out of Martin's car. "I don't think you want the lady going in there. Johnson lost his lunch when he saw it."

"I've already seen it." Helen said as she walked past him toward the apartment.

"You heard the lady."

"What does she mean, she's already seen it?"

"I don't know how, but she told me it had happened before we got the call." Martin watched the red head as she walked into the apartment. He braced himself for what he was about to see. Johnson was no lightweight not with ten years on the job. There had to be a reason for him to lose it.

Martin had all of his answers when he walked through the door. There was a pool of blood just feet inside the entry. Blood sprays covered the wall, mirror and telephone table. The dead woman had fought hard for her life.

"Detective." A young officer called to him from the small glass table by the balcony doors.

Martin walked over to the officer.

"She was stabbed before and after she died. Hacked up bad." The officer shook his head as he took off his hat. "This guy's a real psycho."

Martin studied the crime scene before joining Helen by the window. "I don't think it's the same guy, Helen."

"It is."

"He didn't...it isn't the same type of crime scene."

"It was him. He knows what you'll look for. He understands how you work. It was him. He needed to kill and he doesn't want to get caught so he killed her quickly. He knew the neighbors would hear her screaming. He knew he had to-." Her face turned white and she knelt down.

"What is it?" Martin helped her up into the chair.

"I'm not used to getting hit with these things. Do you still have your men over at Scholar's Studios?"

"I, well…" Martin looked out the window at the police cars crowded in front of the apartment building. "The chief sent them here."

"Get them back there." Helen cried.

"We need them here to find this guy. He could still be in the area."

"He's gone." Helen shook her head. "This is sport for him. He's not done."

Martin knelt down next to her, looking around the bloody room. "What are you seeing?"

"I have a feeling he isn't finished. I, I think he wanted you here for a reason." Helen rubbed her upper arms. "Your chief screwed up." She said as she closed her eyes.

"Martin." Detective Stalls called from the door. "We've got a problem out at Scholar's."

"No." Martin rushed to the door.

"Two victims, one made it out alive, barely. It's sketchy. Seems one girl was home, the second arrived rushed inside when she heard the scuffle. The man attacked her, the first victim tried to help, when he turned his attention back to the other, she managed to get out alive, she called the police on her cell. The man ran off. So far, no description."

"Johnson, take this lady home. Helen, I'll call you later."

"I'll be fine."

"No." He waved an officer inside. "Take her home."

"My car's at the station."

"Give me the keys. I'll get it to you later." She looked as though she'd pass out as the Johnson led her away.

As much as Martin had wished he could see her again, he never expected she'd be brought back into his life by murder. He walked outside and stood in the middle of the lawn watching as she disappeared down the road. He was in for a long, hard few days. Two separate crime scenes in one night were a detective's nightmare. Several victims and he still had no clue as to how to find the killer.

Martin scowled. He thought that maybe Helen would be the key but the idea of the quiet psychic being involved in the murders didn't please him. He didn't know how he'd react to her helping on the case. He shook his head as he walked across the grass wondering how she could see these things before or as they were happening. Even after working with her on the kidnapping case, the logical side of him was still trying to get a handle on her ability.

✷   ✷   ✷   ✷

Helen took a long hot shower and made a pot of coffee as lightening pounded up the coast. She thought about all Martin must be going through, as the minutes ticked to hours. It was a frightening, painful day and it wasn't over yet. She prayed for the survival of the victim. She was the one person who may have seen the killer's face. He wasn't wearing a mask. Sue Tillis hadn't felt threatened by him when she opened the door. That part of the vision was stark.

Helen was stirring the cream into her third cup of coffee when Martin arrived. She walked to the door to greet him and could sense the weight of his heart. His dark eyes were bloodshot and his color, ashen, as he walked into the kitchen.

"Here you go." Martin handed her the keys. "A couple of the guys are going right by here in an hour or so. They'll drop off my car."

"How's the girl?"

"Touch and go. She's unconscious, severe shock."

She could feel his eyes on her as she poured him a cup of coffee.

"Can you read my mind?"

"What kind of a question is that?" Helen turned to face him.

"I'd like to know. I've thought about it before and all but ruled it out."

"And why is that?"

"You answer mine first." He said, putting his large hands around the hot mug.

"No I can't read your mind, as such."

"Why the qualifier?"

Helen smiled. "It's not mind reading. I can't always feel things and then sometimes even when I don't want to, I get it."

"I'd like to understand what it is."

"So would I." Helen lit a cigarette. "My mother called it a gift but I know that even though it paid the bills, she would rather have not had it. She had bad visions and fought them until they went away. She was strong at blocking. I'm not, not at all. My mother could focus in on those feelings, I don't. I take whatever comes my way. It's only if I find the person interesting, that I'll see what else I can draw in. That doesn't happen often."

"How many people do you read a week?"

"Fifteen to twenty a month. I have a full schedule two days a week."

"Are there people you won't read?"

"There have been a few."

"What happens to make you refuse?"

"I get a bad feeling and politely explain that for whatever reason I can't read them. I can usually tell by the sound of their voice and say my schedule is full for the next year." Helen scowled. "There are a lot of weird people out there."

"I know." Martin nodded. "If you can block them, why can't you block these, ah, images?"

"I don't know. Things have been changing. It's hard to explain." Helen didn't understand what was happening to her, how could she explain it?

"Some days I think I must be crazy to subject myself to all of this. Days like today really test me. I'm actually beginning to look forward to retiring in a few years. I've got a decent sized boat, I'm going to pack for a month and sail away the day I retire. I don't even want to see a newspaper for a year." Martin raised his coffee cup.

"If you feel that way, why don't you change careers now?"

"I'm good at what I do. I wouldn't know how to do anything else. Not right now anyway."

"Do you have any hobbies?"

"I don't have the time. Yourself?"

"I paint a little. Dabble in other crafts. I'm not very good but it's therapeutic."

"I hate to ask but have you seen anything else about this guy or the case?"

"No. I'm sorry."

"That's fine. You take the night off and we'll get to work on this in the morning. I'd appreciate it if you could meet me by eight. I'll be down there by five. I have to go back to both crime scenes. The technicians are just finishing up at the second. This is as much of a rest as I'll get tonight."

"How can you think without sleep?"

"Instinct. That's ninety percent of this job. Gut feelings."

Helen smiled. "I'll be there early. Would you like another cup?"

"I'd love one. I'm glad you'll be working with me again."

"I'll be glad when this is over."

Martin nodded, reaching for the cup. "I've seen all of this gore before. It must be hard on you."

"Not exactly my idea of fun."

The headlights shined into the kitchen windows as the officers pulled into the driveway.

Martin drank down the cup and headed for the door. "I'll see you in the morning."

Helen wrestled with her thoughts but finally spoke up. "Call me if you learn anything, well, please, if you aren't too busy."

Martin smiled at her. "Sure, you do the same."

Helen fell asleep waiting for the call. Bright rays of a new day brought her out of her slumber. The four hours of sleep had recharged her. Helen knew the importance of solving these cases within a day or two. She wasn't up for a repeat of the long tense days she'd spent on the last case.

She'd just filled her thermos when the phone rang.

"Is this Helen? Helen the psychic?"

"May I ask who's calling?"

"Stay out of it. Walk away while you can."

"Who is this? Walk away from what?"

"You aren't much of a psychic, are you?"

Helen hung up the phone, the hair on her arms standing straight up. She'd gotten calls like that before but this was different. Something about his voice made her take notice.

She headed to the police station, eager to hear what Martin had learned.

"I'm glad you're here." Martin looked up from his desk. "It's been one hell of a night."

"What did you come up with?"

"Crime scenes are similar. No doubt it's the same guy. I interviewed the victim at the hospital. She's hanging in there, very weak but eager to talk to me. She said the man was wearing a suit with a badge pinned to the chest pocket."

"Could she read the badge?"

"No. She said it was silver."

"Did she describe the man?"

"Yes, tall, light brown hair, tanned and strong. She's a fighter. She said she clawed his neck, the fingernail scrapings being analyzed now. It's the only evidence we have so far. He was wearing surgical gloves."

"Do they think she's going to make it?"

"She lost a lot of blood but she's strong." Martin looked down at the pictures on the desk. "Can you have a look at these?"

Helen nodded and stood beside him, looking at the gory photos. "Let me read through these files. I didn't get a chance to yesterday."

"Go ahead. I want to get down to the lab and check on a few things. I'll be back in a while." Martin stood and motioned to his chair.

Helen studied each case file and over the next two hours she developed a feeling for the killer's history. By the time she closed the last file she was eager to speak with Martin.

"He's not from around here." Helen said as he walked into the office.

Martin studied her as she spoke.

"He's from the Midwest. He's been here for about a year. He's done this before. Many times." Her body trembled as she walked to the chair on the other side of the desk. "You have to do a search out there. He came here alone but he left a family behind."

"Where in the Midwest?"

Helen shook her head. "He wants to make a name for himself, not just as a serial killer but as a genius. He wants to kill as many as he can before he gets caught. It's different from the last time. He's on a mission."

"Why is he choosing young blond victims?"

"He feels they draw more media attention than a plain Jane. They are targeted for their looks, their size, their near-perfect appearance." Helen rubbed her hands over the tops of her arms. "You've got to find him fast. You should alert the public. He's not going to stop."

"The chief is giving a press conference at nine." Martin pressed the extension button and called Detective Chambers. "Put in all the stats we have on the murders and send them out, target the Midwest...Yes...Call me as soon as you get any feedback."

Helen took a few deep breaths as the impressions slowed. "Damn. This animal is pure evil."

An hour later as they sat studying the files, Detective Noel Chambers burst into Martin's office making both of them jump.

"How did you know?" He asked as he rushed to the desk. He handed Martin a file. "It was you, wasn't it?" Noel asked as he studied her face.

"What did you find?" Helen went to look over Martin's shoulder at the information.

"Kansas City, Kansas. Ten homicides in the same area, college students, the murders stopped eleven months ago." Noel puffed out the words and took a deep breath. "I circled the lead detective's name and number."

Martin's square jaw twitched as he dialed the number and hit the speakerphone. "Go ahead detective." He said, nodding as Detective Hamilton and Detective Grace walked into the office.

"It started in September, one murder after another. We had very few leads. The guy was a pro. Our profiler said he had experience in criminal justice, ex-cop or something. We had a team of men on these cases and as quickly as they started they stopped."

"I need everything you've got." Martin said, nodding at Helen. "Our profiler came up with the same."

"When did it start?"

"Ten days ago. Four-."

"It's five now. I just got the call, the witness didn't make it." Detective Grace offered.

"Shit. Make that five."

"I'll send you our files."

After hearing several minutes of gruesome details of the killings hundreds of miles away, Helen left the building for some fresh air. She walked around the block and as she walked up the steps an officer called to her from the door.

She went inside and answered the phone. "Helen Staples here." She pushed the button for the speakerphone as a wave of dread swept over her.

"I told you to butt out."

Helen signaled for the officer behind the desk to get Martin.

"Butt out of what? I don't understand what you mean."

"My case. I know you helped them, I've read about you. Get out or you'll be next on my list."

"Sir, are you sure you have the right person?"

The line went dead as Martin came down the steps. "What is it?"

"He's watching me. He wants me out."

"Who?"

"The killer."

"The killer? What are you talking about?"

"He called me this morning. I didn't know who it was. I get these calls sometimes from clients or more often their spouses when my readings get too close to the mark. Now I know it's him." She stared up into Martin's eyes. "He said I'd be next if I don't back off."

"Son of a bitch." Martin glanced down at the newspaper on the desk and hit it with his fist. "I don't believe this." He pointed to the open page. "This is why. And it came from an anonymous source in the department." He looked down at her. "I'm sorry."

"I'm scared…but in a way, I think it may be a good thing."

"Gees." Martin slapped his forehead. "No. Out of the question. You're off this case as of now."

"And if he comes after me anyway? No. I'm not going to cower for this son of a bitch, not in this lifetime. If he's following me, thinking about me, it will serve as a distraction."

"I won't allow it."

"Allow it?"

"That's what I said." He growled, grabbing a hold of her elbow. He dragged her up to his office and closed the door before storming over to his desk. "Look at this, damn it." Martin pointed to the files spread across his desk. "This guy got away with it in Kansas and so far he's gotten away with it here. I won't have you in this kind of danger. No."

Martin snarled when the phone rang. "What is it? Shit. All right put it through." Martin waved her over to the phone and hit the speaker button.

"Hello." Helen said as she sat down at the desk.

"I'd better read the same source saying you're off the case in tomorrow's paper or I'm coming for you."

"The police don't need me to catch you." Her voice caught in her throat.

"I meant what I said."

The line went dead.

When she looked at Martin his temples were pulsing.

"I don't like this." Helen said as she broke into a cold sweat.

"Good because you're out."

"Not happening."

"Damn you're hard headed." Martin opened a file and pointed at the gory photos. "I'm not going to let this happen to you."

"It won't. I'm in danger." Helen smiled up at him. "But I know you'll protect me. Now you need to contact Kansas and see who their suspects are. Maybe we can narrow it down."

Helen walked over to the window. He was out there, watching her now. She could feel his presence like a dark cloud. He'd made her a target. And with her name in the news it made her that much more appealing to him.

Helen looked at the calendar by the window. "Shit. I have to pick up my dog from the vet. I forgot all about her."

"I didn't know you had a dog."

Helen smiled. "My best friend. She's still a pup, not even a year old. I had her fixed and they had to keep her for a few days."

Helen called the vet and was relieved to hear China would be ready that evening. Helen's mood was lifted by the thought of her lovable companion coming home. It was exactly what she needed now.

"Fine, pick up your dog. I'll get someone to follow you home."

"No. We'll be fine." Helen needed some space. She felt she was being smothered by the intensity of the case.

When she walked out of the veterinarian's office with China, Detective Osborne was standing outside his undercover sedan wearing a big smile.

"I thought you'd come to pick up your puppy." The tall detective laughed. "Not a horse."

"Hey, you'll give her a complex." Helen said as China's floppy ears perked up. "What is it?"

"She's a Great Dane and very sensitive, I might add." Helen smiled.

"Great Dane, huh? Well it looks like you'll have plenty of protection."

"She's actually quite friendly."

"I wouldn't want to get on her bad side." Osborne laughed.

Helen opened the door for China who took her seat on the passenger's side. "I'm feeling better all ready, baby." The dog turned and gave her a long lick up the side of her face. "I guess you are, too."

When she arrived home there were five messages on her machine, four from customers and one from him.

China ran to the small table, barking at the machine when she heard the killer's voice. "Yes, China, yes, he's bad, he's very dangerous. Remember that voice girl."

"You can't hide from me. They can't help you. I think I'll switch from blondes to red-heads for a while."

Helen looked out the window as a cruiser pulled up and parked across the street and Osborne drove away. She was suddenly grateful that Martin had followed through with protection for her.

Helen had two days of calm before the visions returned. A wave of terror came over her as she felt he'd killed again. She closed her eyes, a feeble attempt to block out the images that flooded her mind. The slashing, the blood, the screaming all came crashing into absolute focus as though it was happening right in front of her.

China licked her hand as Helen stood shaking by the window. When the images subsided she slumped onto the kitchen chair. He'd changed the rules. He'd changed his target.

Helen reached for the phone and dialed Martin's cell number. "I…he's killed again…a woman with red hair…a mother. Her kids are home. You-" Her hysterical voice was cut off by Martin's two words.

"I know."

"The children. They're-." Helen stopped to catch her breath, her heart pounding furiously.

"They're in shock but alive. The oldest, an eight-year-old climbed out the window and went to the neighbor's for help. He got a plate number, Helen. We're going to get him."

Tears ran down her face as she leaned back in the chair.

"I'll be over once I get this scene wrapped up. Stay put."

Helen nodded, looking out into the darkness as the sound of the ocean filled the house. She hung up the phone and walked out onto the deck, pondering her connection to Martin in an attempt to escape the fear.

She thought about the morning they'd met. It was raining hard and Helen was crossing the parking lot on her way to the bank. Martin had pulled into the lot fast enough to cause a wave that covered Helen with muddy water. He stopped the car and rushed toward her apologizing.

Helen was completely caught off guard by her reaction to the handsome stranger as he wiped her arm and side with the dark towel. At the first touch of his strong hand, Helen knew they would meet again soon but had no idea as to how or why.

CHAPTER 3

▼

China brought her out of her deep thoughts, barking as she rushed to the door, her big paws clomping across the kitchen tile.

"It's Detective Hamlin…Martin." He called through the door.

Helen grabbed China's collar as she opened the door. "It's okay girl, he's a friend."

"Don't tell me this is your pup." Martin said as he stared at the huge brindle beast.

"She is. Be nice, China, be nice." Helen released the dog's collar and watched as she sniffed his shoes and pants, finally licking Martin's hand.

Helen closed the door behind him. "Would you like some coffee?"

"Sure." When Martin sat down at the kitchen table, China sat beside him, staring.

"Pet her, be friends." Helen said as she walked to the counter.

"Sure. Look, I found a couple of things at the last murder scene that I'd like you to take a look at."

Helen's feet felt like they'd been cemented into place as she continued filling the coffeepot. She didn't like the idea. Touching items could sometimes open a channel to the person who owned them. In this case it was a prospect that held her frozen at the counter.

"That's how you do your readings. I think these belonged to him."

Helen slowly turned to face him. She saw the empty business card holder and the large black button in the plastic bag on the table but didn't move. "The coffee will only take a few minutes."

"Why is it in all the time we worked together, you never told me you had a dog?"

"I didn't think it was appropriate to talk about our private lives." Helen scowled, still staring at the bag.

"You look frightened."

Helen glared into his dark eyes. "Frightened. More like scared shit at the moment thank you. Even China started barking when she heard his voice on the machine. That's never happened before and I've had thousands of calls recorded since I got her. I'm terrified and I have a right to be."

Martin jumped up and rushed to the small telephone table. "You should have told me. It's evidence."

"It's the third message."

As soon as his gravelly voice came on, China rushed to the machine, barking and growling.

"See what I mean?" Helen was relieved when the coffeepot gurgled to a stop.

"Do you have another tape?"

"Yes, there's one in that drawer." Helen served the coffee and sat at the table, the plastic bag daring her to touch it. Helen reached for a cigarette.

"Oh, good. I didn't want to ask."

"You smoke?"

"With smokers."

"How could I have worked with you and not known?"

"Touché."

"But I've smoked around you?"

"It's not the image I like to project."

Helen studied him. "Tough cop?"

Martin shrugged. "It's hard to explain, learned it from my Dad. Now that man could smoke but it was something he did behind closed doors. Drinking, same thing. The most he'd have in public was one beer. If you are going to make a fool of yourself the best place to do it is in your own house where the people already know who you are. My father used to say that every time he lit a cigarette or cracked open a bottle of beer." Martin lit a cigarette and put the cassette into his pocket. "It's been a long week."

China let out a low growl as she lay down in front of the French doors.

"I'm going to keep the officer out front and maybe get a couple more guys down here to do a local patrol."

"Please don't. They need to be looking out for this freak not watching over me. I'll be fine."

Martin walked around the two rooms closing the curtains. "I wouldn't put it past him to shoot you from the beach. He wants you out of the way. How are the other rooms?"

"Wide open."

"I'll be back."

"I can do it."

"Stay where you are." Martin went down the hall.

"I'd like a handgun license and a gun." Helen said as he walked back into the kitchen.

"We can do that." Martin smiled. "I've got everything in my car. Can you shoot?"

"Trust me, if someone comes in this house, I'll hit him." Helen took a deep drag. She wouldn't have a choice. She'd have to use it. Her eyes were drawn to the bag just as Martin returned with a large box.

"I'd like you to handle those things. They've already been dusted for prints and they're clean. Go on while I get this set up for you. Here's the license. We had your photo on file. Snub nose.38 and a full box of ammo. I've got a lock here but I don't think you should use it right now. These are speed loaders. I've got four filled for you."

Helen watched as he loaded the gun with a press of a button and closed it.

"It's that fast." He emptied the gun and refilled the speed loader.

"And what is in that bag you left beside the door?"

"Shaving kit, change of cloths, the usual overnight bag. Now if you'd be uncomfortable, I can sleep out in my car but I'd prefer your couch." Martin smiled at her as he set the gun on the counter and sat down across from her. "Thanks for the coffee."

"It just seems so insane. I've had nightmares, but nothing has ever come close to the last few days. You can stay on the couch. Feel free. If I'm not safe with the three of you than it just isn't meant to be."

"You're safe." His dark eyes made a line from hers to the items on the table as he sipped the hot coffee. "We have to get this guy. Please. Maybe you won't feel a thing."

Helen took a last long drag of her cigarette before reaching for the bag. "It's his." She said as she pulled the business card case out of the bag. The leather seared her fingertips as images exploded in her mind.

"He's been doing it all of his life. He attacked an elderly woman when he was young and got away with it. She was a neighbor." Helen dropped the case and stood up. China was immediately at her side. "He's a monster."

"What else?"

"He's staying with someone…a relative. The person is old and very rich. He's got a circle around him. They have no idea what he is and he thrives on their ignorance. He's close." Her voice trailed off to a whisper.

"What else?"

Helen put up her hands. "I need a few minutes."

"You won't forget anything?" Martin leaned closer.

"No. I wish I could." Tears streamed down her cheeks as she spoke.

"I don't mean to be insensitive." Martin sat back in his chair. "I want this guy."

"It's so horrible. I turn people away with the slightest bad energy. I…this is hard. I'm sorry." Helen wiped her cheeks and reached for another cigarette as the butt of the last smoldered in the ashtray.

"You need to look at the rich in the area. Find out if anyone appeared on the scene lately, living with an old aunt or something? Ask those types of questions. It won't be easy. They can be very tight-lipped. And they will be."

"Relax for a few minutes. Would you like another cup of coffee."

"Yes. Thank you."

"You will use the gun if you have to."

"Yes."

"Good. Two sugars and milk?"

"Please." Helen studied him as he stirred the coffee. "How close do you think we really are?"

"This close." Martin held up his fingers. "I know we're going to get him soon."

*   *   *   *

Donald Abington sat by the indoor pool, reading the morning newspaper as he sipped espresso. The only leads they had were the leads he'd given them. Donald smiled as his niece dove into the other end of the pool wearing her tiniest black bikini. He watched her do her usual ten laps, admiring the way she glided through the water effortlessly.

"Good morning, Tara." Donald said as she emerged just a few feet from him.

"Good morning, Don. Are you reading about those murders?"

"Terrible isn't it?"

"They haven't gotten anywhere. I don't think they'll ever catch that guy."

"Are you frightened?" Donald knew the answer and relished hearing it.

"Not when I'm home. But when I go out into the real world I'm scared." She grabbed a white towel off the stand by the steps and dried her blond hair. "Most of those women were my age. It's horrible. I can relate to how terrified they must have been. How helpless they must have felt."

Donald studied her, thinking how close she was to the truth and the killer. "Maybe it was their time to go. They say we all have a time, whether its getting hit by a truck, struck by lightening or-."

"Or being murdered? You can't be serious, Donald."

He shrugged his broad shoulders. "I don't know. Who can figure these things out? It's beyond me."

"I don't think they should be putting such gore in the paper to begin with. Damn, it's gotten to me." Tara said.

"Don't you worry. He doesn't seem to be traveling in our circles."

"I go to the mall, the stores, the theatre. And I fit the profile if you haven't noticed. Blond, twenty-something, thin and single."

"That you do, but the last one was a married red-head with children."

"Let's change the subject."

Donald's mind raced with his narrow escape from the scene. While he was going out the back door, a kid peeled out on the street. Donald could hear someone yelling that they got the plate number as he hopped the fence. His heart started to slow as he walked the two blocks to his car. He'd done his work and gotten out of there clean. He tossed the surgical gloves and the knife down the gutter as he approached his car, sirens waling in the background.

How easy it had been from there on out. After taking a nice slow drive by the shore to catch his breath he headed home to dear auntie's estate.

"What do you think about the psychic?" Tara asked.

"I thought you wanted to change the subject?"

"She helped them with that kidnapping case. Maybe she's for real."

"I don't believe in that shit." Donald scowled.

"What's wrong?"

Donald put the paper down and lit a cigarette. "She's had a few lucky guesses."

"It was more than that. I followed that case. She was good. Even the chief of police said they wouldn't have found that boy in time without her. He said she's on the payroll now as a profiler."

"Like I said, I don't believe in that shit." Donald growled.

"Okay. We'll change the subject."

Donald buzzed for more espresso as he sucked on the butt, crushing it between clenched teeth. He despised being threatened by a woman. If she was really good, he'd have been caught by now. No, she was sucking money from the system in the gypsy tradition. She was nothing but a cheap fortuneteller.

"Are you going to the benefit? Everyone who's anyone is going to be there." Tara smiled. "I've got the perfect dress. Julius did the fitting himself."

"Julius?" He raised his eyebrows. The man never did a fitting unless the gown was over a grand. "Must be one hell of a dress."

"There's hardly anything to it. Mother almost fainted when she saw it. I'm only getting away with it because she can't make it. She's leaving for Palm Beach this afternoon." Tara grinned.

"Lucky you." Donald nodded. "Yes, I don't have a Julius original, but I'm looking forward to it. I've had my eye on Gloria Fritz and she's agreed to accompany me."

"Gloria Fritz. Are you serious?"

"Yes. She is a nice quiet lady."

"Quiet? The woman is wallpaper."

"Very rich wallpaper."

They shared a smile and a nod before Tara excused herself to get ready for her afternoon at the spa. "I'll see you tonight." She kissed his cheek and rushed into the mansion.

Donald leaned back and thought about Gloria. She was a composed woman worth hundreds of millions and with his divorce papers finalized, he was ready to return to his roots. Money was the key and with a fat purse like Gloria's, he wasn't going to waste much time making it his. He'd made his plans the minute he'd been introduced and he'd pursued her calmly and steadily. Donald knew he had her where he wanted her. A quick marriage, a quiet death over a cliff or something and he'd be in charge in a way he'd only dreamed about.

*   *   *   *

Helen dropped the newspaper on the kitchen table. "You need to go there."

"Excuse me?"

"The charity ball. It's tonight. You should go." Helen looked out at the cruiser parked in the driveway.

"He'll be there?" Martin looked at her. "You'll come?"

"I'd rather not, but yes."

"Let's do it. I'll make a few calls. I have to go home for my tux."

"You own a tux?"

"Long story." Martin shrugged. "I'll get Osborne to come out here while I go-."

"Don't. I'll be fine. There's already an officer outside. I've got China here."

"You'll call if she raises an ear?"

Helen smiled. "You catch on quick."

"I'm a trained observer." Martin stood and kissed her cheek. "I'll be back within the hour."

Helen's mood darkened as the heat rose to her cheeks.

✳   ✳   ✳   ✳

Martin walked over to the young officer parked across the street from Helen's. "I'm going home. Keep your eyes open. If you hear that dog bark, get in there and radio for help immediately."

"Yes, sir."

Martin thought about her as he drove to his apartment. Helen was a beautiful, intense woman and all though he didn't like the idea of her being mixed up in such a horrific case, he was counting his blessings that fate had brought her back into his life.

On the ride over he made a few calls and arranged to have another three detectives at the ball. Two captains and the chief were already planning to attend, making the evening that much safer for Helen.

Helen. Her name floated around in his head as he unpacked his overnight bag and pulled the bag containing his tuxedo out of the closet.

Her eyes were as green as the emerald ring she wore. He saw a future in those eyes. A smile took over his face as he thought about kissing her goodbye. His next thought was of the passionate kiss that they'd shared months before. It was like nothing he'd ever experienced. He belonged with that woman. He would share a thousand more of those moments with her, he just had to find a way to win her over.

Martin was blind-sided when he returned to her house an hour later. He opened the kitchen door to see Helen sitting at the table scowling.

"What's wrong?" Martin asked, setting down the bags.

"We need to talk."

"More visions?"

Helen shook her head, her tone low. "We obviously need to set some ground rules."

"Excuse me?"

Her cheeks turned bright red. "I don't want...I'm not interested in getting involved personally. I don't appreciate being kissed by...by someone I'm working with...a co-worker...that's what we are."

Martin closed the door, his hopes challenged, and sat down opposite her. "What you're saying is wrong and you know it. There's something compelling between us. Why try to say otherwise? Are you a game player? Do you want me to pursue you in a certain way until you deem it appropriate for me to kiss you?" Martin took a deep breath, sucking the anger back into his chest as her green eyes darkened.

"This is just what I didn't want to happen. I explained that to you before." Helen twisted the emerald ring.

"So you've been hurt. Who the hell hasn't? Some guy hurt you and now you won't give another man the time of day."

Tears welled in her eyes as she reached for a cigarette. "Right. End of story."

"End of story?" Martin lit her cigarette and then his own. "We've got something, lady. It's something that doesn't come along everyday. I know you feel it. Shit, you can't deny this. It's just as strong as it was months ago. The fact that we didn't see each other doesn't mean we haven't been thinking about each other all of this time." Martin was angered by her shocked expression. "You didn't ask to see the chief or Osborne, you came straight to me. I think this gave you a chance to see me again without having to say you were wrong."

Helen shook her head. "I'm sorry if I gave you the wrong impression."

"It's not an impression. We're connected."

"Connected by kidnapping and now murder."

"That's not true."

"Oh?"

"I don't think one has anything to do with the other."

"Then you're wrong." Helen got up and walked down the hall. China followed her to her room and she closed the door with a thud.

"You handled that well." Martin mumbled as he brought his things into the guest bedroom.

CHAPTER 4

▼

The moment they entered the crowded ballroom Helen began scanning the many faces. The room was loaded with energy of all kinds. Images of a demure woman in her early forties entered Helen's mind. She walked through the room to the wide balcony doors and decided to stay there and clear her senses.

Helen's nerves tingled when she spotted the woman in the images walking through the crowd. They exchanged a glance before the woman disappeared.

After an hour of looking Helen was about to give up hope when she touched the handle of a balcony door. Helen released it, instantly knowing the killer had touched the spot. She scanned the area and within moments Martin was by her side.

"What is it?" Martin whispered.

Helen nodded. "He's been here. Right where we're standing."

"Let's walk around together." Martin hooked her arm and they zigzagged the length of the room twice.

"I think he's already left." Helen said as they walked out onto the patio.

"It's early." Martin lit a cigarette staring into the ballroom.

"He's gone. He left right after we arrived."

Martin nodded. "OK then. Let's relax and mingle. Maybe we can pick up on some helpful gossip." He looked at the cigarette and cringed. "You're a bad influence on me." He said butting it out.

They wandered through the crowds for hours before calling it a night. They were waiting in line at the coatroom when she felt his presence. She turned to face Martin the blood draining to her toes.

"He's back." Her eyes scanned the area as Martin pulled her aside.

"You're white as a sheet." He held her arm and walked her to the bar. "Sit. Brandy please."

Helen sat on the stool her eyes darting from one face to the next until the feeling subsided.

"Drink this." He handed her the snifter. "Drink it all…damn it woman."

Helen glanced up at him as she drank the warm brandy. "It scared the shit out of me Martin. I'm sorry."

Helen set down the empty glass as Martin ordered two more. "I'm fine. Thanks." Helen held up a trembling hand and he reached for it.

"No, you're not. We're done for the night. Officially off duty. We'll drink this and I'm taking you home."

Helen wasn't about to argue with his last statement. She needed to feel the safety of her cottage. She drank the second brandy slower than the first and as promised he took her home. Helen wasn't ready to call it a night. The brandy had helped to take the edge off but her mind was running the case through like a horrible movie that wouldn't end.

"Would you like me to make some coffee?" Martin asked as the pup greeted them in the kitchen.

"I'd prefer a nightcap." Helen patted her furry companion. "I'm going to change first." Helen headed for her room and put on her sweats before joining Martin in the living room.

"I was going to offer to make those." Helen eyed the drinks on the coffee table.

"I was thinking about a conversation we had…the one about changing my line of work."

"Oh, really?" Helen sat on the couch with a full cushion between them.

"I'd have to make a few changes in my life…incentive type of things."

Helen studied him, before asking the expected question. "What type of things?"

Martin raised his brow and smiled. "I want to get to know you better."

"We've been through this."

"You haven't given me a chance."

"I'm not ready."

"When I saw the look of horror on your face tonight, all I could think about was getting you out of there…protecting you." He caressed her cheek with his large hand and looked into her eyes. "I love you, Helen."

"I'm not ready."

"Tell me how you feel about me."

"I don't know…I…don't know." Helen took a deep breath and sipped the drink. "I don't know how else to put it, Martin. I like you but I'm not interested in getting involved with anyone."

"You like me…Do you think I'm blind?" Martin scowled. "I see the way you look at me when you let yourself relax…you aren't as careful as you think."

"What I think…it's none of your concern."

"Of course it is. I'm not going to hurt you."

Helen finished the drink in silence and set down the glass. "I'm not trying to hurt you. Yes, I'm attracted to you. Yes, I like you. I am happy with my life just the way it is. Once this is over that will be it…we'll go our separate ways."

"Until the next case? Are you really willing to torture me that way? Torture us? Whatever this is, baby, it isn't going away. I'm no psychic but even I know that."

Helen was softened by his words, knowing full well that he was right. "I'm not up to thinking about this right now."

"Fine then just sit here with me for a while and see what you think." Martin said as he moved closer. He wrapped his arms around her, cradling her head on his strong shoulder.

Helen gave into his comfort and woke hours later in the same position. She looked up at his smiling face. "I guess it was the brandy."

"I don't think it had anything to do with the brandy." Martin stroked her hair.

"I'd better go to bed." Helen stood and studied him for a moment, caught up in the warmth of his tender embrace. She fought the urge to invite him to join her as she walked to her room.

"Good night. And thank you."

"Good night, Martin." Helen said as she closed the bedroom door.

Helen woke in a cold sweat as Martin burst through the door. "What is it?" He yelled as he flipped on the light.

"I…I…was having a nightmare."

"I heard you scream and the dog ran to your door." Martin set his gun on the nightstand and sat on the edge of the bed. "You scared the hell out of me." He said as he pushed her long auburn hair from her eyes. "Are you okay?"

"I'm sorry I woke you. I'm fine. Can you shut off that light?" Helen shielded her eyes from the bright beam.

"Sure." Martin flipped the switch and returned to the bed. "I'll sit here with you while you fall asleep. I almost killed myself tripping over the ottoman." He said as he rubbed his shin.

Helen's mind was filled with pained images but they didn't connect with the murders. It was someone young. A girl. She stiffened and sat up.

"I won't be able to sleep now."

"The nightmare?"

"I think it was more than that."

"Another murder?"

"I don't know." Helen turned on the small lamp by the bed. "I need some coffee." She said as she got out of bed.

They walked out to the kitchen as the newspaper hit the door.

"I'll get it." Martin said, holding up his hand.

Helen started the coffee and sat at the table. As soon as Martin put the paper in front of her the images reappeared.

"Oh, shit." Helen grabbed it and scanned the headlines. When she turned the page her eyes settled on the picture of a six-year-old girl. "We have to get to her."

Helen ran into the bedroom and threw on jeans and a sweatshirt. She was putting on her sneakers when Martin walked in holding the paper.

"Is this what woke you up?"

"She's running out of time." Helen looked up at him. "It's her father...no...stepfather...get someone to follow him."

"Helen, take a breath."

She shook her head. "We have to find her now...the stepfather, where does he live?"

"They live about four miles from here." Martin studied the article.

"Let's go. She isn't far...please, get someone to watch him." Her heart was hammering against her ribs as she grabbed her jacket out of the closet and headed for the living room. She let the dog out and turned to Martin. "She's in a vacant cottage...I'm..." The Dane ran back inside and Helen locked the door. "We'll be back, girl."

"Would you take a deep breath?" Martin followed her out the door.

"Let's go." She rushed to his car as he ran across the street to the patrol officer. Helen stood by the door, hearing the girl whimpering for help in her mind.

Martin returned, calling in for someone to get to the girl's address.

"Where are we going?"

"She's not far from home...it's gray...for sale...rundown...we have to get there now."

Martin sped onto the two-lane highway and turned right onto the girl's street. "Okay, that's her house." Martin pointed at the cheery white cottage.

"Keep going…shit…shit…" The fear was getting worse. "Is the stepfather home?"

"I don't know that yet."

"Stop. Back up…Go right."

Martin followed her directions and they headed down the dirt lane. As they rounded the corner she saw it.

"She's in there." Helen pointed to the shingled cottage and Martin hit the brakes. She jumped out of the car and ran toward the building.

"Wait damn it." Martin yelled.

Helen couldn't stop. She burst through the front door and ran toward the back of the vacant house. When she pushed open the door she stopped, shocked to see the empty room. She turned to the sound of whimpering and opened the closet door to find the little girl, naked and beaten, scratch and strap marks covering her frail body.

"Oh, my God." Helen removed the blindfold from the child's eyes and untied her hands and feet. She took off her jacket and wrapped it around the girl. "It's okay, Cathy…you're safe now."

"Daddy's coming back." The girl cried.

"He can't hurt you anymore." Helen looked up as Martin came into the room. "You need to arrest her stepfather now." Helen cried. "We need to get her to a hospital."

Martin reached for the child and she screamed clutching Helen and he pulled back. "It's all right. We're here to help you."

"I'll carry her." Helen lifted the child and followed Martin out of the cottage as he called for assistance. She sat in the backseat of his car holding the weak little girl.

"You're going to be fine now. You're a very brave little girl."

"I was calling you." The girl cried against her.

"Calling me?"

"You helped that boy…I remembered." The girl fainted against her.

"Martin. Martin. She's passed out." Helen moved the coat to make sure she was still breathing. "She needs-." The sirens in the distance interrupted her thought.

Martin rushed to her as the ambulance rounded the corner.

Helen rode with the little girl to the hospital and stayed with her in the emergency room until her mother arrived.

Helen stepped back as the woman rushed to her child, crying as she wrapped her arms around her.

"I was so scared, Mommy…Daddy said I was bad."

The woman's sobs filled the room as Helen walked out into the hallway.

An hour later Martin arrived. "How is she?" He asked as he sat down beside her in the waiting room.

"She'll be okay physically but it'll take a long time for her emotionally." Helen looked up at him. "Did they arrest the stepfather?"

"Yes. They got him coming out of his house."

Helen stared into his dark eyes. "She said she was calling me. She told the nurse she tried to remember my name and when she did, she called me to help her."

Helen shook her head and walked to the window. Things were getting out of control. She wasn't ready for the changes in her gift. The intensity of emotions threatened to overwhelm her.

Martin walked up behind her and placed a warm hand on her shoulder. "The stepfather had a butcher knife and a meat cleaver in a bag…he was going to kill her."

Helen turned toward him, rocked by his words. "I didn't think we were going to make it." Tears rolled down her cheeks. "I thought he'd get there first."

"We did make it. She's alive because of you."

"Excuse me? Are you Helen?" The girl's mother trembled in the doorway.

"Yes."

The woman rushed to her and embraced her, sobbing. "Thank you. I…can never thank you…enough."

"I'm glad I could help her. How's she doing?" Helen asked still feeling the girl's pain.

The woman released her and took a step back, wiping her eyes with a soggy tissue. "Nothing's broken…she's dehydrated…he raped my baby." She cried as she reached for the chair. "We've been together for years…he's never spanked her…he never hurt her before…I asked her."

"Why now?" Helen asked.

"She said she knocked his beer bottle off of the table with a toy…he took off his belt and beat her." The woman sobbed.

"They have him in custody." Helen said, patting the woman's back. "She's safe now."

"Thanks to you...she's asking for you." The woman stood and took a deep breath.

"I'll go." Helen started for the room, wishing the visions had come sooner.

"How are you doing?" Helen managed a smile for the girl as she entered the room.

"Better." The girl nodded. "Thank you for helping me."

Helen touched her chestnut hair. "I came as soon as I could."

"I couldn't remember your name at first. I'm glad I did."

"I'm glad you did, too." Helen fought to keep the sadness she felt from the girl. "I have to go home but I was wondering if it would be okay to come and see you tomorrow."

"Please, do." The girl's green eyes widened as they scanned the room. "Are you sure you have to go?"

"You're safe now."

"I don't feel safe."

"I know. It's going to take a long time...but you're smart and strong. I'm sure you're going to be just fine."

"What if I couldn't remember-"

Helen stopped her mid sentence. "You did and I found you." Helen pulled the covers up under her chin and glanced toward the door at her mother. "I'll be right back."

"Promise?"

"Yes." Helen kissed her forehead and walked out of the room.

"What are you up to?" Martin asked, walking beside her as she headed down the hall.

"Shit. I don't have my purse. Can I borrow some money? That kid needs a teddy bear."

"Teddy bear?" Martin said as she hit the elevator button.

"She needs something to hold onto."

They went down to the gift shop and Helen picked out the largest, softest teddy bear they had and returned to the girl's room.

"This is your new best friend. What do you think?" Helen smiled as she handed the bear to the girl.

"What's her name?"

"Faith."

"I like it. Thank you." Cathy clutched the bear to her chest.

"I do have to go now. I'll be back to see you tomorrow."

Helen walked out of the hospital drained. They rode to her house in silence. Once inside, they sat at the table, staring at each other.

"You are amazing." Martin shook his head.

"I thank God for helping me find her…this doesn't come from me. It's channeled through me, somehow." Helen took a deep breath and walked to the slider to let the dog out. "I'm glad we got there in time."

The phone rang and she let the answering machine pick it up. She looked at the blinking red light as the reporter left a message looking for a comment on the girl's rescue.

"I'm sure it's only the beginning." Martin said as he poured the coffee.

"I'm not interested in talking to reporters."

"Can't blame you. The department will put out a press release. Don't worry about it…come, have some coffee. We need to think about having lunch…" he checked his watch. "Dinner."

"I'm not hungry."

"Sit. Relax. Please." Martin pulled out a chair for her and smiled as she walked over and sat down.

"What a day. I feel like I've run a marathon." Helen lit a cigarette.

"You have. More than that." Martin studied her. He answered his cell phone, still staring at her. "Yes…okay…thanks…yes…alright, bye."

"What is it?"

"The bastard hung himself with his pants in the holding cell."

"Cathy's stepfather?"

"Yes."

Helen nodded. "At least she'll never have to worry about him getting released."

Martin ordered Chinese food and after dinner he left to go to the station. Helen was relieved to be alone for a while. She sat on the couch with the dog at her feet and turned on the TV. Her whole body was feeling the strain of the horrifying events. She thought about the pain Cathy had endured and pulled the afghan off the back of the couch, wrapping it around her. The child was safe but she'd have to live with the savagery put on her by a person she was supposed to be protected by.

Helen was glad when Martin returned. "You must have thought I'd lost my mind this morning." Helen shook her head. "It all hit me so hard. It was as if I was gripped by the visions. I had to respond." Helen scowled. "I wish I could make you understand."

Martin sat beside her on the couch and she stared into his warm brown eyes.

"I can't say that I've understood but I know what I see. I know you were in a panic but it was warranted." Martin took a deep breath. "All I would ask is that you not leave me in the dust again. Shit woman, when I saw you run into that cottage my heart shot out of my chest. The bastard could have been in there waiting for you."

"I knew he wasn't."

"But I didn't." He put his large hand on her shoulder. "I believe in what you can do. I just need for you to take some of the rules into consideration. Some protocol."

Helen nodded. "I said I'm sorry. It was as though her panic became my own. I wasn't thinking clearly. I'm going to work on that."

"I'm glad to hear it."

"It's like these visions are my personal path to danger. I'm propelled in a direction and I can't turn away from it." Helen cringed when she thought about how Cathy looked when they'd found her.

"Well, lady, you once told me these visions could change. If that bastard had been there, well, I hate to think about what could have happened."

CHAPTER 5

▼

Two weeks past without a murder or a threatening phone call and Helen began to relax. She spent her days going through the murder files but nothing new came through.

Helen was frustrated by the statistics that said that the more time that went by the less likely they were to catch him. There was no such thing as a perfect crime. There had to be clues they were missing.

Helen looked up when the office door opened. She smiled as Martin walked in and she set the files back in the tray.

"He's stopped for a while. I don't know why...it isn't because he's afraid of getting caught. I think it's something in his personal life. He doesn't have the time right now." Helen leaned back in the chair.

"Excuse me." A young officer appeared in the doorway. "There's a woman here to see Miss Staples. She said it's urgent."

"Did she say what it's about?" Martin asked as he walked over to the officer.

"Just that she needed to see Miss Staples immediately."

Martin looked over at Helen who stood and nodded. "Show her in."

A few moments later a tall, thin woman walked into the room holding a file. She gave them both a long hard look before setting the file on Martin's desk. "This is my son's history." She glanced over her shoulder at the officer standing in the door. "The police can't find him. I need your help. I'll pay whatever...his name is Tyron, he's only five."

"Please, have a seat." Martin said as he stood by the desk.

"He's been gone for three days. He was taken from my back yard while I was vacuuming. No one heard or saw anything."

"I'm sorry ma'am but I don't remember hearing about this case." Martin said.

"She's from Boston." Helen said, staring at the woman.

"Yes, I am." She reached into her purse and pulled out a piece of blue fabric. She held it out to Helen. "This is all he left behind. They took him over the fence and ripped his shirt."

"The police have been searching for him?" Martin asked.

"Yes. Volunteers from my neighborhood and the police."

Helen took the piece of cloth and sat down. "Can I see his picture?"

The woman opened the file and handed her the picture of the little boy. His round happy face contrasted what she was feeling. She looked up at Martin. "I have to go."

"To Boston?"

"Where is his grandmother?"

"His grandmother?" The woman cocked her head. "My mother?"

"No, his grandmamma?"

"She..." the woman's eyes widened. "She was my neighbor, her...she just moved."

"Where?"

"She broke her hip and her children decided it was time she go live with them...somewhere on Cape Cod."

"I need a map...he's lost...he climbed the fence...he took the T." Helen could see the little boy making his escape.

"The T?"

"I see a bridge...I've seen it before...he's made it to the canal...he's near the canal." Helen fingered the fabric. "He knows he's lost...I see the bridge overhead and a swing set...playground...set in sand...it's a campground."

"Hold on. There's a campground, a state park, in that area." Martin picked up the phone. "Get me Bourne P.D. Hello, this is Detective Hamlin from the Worthington P.D. Look I just got a tip that a missing boy may be at the campground by the bridge. Can you send a unit by to check it out? Sure."

Martin reached for the file and began listing the details of the boy's appearance and circumstance surrounding his disappearance.

He hung up the phone and looked at Helen.

She shook her head. "He's going to hide from them." Helen turned to Tyron's mother. "We'd better head down there."

"You need an escort." Martin said as he followed her to the door.

"Drive us...you have the blue lights." The woman scowled at him.

The siren wailed as they raced down the highway. Helen's pulsed increased with every passing moment.

As they turned off of the highway onto the rotary the woman leaned forward and touched Helen's shoulder. "There's no way you could know about Grandmamma."

"But I do...he's going to be fine." Helen said as they turned into the campground.

Martin flashed his badge at the man in the gate shack and showed him the picture of Tyron. The man's eyes widened.

"He's here. I saw him this morning."

"Thanks. We're going to have a look around." Martin said and looked over at Helen.

"Go straight." She said, looking over at the bridge. "He's down there."

They drove a short distance and came to the play area Helen had seen in the vision. Martin stopped the car and they all walked over to the swings.

"He's here." Helen said. "Call him."

"Tyron. Tyron. Please answer me baby." His mother called as she turned in a complete circle.

Helen saw the cruiser approaching and put up her hand. "Martin, please tell him to stay back. The boy thinks he's in trouble."

"You aren't in any trouble baby. I know you just wanted to see Grandmamma. I'm sorry I didn't take you. Please...Please...Tyron..." The woman dropped to her knees sobbing, calling his name.

Helen scanned the area and spotted the small boy as he walked out of the brush behind the swing set.

"Mom. Mom." He said as he broke into a run.

"Oh, Tyron." She wrapped her arms around him. "Tyron you scared me so bad, baby." She sobbed as she rocked him on her lap. "I love you baby. I love you."

"I'm sorry Mom."

"I was so worried."

"I was going to see Grandmamma. I miss her Mom."

"I know baby." She smoothed her hand over his black curly hair as she looked up at Helen. "Thank you."

Helen nodded and walked down to the edge of the canal. She looked down at the whirlpools rushing by as her mind began to clear.

Martin joined her a few minutes later. "Are you okay?"

"Yes. How's he doing?"

"Fine. Are you ready to head back?"

"Yes."

He put his arm over her shoulder as they walked back to his car. "You are good."

"Lucky."

"Right."

"I'm beat."

"Hey, another happy ending." Martin said as he pointed to mother and child in the back of his car. "Maybe I should change my line of work."

Helen looked up at him. "Nothing like this has ever happened to me…I mean, well, when I helped you the first time…" Helen could feel them staring out at her. "Maybe we can talk later."

"I'd like that."

Helen got in the car and the little boy touched her on the shoulder. "Thanks for helping my mom find me. I was starting to think I was lost."

"You're welcome. Can you do me a favor though?" Helen smiled at him. "Don't get lost again."

"It's a deal. I'll only go with my mom to see Grandmamma."

"Glad to hear it." Helen leaned back in the seat and closed her eyes as they drove out of the campground.

Helen got out of the car at the police station and asked Martin to get her a ride home. She was through working for the day. Martin agreed to bring her home if she'd allow him to take her out to dinner first. She was too drained to argue and waited by the car while he escorted Tyron and his mother into the station.

When Helen saw the television van pull in across the street she jumped back into the car and ducked down. A few minutes later Martin walked outside shaking his head.

"They knew about it before we could get back here." Martin said as he started the car. "They sent an extra cruiser to your house to keep the reporters away."

"We have to come to some kind of agreement about this. I don't want my name out there."

"You can't say that, Helen…not after what that girl told you…remember, you're under constant guard."

"And we both know it can't last forever." Helen took a deep breath. "Enough shop talk. Let's go eat."

"Deal."

They enjoyed a nice long meal before returning to Helen's house to face the excitement. Her street was a zoo. Three television vans, and another four cars were lining the road in front of her house. The officers held the reporters at bay as they parked and walked inside amid the shouted questions.

"This is horrible. I can't live like this."

"It'll die down." Martin pulled out a chair. "You have to admit it's pretty wild…shit…first you save some girl then locate a kid from Boston under the Bourne Bridge. That's as wild as it gets…plus they know about the other boy and that you are working on the murders with us."

"Stay." Helen put her hand up to the dog and walked outside.

"What are you doing?" Martin rushed out behind her.

"I'm going to make a statement."

"You're what?"

She walked down the driveway to the barricade the officers had set up.

"I'd like to make a statement." Helen watched as the reporters scrambled toward her. She waited until they were all in place.

"My statement is, I do not now, nor will I in the future, have anything to say about any cases you are reporting about. My neighbors and I would appreciate it if you would leave us alone. You are blocking the road and being a public nuisance. Thank you." Helen turned and walked back into the house as they called questions after her.

Within two hours the reporters had cleared out, finally taking the hint. In spite of her statement, her name was plastered all over the evening news and she had so many messages that she turned the ringer off on the phone.

"You need a new line of work." Helen said as she sat down on the couch.

"Is this what you were talking about before?"

"In a way. The first time I had these visions was after we met. What happened with Cathy was one thing but with Tyron today…it was so clear…I knew exactly where he was and how he was feeling…I felt like I was there with him." Helen shook her head. "I don't really know how to explain it…I was drained after the first case. This isn't something I can keep doing."

"But it's such a gift. Any cop would give his eye teeth to be able to do what you do."

"That's because they don't know what it's like. I feel the fear…when that little girl was calling out for me, I felt her terror…my heart felt like it would explode it was beating so fast."

"I'm sure it must be hard on you but you have to think about the fact that you've rescued three children."

"That's all that keeps me going but I can't help but think about the ones I can't help…like those young women. It was terrifying but it wasn't clear, it was as blunt…I can't explain it…I'm tired."

"Why don't you get some sleep. We'll talk more in the morning." Martin said.

"That's another thing, I don't think you need to stay here. With the guys outside and China in here, I-."

"We've already discussed this. It's not like there's anyone waiting for me. I'm taking the rest of the night off. I want to get an early start tomorrow."

For the next three days they sifted through the files on the murdered women, searching for anything they might have missed. The peace in Helen's mind nagged at her. There was a reason he'd stopped. She had to find the answer. She went through the files they'd gotten from Kansas City.

"I think he's on an extended vacation." Helen said as she watched Martin shoot three darts into the bull's eye.

"Makes sense." Martin walked over to the desk and sat down.

"I've needed these days to recover…I'm feeling much better…thinking more clearly." Helen reached for the first file. "I'm going to start from the beginning."

"Oh, no. I think we've done enough for one day. It's after six." Martin put the file back on the stack. "I need food."

Helen nodded. "I give. But you know it's in there." Helen pointed to the files. "You know." Helen stood and put on her jacket. "You never did show me the photos from the charity ball."

Martin's face dropped. "I didn't? Shit." He looked at the top of his desk. "They're in my briefcase. We can go over them after dinner."

"Okay."

As they walked past the front desk the young officer manning it stopped them.

"Here are your messages, Miss Staples." He handed her a stack of yellow slips. "You've kept that switch board busy."

"Thank you." Helen put them in her purse. She'd expected the calls once she'd made national news. The reporters called her so often she'd changed her number leaving the only contact the police station.

"Thanks for dinner. I enjoyed myself." Martin said as they walked into her cottage.

"Now I have to go through these." Helen took the slips out of her purse and set them on the table.

"If you're going to work, I'll get those pictures for you."

Helen thought about the first case they worked together and how comfortable she'd become with him as he left to retrieve the pictures. She was thinking about their only kiss as he returned to the room.

"Are you all right?"

"Yes." Helen shook her head and reached for a cigarette.

"Anything interesting in those messages?"

"I haven't looked." Helen could feel the heat rise to her cheeks as she took a drag to calm her nerves. She was glad he couldn't read her thoughts. She flipped through the papers as he sat down beside her.

"My aunt...I didn't think to call her with my new number." Helen thought of their last visit. "Excuse me."

She went to the living room and settled on the couch for a long call.

"Oh, dear, it is so good to hear from you."

"I'm fine. Things have calmed down."

"Calmed down? Oh, Helen, I've been so worried. Are you eating?"

"Yes."

"You looked so thin the last time I saw you."

"I'm fine, really."

"You're amazing. I was talking with the girls, they can't believe the strength of your gift. When will you come to see me? I have so many questions, dear." Madeline took a deep breath. "Are you focusing? How is it all coming to you?"

"Slow down, auntie." Helen stood and paced the floor in front of the couch.

"You must be ecstatic to realize your potential. I'm so glad for you."

"I'd rather not talk about it right now."

"When will you come for a visit?"

"I'm not sure...soon."

"I'll be waiting."

Helen hung up the phone and walked back to the table. "That woman wears me out. She has more energy than a five year old." Helen shook her head and reached for a cigarette. "Question?" She asked looking into his brown eyes.

"Does your aunt have the, ah, gift?"

"To a degree. I think that's why she's so fascinated by me." Helen sat down and leaned her elbows on the table still staring into his eyes. "She sees dollar signs...has since the first case."

"Envy?"

"That and pride. She's a good woman…just different. More like a fortune teller."

"I don't understand any of it. I never used to believe in all this stuff, you changed that."

"Is that good or bad?"

"Both. It makes things less cut and dry. Makes that gut feeling more important."

"It is important. Everyone has the gift to some degree." She realized she was staring at his handsome face too long and straightened in her seat focusing her attention on the messages. "All of these people want my help and I don't feel anything." She said as she came to the end of the pile.

"Take a look at these." Martin slid the pictures in front of her.

Halfway through them Helen handed him the one of the woman she'd seen at the ball. "There's a connection here. I felt it when I saw her." She went through the rest and set them aside. "She doesn't fit the profile but she's around him and in danger."

Martin nodded. "I'll ask around, see if anybody can identify her."

"I need a hot shower." Helen stood and smiled. "I'll be out in a while."

Helen returned a short while later to the low lights and a blue TV screen. Martin was sitting on the couch with the Great Dane sleeping at his feet. She wanted to tell him he looked like he belonged there, but didn't dare. Helen went to the kitchen and poured them a glass of wine. The day had taken its toll.

"Thanks." Martin smiled up at her. "Mm. This is good."

"One of my favorites." Helen raised her glass as Martin's beeper went off on the coffee table.

"Shit." Martin scooped it up and read the number. "Watch the movie, I have to call in." He walked into the kitchen to make the call.

Helen was deep in thought when he returned.

"Helen…Helen…are you there?" Martin waved his large hand in front of her.

Helen looked at him. "Sorry. What did you say?" She asked, setting down the empty glass.

"I have to go to the station for a while. They've got a witness to the last murder. I should only be gone an hour or so."

Once she was alone, her mind drifted back to their meeting and their closeness that first month. She'd been so quick to pull away from him after that one kiss.

She hadn't been ready for a relationship then even though she understood what was holding her back.

It was the loss of Tim that kept her from Martin. Feeling the pain of his death had been devastating. She'd warned Tim not to take that flight. She'd pleaded with him to delay the trip even an hour but he wouldn't do it. Instead he attempted to satisfy her concerns by leaving the house ten minutes later than he felt he should. Helen didn't have a vivid picture of the impending crash, only a sharp feeling of dread about the trip.

She'd held onto his strong tall body for the last time and felt his death two hours later as an engine burst into flames and then exploded sending the aircraft spinning back to earth.

Helen had been overwhelmed by grief. They'd planned to marry in the spring. Her whole future became dark and grim. She'd stopped seeing clients for months and holed up in her cottage, leaving only by necessity.

She thought of those empty, lonely weeks following his death. She'd been able to get through it by drawing on the seemingly endless memories of their days, their moments together. A certain smile on his face, the sound of their laughter during one of his story telling moods. The time they'd been blessed with kept her going.

It took nearly a half year for Helen to pull herself together and start living her life again but she never imagined, even more than a year after his death, that she'd be thinking of another man's company.

Helen thought about Martin as she refilled her glass. She'd explained to him how she felt the night he'd kissed her. Explained her love for Tim and the loss she'd felt after his death. She'd told him she didn't want a relationship with him or anyone else and she'd been firm about it.

Still, she knew Martin was in love with her then and now. He was growing on her, inching his way into her life and making her rethink her position. It was fear of getting too close and then losing him that she couldn't come to terms with.

Martin tapped on the door, startling her and the Dane, before walking inside. As his dark eyes studied her, she tied the sash on her robe and smiled.

"How'd it go?"

"Good." Martin patted the dog on the head. "We've got an artist working with him."

"That's great." Helen dropped the empty wine bottle into the trash. "I was about to open another bottle."

"Have you been crying?" Martin moved toward her.

"I…well, yes…I'm fine though. I was thinking about Tim."

"Oh? Anything you want to talk about? I'm a good listener."

"Not really."

"Okay…well, go ahead and sit down. I'll open this for you. Did you finish the movie?"

"To tell you the truth I was lost in thought. We can start it over if you like."

"That's okay. It's kind of late now." Martin opened the bottle and followed her into the living room. "What line of work was Tim in?"

"Corporate lawyer."

"He must have flown a lot." Martin sat beside her.

"Probably ten times a month."

Martin nodded. "Why didn't he listen to you?"

"I don't know…maybe because everything in his life was logical, clear. He thought what I did was silly in a way. He didn't understand it and we didn't really talk about it. You have to understand, things, my gift or senses changed when I met you."

"I wonder why?"

"No clue."

Martin lit her cigarette staring into her eyes. "I'd like to understand it."

"So would I." Helen smiled. "I stopped trying. It's…" she tapped on the coffee table. "For me the feelings have become as tangible as the wood this is made of. When we were trying to find Cathy it was like following a trail of pebbles to the door of that old cottage. It was the same with the boy only not as scary."

Helen took a long drag. "How do you deal with it?"

"With?"

"The things you see, the evil you're exposed to?"

"I don't know. It's part of the job."

"I wish I could feel that way about it."

"I didn't always. I've cried my fair share and I'm not ashamed to admit it. I wouldn't be human if I didn't." Martin took a deep breath. "The thing of it is, it doesn't end. One case is solved and another comes across my desk."

"You need a new line of work." Helen smiled.

"I believe you've mentioned that before."

Helen thought about the flurry of cases that she'd been able to help solve. "I have to believe we are going to catch the killer."

CHAPTER 6

▼

Helen woke with a start as China barked her warning. She rushed out to the kitchen where Martin was attempting to quiet the distressed dog.

"China, it's okay, girl. Come." Helen patted her thigh and the dog came to stand at her side. "What's going on?"

"It was a messenger." Martin walked over and handed her the envelope.

"All of this excitement before coffee." Helen said as she sat at the table. She opened the envelope her eyes grazing over the ten thousand dollar check before setting it aside and reading the letter. "It's a reward for finding the little boy." Helen handed him the letter.

"Must be nice."

"I'm sending it back, it must be a conflict of interest."

"Not at all. You aren't a police officer. I can clear it with the chief if you'd feel better."

"I need some coffee."

Helen and Martin were in his office by nine and worked through the day, reviewing the files. They were both disappointed when Helen saw the sketch of the man the witness had seen. Helen studied it but it meant nothing to her. It could've been anyone but it wasn't the killer. The witness had said he saw the man fleeing the area after one of the killings.

When Martin announced he was done for the day Helen had a thought. She picked the sketch off the desk. "Maybe he's a witness. Maybe he was running because he saw something or someone that scared him."

"Did you say maybe?" Martin smiled.

"It's a hunch. I don't have a clear feeling about it."

"Okay. I was thinking the same thing."

They headed down to the Scholar's apartments and walked around the complex. After showing the sketch to several residents they went across the street and asked a few locals. None could identify the man.

Helen was getting discouraged when a man up the street caught her attention. "Hey, it's him." Helen slapped Martin's back and pointed at the man.

Martin bolted for him and grabbed a hold of his thick arm. "Police. We need a word with you." Martin looked at Helen. "Which him?"

"The witness."

The man's thin face became longer as he recognized Helen. "You're that psychic lady."

"And you're our witness." Martin smiled. "Good work, Helen." Martin said as he escorted the man to his sedan.

"You aren't taking me to the police station are you?" He asked as he got into the car.

"We need a statement."

"I'll give it to you here. I don't want to be involved."

"Why?"

"A million reasons."

Martin sat in the driver's seat and turned to face him. "Tell me what you saw."

The witness took a long deep breath and described the scene. It was the night of the second murder. He was at his girlfriend's house for dinner. When he left he walked around the corner to his car. He freaked when he saw a man in a blue suit running toward him. The man was holding a large knife at his side and there was blood running down his hand and fingers.

"He tossed the knife in that sewer drain and kept on running."

"Would you recognize him?"

"Maybe…I don't know…I only saw his face for an instant, I was looking at the knife and his arm when he went by me. His back was to me when he tossed the knife. I didn't know. It didn't mean anything to me until I heard about the murder the next day."

"What sewer?"

The witness pointed to the one directly across the street from the parking lot. "That one. I'm sure because as soon as he did he ran around the corner."

"How big was the knife? What type was it?"

"It looked like a hunting knife but I can't be sure. That's one reason why I didn't call. I really have nothing to say."

"Have nothing to say?" Martin's jaw twitched. "You saw an injured man drop a bloody knife into the sewer and didn't think it was important?" He turned and started the car.

"Oh, come on. I've told you everything."

Martin ignored him as he backed out of the space and headed toward the station.

Helen took her messages from the young officer and walked up to Martin's office as he disappeared down the hall with the man. He joined her a few minutes later.

"They'll see what kind of sketch they can get out of this guy, then go through the books with him. He's in for a long night and so am I. If you're ready I'll take you home."

"Sure. I'm glad we found him."

"It's a huge break. You're getting a couple of days off." Martin smiled at her. "The chief pointed out that you've worked ten straight. He doesn't want to get billed for overtime. He's got you on a forty hour a week contract. You're making him nervous."

Helen laughed. "I'd love to have two days off. And what about you?"

"I've got a lot of work to do. Two other cases came in this morning. They need my attention."

"How can you work on so many things at once?"

"I've asked myself that. These are more routine investigations. I'll be staying at my place tonight and tomorrow night but don't worry you'll have an officer outside."

"I don't think it's necessary. Not right now."

Martin let out a laugh. "I need to focus on my work, not on what's happening at your place."

"Fine, Mister Detective sir." Helen put up her hands. "I need to grab some groceries on the way home."

"Not a problem."

*   *   *   *

Martin helped Helen with her groceries and rushed back to work. He was eager to plow through the new cases without Helen as a distraction.

Martin finished things up early the following night and was headed home when she popped into his mind.

He thought of her sitting on the couch beside him. She looked so vulnerable almost childlike as she spoke to him. He'd wanted to wrap his arms around her and stroke her long auburn hair. Martin had felt an instant attraction to her. His desires for her were growing stronger.

"Ugh." He moaned as he walked into his apartment. He wanted to be there, with her. He turned on the television, sat on the couch and thought about the way she seemed to have softened with him. He was sure she was more comfortable with him.

Martin flipped through the channels, stopping when he saw Helen's house. He turned up the volume and listened as the narrator described the fascinating rescues by the recluse clairvoyant.

"They make her sound like a freak." He said as he shut off the program. But Martin knew it was inevitable.

Martin had felt the same about the whole psychic thing when he'd gotten that first call from Helen. He'd rolled his eyes and leaned back in the chair when Helen told him who she was. He'd recognized her voice at once. "Have we met?"

"Yes. You almost ran me over when you pulled into the bank parking lot this morning."

"I knew you sounded familiar. What can I do for you?"

"It's about the missing boy. I'm seeing his shirt near a sign that says Timberland…or Timber world. It's a blue and white striped shirt. I sense the boy is near there and he's in danger."

"Is that all?"

"Well, can you tell me if it means anything to you?" Her voice was suddenly shrill.

"I can't give out any information. I thank you for your call, Miss…"

"Staples. Helen Staples."

The line went dead and he let out a laugh before calling the desk. "Hey, screen my calls. That was a fortuneteller. I don't have time for crackpots. Weed them for me."

An hour later she walked into his office. She was a striking vision with a burning in her green eyes that made him straighten in his seat.

"I'm sorry sir." The deskman said as he followed her in. "She insisted on seeing you, and…" He looked her up and down, then smiled. "How could I say no?"

Martin waved him off. "Miss Staples I'm very busy."

"Did you find his shirt?" She stopped on the other side of the desk, glaring at him.

"No."

"Fine. You can think...I am trying to help that boy."

"So are we. Now if you'll excuse me."

"You don't look too busy at the moment. Tell me, do you know where Timberland is?"

"No."

"And you aren't looking?"

"I need something more tangible than some feeling, lady. I'm sorry." He watched as she turned and walked out of the office. He heard her speaking with the officer at the desk and the door close after her. Martin walked down the stairs and smiled at the young officer.

"What did she say to you?" Martin looked out the glass door as she got into her car across the street.

"She wanted to know if the names Timberland or Timber world meant anything to me."

"And what did you say?"

"Timberland is a cabinet making business down in the industrial park."

Martin stiffened. "It is?"

"Yes. I used to drive by it every night when I was on patrol."

Martin was torn between dismissing it as foolish and racing after her. "If she calls, put her through."

He returned to his office but after ten minutes of wondering if she was on to something, he headed out to the industrial park. His heart was racing when he found her sitting in her car, the headlights shining on the sign and a little blue and white shirt on the ground beside it.

Martin stood by his car staring at the shirt for a long moment, not sure how to figure out what he was seeing. Was she some nut who'd planted the shirt there in a warped attempt to get some attention? Martin went with the thought as he approached her.

"What the hell are you up to lady?"

"I'm trying to help this boy...he was here...he was taken through those woods." She covered her face and cried. "I don't know why I knew his shirt was here...or why I know he was taken through there." Helen pointed to the woods past the sign. But it is true. He's being held somewhere. Bound."

"By who?"

"I don't know…these images started coming to me. It's never happened before."

"I'm going to get some guys out here. Stay in your car so you don't contaminate the crime scene."

Martin took a deep breath as he walked back to his sedan. There was something about her that told Martin to listen. The shirt was there and it matched the description the boy's mother had given. He called a team out to search for the boy and bag the evidence.

While he waited, he watched the woman sitting in the car. Her expression was one of panic and fear. He wondered if she really was seeing something but shrugged it off thinking it was a shame someone that pretty was so loopy.

His feelings about her took a drastic turn when an officer found a boy's sneaker an hour later in the direction she'd said they'd gone. He walked toward her car and she got out when she noticed him approaching in her rear view mirror.

"They found a sneaker." Martin took a deep breath. "Can you tell me anything else?"

"I don't…" she searched his eyes. "Can I touch the shirt?"

"It's evidence."

"Let me walk back there." Helen closed the car door.

"Fine, come with me." He led her past the officer and up the hill into the tree line where she stopped and looked off to the left.

"He's not around here. There must be-." She continued on until she came to a clearing. "The kidnapper parked over there. Do you see it?"

Martin followed her eyes to a dirt road on the other side.

"He put him in his van. It was parked right there."

Martin took out his notebook and wrote van, change of vehicles, and waited for her next sentence as they walked over to the dirt road. He couldn't believe it when he saw what appeared to be fresh truck or van tracks. He called the team over still waiting for what she would say next.

"He's taken him far from here. The boy is in serious danger. You must believe me." Helen turned toward him. "What I'm saying is true."

"Where did he take him?"

"East." Helen took a deep breath and headed back to the parking lot.

Martin followed after her, stopping her as she got to the car. "Look lady. I don't know what to think about all this. Do you think the kid is still alive?"

"Yes…but he won't be if you don't find him soon."

Martin wrote his cell and home numbers on the back of his business card and handed it to her. "Please call me if you think of anything else."

"I will."

Two hours later he returned to the station to find her in his office studying a map on the wall.

"I was waiting for you."

He nodded at her. "What is it?"

"I've narrowed it to this area."

"That's about five square miles."

"I know. It's the best I can do. Did you find his glasses?"

"You…we didn't publicize that."

"Did you find them?"

"Yes. They were by the side of the dirt road."

"He can't see without them."

"I know." Martin sat down behind the desk.

"That's all I know." Helen walked over to the door. "I hope you find him soon."

He didn't hear from her for two days and when she called she sounded frightened.

"You have to do something. I don't know how much longer he can last."

"We've beefed up patrols in the area."

"What do you think, the son of a bitch is going to take the kid out to an ice cream parlor? You have to look for him."

"Please calm down, Miss Staples. I assure you we are doing everything we can to find him."

"Well you're running out of time."

He looked at the phone as the line went dead. He didn't know how but he believed she was right. The boy was running out of time.

Martin went to the map and looked at the area she'd pointed out. To the south was a thick residential area but most of the northern section was scattered businesses and warehouses and acres of vacant woodlands. The boy could be anywhere.

Martin couldn't deny the fact that none of the usual procedures had yielded a clue yet this woman had given them leads to the only hard evidence in the case. She'd returned to his office daily asking if he'd heard anything new and seemed more angry and upset each time he told her no.

The days blended together and she again came into his office, catching him shooting darts as he puzzled over the case.

"You can't expect me to find him alone."

"I don't. Believe me."

"Then what are you doing?" She waved her arms. "You aren't going to find him on the damn dartboard?"

He managed to calm her down and they sat together reviewing each piece of the case.

The next day he decided to drive around the area she'd suggested and past her on old highway one. He hit his horn and spun around after her, pulling her over.

"What are you doing here?"

"I'm trying to find that boy."

He noticed that her face looked thinner than the day they'd met. She appeared to be under a great strain. "Are you feeling okay?"

"No. I'm scared, damn it. The kid is running out of time and you guys don't seem to be able to help him."

"So you're out here looking."

"I don't have a choice."

Martin scanned the area. "Do you think he's around here?"

"I'm closer to him than I was at Timberland…we are wasting time." She put her car in drive and headed down the road.

Martin couldn't resist following her. She came to an old abandoned farmhouse and stopped. He pulled up behind her and watched as she covered her face.

Martin took a deep breath and got out of the car. "What is it?"

She moved her hands from her face and cried. "He's in water…somewhere…" she opened the car door. "You have to get help…he can't keep holding on."

He watched as she bolted from the car and ran around the back of the house.

"We are here to help you." She screamed. "Let us help you." She stumbled and fell to her knees taking gasping for air.

Martin stopped dumbfounded by what he was witnessing. "I'll check the house."

He went into the condemned building and noticed food wrappers on the floor just inside the door. Martin whipped out his revolver and crept through the house. Adrenaline moved him from room to room with no results. There was old rope tied to a pipe but other than the food wrappers it looked like just another abandoned building.

He walked outside to find her gone but didn't dare yell for her. He scanned the area without results and started toward the back of the property.

"Hamlin." Her scream pierced the wind.

"Where are you?"

"Over here, by the shed. Quick."

When he found her she was laying on the ground holding a rope that went into a hole.

"Help me! He's going to drown."

Martin grabbed the rope and looked in the hole to see the shivering boy up to his neck in water in the old well. "Hold on, kid." The boy nodded and Martin pulled him up. "My God." Martin said as Helen reached for the boy and set him on the ground. "My hands are covered in oil."

"That's why I couldn't get out...I kept trying and slipping." The boy held up his raw hands.

"You're safe now." Helen took off her coat and wrapped him in it.

From the moment she found the boy, he was a changed man, a believer. The following day she was offered a position by the chief which she flatly turned down. That evening after a delightful dinner with her, Martin had made the mistake of acting on impulse as they stood by her door. He'd kissed her, she'd responded, and then shut him down.

Martin couldn't believe his luck when she showed up at his office months later but he wished she'd come there to see him rather than being forced there by her visions.

CHAPTER 7

▼

For two days Helen worked around her house wondering what was happening in the case. She thought about calling Martin but held back and waited for his call the next morning.

"We've put a name to the woman in the picture. Gloria Fritz."

"Great."

"I'm on my way over."

Helen sat back and said the name aloud. It didn't seem to suit the woman. She puzzled over it for a minute and let it go hoping he'd have plenty of information for her. The only sense she'd gotten from the woman was the fact that she was surrounded by danger and somehow connected to the killer.

Martin was in an upbeat mood as he greeted her. "I'm ready for some good coffee. The one I got in town was horrible." He said as he patted the dog's head and sat at the table.

"What do you know about her?"

"Tons. She's big in the high society scene." Martin took a folder out of his briefcase and set it in front of her.

"Have you contacted her yet?"

"No. What are we going to say? Anyway, she's out of town right now." Martin pointed it out on the second page. "A one month cruise…we've requested a list of passengers."

"He's with her. I'd like to see that list."

"I'm hoping to have it this afternoon."

"This explains a lot." Helen made a note of the return date. The killing would resume then, she had no doubt. "What about the sketch?"

"He couldn't do it. He spent hours with the artist but he wanted to change everything. It was a waste of time."

"What about the knife?"

"No luck, yet."

"Someone is going to have to approach her. She has to be warned."

"My first thought was to get an anonymous message to her before she leaves the ship...problem being if she's traveling with him." Martin shrugged. "Defeats the purpose."

"We're going to have to do something." Helen studied his brown eyes. "Let's take a ride around the area she lives in."

"After coffee." Martin smiled.

An hour later they drove past the gates to the Fritz estate.

"He's been here." Helen said as he slowed the car. "It's frustrating." Helen looked over at Martin. "Why is it that the images of the children and the murders themselves were so clear, yet I haven't been able to get a clear image of the guy?"

"I'm sorry I can't help you."

*   *   *   *

They arrived at the captain's table and Donald held out the chair for Gloria. "Did I tell you how exceptionally beautiful you look tonight, my dear?"

"I believe you did mention it." Gloria smiled up at him as he sat next to her, taking her hand.

"You've captivated me." Donald whispered in her ear. "How much longer are you going to make me wait?"

"Please, Donald, someone might hear." Her cheeks glowed as she looked around the dining room.

"The captain agreed to marry us. Why make me wait, my darling." Donald lowered his head and raised her hand to his lips.

"We don't have the proper papers in order."

Donald fought back the frustration. "What do these papers have to do with our love for each other."

"But you agreed." Her bright blue eyes widened softening her crow's feet and making her look years younger.

"Of course I did. I'll do anything to please you. My dear, I've enjoyed the first half of our trip so much. I found myself laying in bed last night thinking that the only thing that would make this trip better would be if I could introduce you as my wife, rather than my companion. I guess you haven't noticed the raised eyebrows. I have."

"You have?"

"I just loathe the idea of anyone looking down at you. It isn't as though we are sharing a cabin but I believe most of our fellow travelers are thinking we are at least sharing some time in each others beds." Donald lowered his voice as he spoke.

Gloria turned to him. "You don't really. Your room is down the hall from mine."

"I know, my dear." Donald said as she straightened in her seat, looking around the dining room. "My only point is that I think we would both feel more comfortable if we married here, on the ship, for all to see."

"My friends would be so disappointed." Gloria pouted as she considered his suggestion.

"I'm sure they'll throw a grand party for us when we return. You can send telegrams to everyone...my family will be disappointed too, though I know my aunt was concerned about what people would think about us traveling unescorted."

Donald felt like he was on a roll. He put his arm around her and kissed her cheek. "Just consider it for me, for us. And personally, I feel a second marriage, which it is for both of us, should start out in a unique rather than repetitive way. We both had a large traditional first." He kissed her again. "I'll leave it for you to decide and I won't bother to ask you about it again. You let me know."

Donald studied her all through dinner and asked for the first dance with her. He'd never pushed the sex before marriage thing once she'd explained her puritanical views but that was about to change. He needed Gloria to agree. It was the only way for his plan to succeed.

"Why don't you come to my cabin for a night cap?" Donald asked, holding her close as they danced. ·

"How would it look?"

Donald kissed her neck. "Everyone thinks we are tip-toeing around anyway darling. I won't take advantage of you." He kissed her small ear as he whispered.

"I couldn't."

"Let me come to your cabin then."

"Please Donald."

"Sharing all of this time at sea has served to increase my desire for you. Having you so close." He slowly stroked her back and shoulders. "So close and yet so far from where I want you to be."

The song ended but he held her there as the next began. Gloria looked up into his eyes and he kissed her full lips.

"Yes." Gloria smiled. "Arrange it."

Donald kissed her again before leading her back to their table. Within ten minutes the captain was leading them up to his office to prepare the paperwork. Donald had worn a black tuxedo for the dinner and Gloria was dressed in a cream sequined evening gown. A quick call to the florist, a ship wide announcement and an hour later they were standing on deck exchanging vows.

When he said, I do, it was one of the grandest of his victories. He'd instantly become a multi-millionaire and the hard part was over. He kissed her in front of over two hundred passengers as he thought about how he would take her that night. Little miss puritanical was in for a bit of an education.

They drank champagne and danced for hours before he led her to her cabin. He carried her over the threshold and kissed her hard before setting her on her feet.

"I want to take care of some business before we get down to pleasure." He popped open another bottle of champagne and poured her a glass. "I want to make sure if anything happens to me, my papers are in order. You sit there and look pretty while I make the call to my attorney."

"Do you think that's necessary? Can't you take care of it tomorrow?"

"I'd like our personal matters reflecting the fact that we are now husband and wife." He kissed her again and opened his cell phone. "This shouldn't take too long." He dialed the number to his cell phone and his answering service picked up. "Yes, Mr. Austin. I've just married Gloria Fritz…thank you, sir…yes…I want everything to reflect joint ownership, you remember the packet we discussed…yes, I'll hold."

Donald slid a pen and paper over to her. "He'll need your date of birth and social security number."

Gloria nodded and wrote it down.

"Yes, sir…good…yes, I have that right here." Donald thought he'd pass out from the anticipation of hearing her make the call to her lawyer. He rattled off the information she'd written and then ended the call. He set the phone down beside her and wrote his information on the back of the same paper. "I know you'll need this."

Gloria hesitated. "Herbert's number is in my room."

"You relax and tell me where to find it."

Donald's plan swirled through his mind. He'd hold off until the end of the trip, two nights before they were to hit Miami, just in case he had to abort it for some reason. He'd have witnesses, he'd be rich, and he'd live the life he'd dreamed of without someone else holding the purse strings. His aunt had been very generous, even he had to admit that, but it wasn't enough. Donald needed the millions Gloria's estate would provide.

He went down the hall to her cabin, found the address book lying on the desk and quickly returned to her. He set the book down beside her and took her into his arms, his blood pulsing, his excitement was threatening to overwhelm him.

"I'm glad we did it." Gloria smiled up at him. "I do love you Donald."

"I'm sure each and every day of our lives together will be wonderful. You've made me very happy." Donald released her. "Let's get the business out of the way so we can get serious."

Donald moved behind her and kissed her neck as she dialed her lawyer. He had to move away from her as his body trembled with excitement. He listened to her make the changes. The only loose end was the pre-nuptial agreement, which Donald agreed he would sign as soon as they returned home.

"It's done." Gloria hung up the phone and refilled the champagne glasses. "The changes will be made in the morning." She walked over to him. "To us. May our love for each other continue to grow."

"All the days of our lives." Donald took the glass and tapped it to hers. His whole life had changed in less than six hours. He felt renewed, invigorated.

*   *   *   *

"Hey, lady." Martin smiled as she opened the kitchen door. "I've got the passengers list."

"Good morning." Helen fixed him a cup of coffee and joined him at the table. "I'm ready." She took the list and stopped at the third name as images began to flood her mind. "It's him. Donald Abington." Helen nodded. "I can see him now." Tears welled in her eyes. "My God."

Martin was on the phone. "I want everything you can find on one Donald Abington."

His voice was lost to her as the images of the man flashed through her mind like a slide show.

"Helen." Martin touched her shoulder.

"You've got to stop him…he's going to kill her."

"Who?"

"Gloria."

"Why?"

"Power." Helen closed her eyes and wiped her wet cheeks. She took a deep breath and looked over at him. "You have to arrest him."

"We need proof."

"You'll find proof in that storm drain. It's down there." She rubbed her arms as the chill crept into her flesh. "Damn…this guy is crazy but he's smart…you have to warn her."

Martin nodded. "I wish I could. We have to be careful."

"I'll call her then."

"No. You can't chance him getting a message from you."

"Well we have to do something."

"I'll go see her when they get back. I'll just have to figure out what to say."

Helen pondered the issue as she drank the hot coffee.

"I've got to get back to the station. I'll be back tonight. How about I pick up dinner."

"Sounds good."

Martin finished his coffee and left her sitting at the table, looking forward to his return. Helen went to the glass door and looked out at the cold churning waves as she pondered the killer's motivations. It was clear that all Gloria Fritz meant to him was the money. She'd be disposable once he had her wealth.

Martin showed up at six with the data on Donald Abington and a fantastic Italian dinner. After the lasagna, Martin handed her the information and refilled their wineglasses.

"You had this guy pegged. Not only is he from the Midwest, he's a retired police sergeant."

"That's why he's been able to get away with it."

Martin flipped the page. "He was on the task force for the murder of three college girls, six years ago."

"But can you prove it? Can you arrest him?"

"Not yet, but this gives us good reason to question him. We need to let him know we're on to him. It might slow him down."

"I don't think he's going to be killing when he returns."

"You don't?"

"No."

"You said Fritz is in danger."

"I think she's going to be his last victim…for a while, anyway."

"Damn." Martin slammed his fist on the table.

"He's married her."

"Damn…are you sure?"

Helen looked up at him. "Yes."

Martin tapped on the table. "There isn't much we can do with them at sea…damn." He got up and paced the kitchen.

"I have to call my aunt." Helen rushed to the phone and dialed her number. "Hi, Madeline."

"Hello dear, how are you?"

"I need your help. Have you ever done a reading for a Gloria, tall, thin, very rich?"

"Let me think…I do a monthly reading for a Gloria, hold on…yes, she hasn't been here for about two months."

"What's her last name and address?"

"She only gave a first name and C.F. for middle and last…her address, well I only have Longwood as address."

"Is her street considered the Longwood area?" Helen asked Martin.

"Yes."

"I'll be right over, auntie." Helen hung up the phone and picked up her jacket. "We'll have Madeline send her a message. She used to read her." Helen smiled.

"I'm right behind you."

Helen scowled at Martin's reaction to Madeline's parlor as he looked up at the ornate mystical decorations scattered on every wall. She shook her head as she sat on the sofa.

"So what is it? My heart has been racing since you called."

"First I have a few questions. Why did she stop coming?"

"She said her fiancé didn't approve."

Helen nodded. "What was your sense of the relationship? Can you remember?"

"Oh." Madeline went to the file drawer. "I've got it here. I always make notes." She smiled at Martin. "Helps me get ready for the next reading." She flipped through the papers and pulled the last one. "OK. I wrote, too rich, boyfriend not, empty heart, she is happy but he brings darkness." Madeline handed Helen her notes. "Tell me what's going on."

"He brings darkness." Helen said. "You need to get a message to her. She's in danger."

"From him." Madeline's tone was flat. "I hate giving bad news…I remember telling her that he may not be the right one…I should have focused in on it more seriously." She shook her head.

"It's okay auntie."

"Do you have her number?"

"She's on a cruise." Martin opened his notebook. "Here's the line's number. They will get the message to her."

"What should I say?"

"Give your name and say she must contact you immediately." Martin smiled.

"And when she calls?"

"Tell her she's in danger…tell her you have a vision, connected to her husband."

"She married him?"

"On the boat." Helen took a deep breath. "Tell her to get off the boat…you see her drowning…tell her to call the police when she returns and ask for Detective Hamlin."

Helen sat on the edge of the sofa listening as Madeline made the call.

Madeline's expression darkened as she hung up the phone. "You have such a gift…I should have taken more time with her."

Helen reached over and touched her aunt's hand. "Don't feel bad. You're doing all you can now."

"He's going to kill her?"

"He's planning to. Maybe we can stop it with your message."

"Maybe. I don't have a good feeling about it though."

Helen nodded. "Thank you for your help."

"It was good to see you."

"Please call either of us once you hear from her." Martin said as he walked toward the door.

"I will. Immediately." Madeline followed them out and stood in the doorway, waving goodbye.

"Now, see, that's what I expect a psychic's place to look like." Martin smiled as they drove down the road.

"There is no need for that."

"I don't think I've seen your parlor."

"It's over the garage and it's nothing like my aunt's place."

"I noticed the tarot cards. Do you use them?"

"No. I get feelings from personal items, jewelry, pictures, those types of things."

Martin nodded. "By her notes I'd say she was very close to the truth."

"Yes." Helen thought about the people that she'd refused to read in the past. "It's a business for her. Most clairvoyants stay away from bad news, maybe give a caution, but that's it. Bad news is bad for business."

"You two are different."

"Very. So what do we do now?"

"Wait for the call. I'll drop you at your house. I have to go to the station for a while."

CHAPTER 8

▼

Donald covered his sleeping wife's naked body and headed out for a quiet breakfast alone. As he closed the door he noticed a clerk knocking on Gloria's cabin door.

"Can I help you?"

"I have two messages for Miss Fritz."

Donald started toward him. "We were married by your captain. She's Mrs. Abington, now." Donald held out his hand for the messages as he reached into his pocket for a ten-dollar bill.

"Well, I..." the young man hesitated.

"She is sleeping in my cabin, if you insist, I'll wake her." Donald looked at his watch. "It's only eight. She usually doesn't rise before ten." Donald turned and took a step when the clerk stopped him.

"No. It's fine you don't need to wake her." He smiled, holding out the slips of paper.

"Thank you." Donald handed him the ten and watched him walk away. He studied the slips. The first was confirmation from her attorney stating the changes were all in place. The other was from a woman wanting an immediate call. He tossed the latter in the rubbish beside the elevator and put the attorney's message in his pocket.

Time was passing, he thought as he headed up to the dining room. He'd had fun using his prudish wife but knew it would grow old quickly. She'd served her purpose.

After breakfast he took a walk down to the lower deck. He leaned over the side checking for any obstruction that she might be able to grab onto as he searched for the perfect spot for his crime. He knew the deck would be brightly lit until midnight when the band stopped playing. Though he'd thought about throwing her off of his balcony, he wanted to have witnesses after the event. He'd seem more innocent if she fell overboard out in the open, where he could call for help.

The murder plan consumed him for the rest of the day. Gloria awakened after noon and he gave her the lawyer's message.

"Oh, well, that is good news." Gloria handed it back to him, blushing. "I'm sorry I fell asleep on you last night. I think I had too much wine."

Donald wrapped his arms around her. "Are you trying to tell me you don't remember last night?"

"I…" her pink cheeks darkened as she looked away. "The last thing I remember was laying down with you."

Donald laughed. "I assure you, you didn't fall asleep for hours after that."

"You're embarrassing me, Donald."

"I don't mean to. I was very happy with your performance, believe me."

"By that smile on your face I guess I'd have to." Gloria wiggled out of his arms and headed for the bathroom.

Donald walked out on the balcony and took a good look. It would be his last resort. He went back inside and called down for coffee while she showered. He felt like dancing but forced himself to act subdued.

Gloria joined him as the server tapped on the door.

"You look delicious." Donald smiled as he went to answer the knock. He took the tray and set it down on the table.

"Thank you."

"Now, would you like to stay on the boat today? We are going to be docking at Nassau for the afternoon."

"Nassau already?" Gloria picked up their itinerary. "Where has the time gone?"

"We've been busy." Donald grinned, touching her silky hair.

"I can't believe we'll be home in three days."

"Back to reality." Donald nodded. "We can't expect this to go on forever." As he glanced toward the window he saw dark clouds ahead of him and noticed the waves were getting higher.

"It looks like bad weather. Maybe we should do some shopping on board."

"That sounds good. I've hardly been to the stores."

They spent their afternoon mulling about the ship. The captain gave a warning about the weather and rough seas they were heading into as the ship left port. It lightened Donald's mood. High waves and rain would play right into his plan.

Of all the murders, Gloria's would be the most exciting and rewarding. No, he wouldn't be there to see the horror on her face as she died but he'd be able to picture her drowning in the huge dark ocean below.

"Donald...Donald."

He looked over at her standing by the door. She looked radiant in her full length black gown. "Excuse me?" He stood staring at her.

"I said we are going to be late for dinner." Gloria opened the door. "You weren't thinking about work already."

Donald nodded. "Yes. I'm sorry. I have to admit that I was."

"We still have a little time left."

"I know. Let's go enjoy it." Donald straightened his tie and patted his jacket pocket for the sleeping pills he'd ground up early that morning. He got a rush through his body when he felt the small packet. "Let's go."

Gloria held his arm as they walked down the hall, the boat rocking to a slow but steady pace.

"I wonder what the dining room will look like." Donald pushed the elevator button. "The halls are pretty empty for this hour."

"I'm glad we have these motion sickness patches." Gloria said. "It's not bothering me at all."

Donald had a powerful appetite. He finished dinner and ordered dessert for the first time since they'd been on the ship. It was a night to celebrate. As for Gloria, she would never have to face the mirror to see her beauty had abandoned her. For eternity she would be remembered as being in her prime. In the long run he was doing her a favor. She was far to vain to deal with such a loss. Donald studied her face as he sipped the last of his wine.

After dinner he escorted her out to the deck where they were told the band had been moved inside the main lounge due to the weather. As they walked inside Donald sat at the table closest to the door.

He looked out the windows at the lightening in the distance. When the waiter approached he ordered two margaritas and asked about the weather.

"We are expecting to be through the worst of it by two, maybe three in the morning. The rest of our trip looks calm."

"Thank you."

They did more drinking then dancing as the storm rocked the ship. The waves were fifteen feet high at midnight. They ordered a last drink and as soon as Gloria went to the ladies room, Donald put the powder in her glass. He watched as it quickly dissolved in the liquid and leaned back in his seat.

A short while later the band broke down their set and the lounge cleared, leaving Gloria and Donald to finish their drinks alone.

The workers scurried around cleaning up, giving the couple an occasional smile.

"I guess it's time to leave." Gloria frowned. "I'm exhausted."

Gloria stood and lost her footing. Donald grabbed a hold of her arm, steadying her as she reached for the chair for support.

"Maybe we should just…" Gloria glanced around the empty lounge. "Just stay in here…it's so rough."

"I'll help you."

"I'm feeling nauseous." Gloria looked up at him.

"Let's go outside. Maybe you just need some air." His nerves sparked as he walked her out onto the slick deck and led her to the rail.

"I have…to sit down…I feel sick…Donald."

"I'll get you a chair. Hold on." He put her hands on the rail and took a step away. Her hands slipped from the wet metal and she slumped to the deck. "Oh, dear." His heart pumped.

"Do you need assistance?" A young waiter asked as he walked out of the lounge.

"No. I guess she's had too many margaritas. She'll be fine."

"Very well." He turned and walked away.

"Can you stand?"

"No, I'm going to be ill." Gloria said as she rested against the bottom rail.

"Lean over the side." Donald helped her position herself just as she began to vomit. He scanned the empty deck. "You'll be fine."

"Please…I…need help…to get up."

Donald thought about the life insurance, the estate and business and smiled as he looked down at his pathetic wife. The boat continued it's violent rocking as lightening lit up the sky. She vomited again and then slumped over the rail.

"Gloria." He said as her arms went limp. When she didn't answer he looked around, took a deep breath and lifted her hips. The sky opened up and the rain turned into a torrential down pour. He pushed her body through the railings and watched as her head hit the side of the ship and she plummeted into the ocean.

He waited for a full two minutes before he ran into the empty lounge. "Help...help...my wife's fallen over...help."

A young woman ran out from the kitchen area. "Over board?"

"Yes. She needs help."

The young man who had approached them just minutes before came running out as the woman grabbed for the phone.

"I need a life preserver. I have to help her." Donald screamed.

The young man rushed to his side. "Stay calm sir." He said as a whistle blew.

Donald grabbed his upper arms. "Don't you understand she needs help." He said shaking the man. Donald released him and ran back outside to the rail. He started to put his leg through the rails and the man seized him around the waist, pulling him back to the lounge door.

"I have to save my wife." Donald screamed as the ship slowed.

"They'll circle around for her. Relax, please sir."

Searchlights hit the waves behind them as Donald sobbed for the gathering crowd of staff.

"What happened?" The captain asked as he approached the pair.

"My wife was ill." Donald looked at the captain and then at the young man. "I should have taken your offer to help." He cried, covering his face.

"What does he mean?"

"The woman was sitting on the deck by the railing...she was ill...I offered to help them, he said she'd had too much to drink."

"You have to find her. I only left her for a moment...I was going to ask him to help me get her to the cabin and when I got near the door...I looked back...I saw her slip through the railings...oh, please, tell me you are going to find her."

"Help Mr. Abington inside." The captain nodded toward the lounge. "We will do our best. We've already put in a call to the Coast Guard."

"Please, you have to find her...we were just beginning our life together." Donald sobbed as the young man led him inside.

*   *   *   *

"We were too late." Martin said as he walked into Helen's kitchen. "It's all over the news."

Helen sat down, his words hitting her in the gut. She looked at the front page and nodded.

"It's been ruled an accidental drowning. He has witnesses."

Helen shook her head. "The bastard threw her over board and we both know it."

"Knowing it and proving it are two different things."

"What about the knife. Did they find it?"

"Not yet."

"Did they find her body?"

Martin shook his head. "The Coast Guard searched the area but they say they may never find her."

"He can't get away with it."

"I put in a call to the ship's captain. By all accounts it looks like an accident."

"But we know it wasn't."

Their conversation was interrupted by Martin's cell phone. Helen walked out onto the deck and looked up at the cloudy sky wondering how they were going to find the proof of what she knew was true.

*   *   *   *

Donald returned home three days after the murder to set up a service for his newly wed, newly departed wife. A wife whom it appeared they would never find. He went directly to his new home and consoled the staff before calling Gloria's attorney. With the funeral plans in motion he went to his aunt's estate to be comforted by his family.

His aged aunt greeted him at the door, tears flowing down her pale, weathered face. Donald hugged her, crying on her shoulder for several minutes until her private nurse escorted her to her room.

Donald picked up his messages off the table in the hall and headed for his room.

"Donald," Tara called as she rushed up the stairs after him. "I was so sorry to hear." She hugged him as she stepped onto the landing.

"Thank you. It was quite a shock."

"I'm sure." Her eyes widened. "What happened? Or is it too soon to talk about it?"

"Let's talk in my room. I'm exhausted. I need to sit down." Donald walked down the hall, controlling the smile that threatened to give away his mood. He held his hand out for her to enter his sanctuary first and followed her inside taking a seat at the small table by the balcony door.

"I was so shocked. It's been all over the news."

"I know." Donald shook his head. "We got married...everything was great...we had dinner..." he took a deep breath. "She liked her booze...we'd been dancing and she got nauseous and leaned over the rail to vomit. I went to get someone to help me get her up to the cabin and when I looked back." Donald looked out the window. "She was gone."

"My God."

"They tried to find her...even did a room by room search of the ship in case she'd made it inside...I knew she'd gone over board...she disappeared in a flash."

"Did you hear a splash?" Tara leaned closer.

"No...we were going through some rough weather...I didn't hear anything."

Donald relived the experience as he spoke, picturing the spotlights, hearing the whistles. He shook his head. "I was just getting to where I wanted to be. I still can't believe it."

"I am so sorry. What are you going to do now?"

He shook his head. "I'm having a service for her on Friday. I can't think past that."

Tara stood and patted him on the shoulder. "I'll let you get some rest. If you need to talk you know where to find me."

"I appreciate that." He watched her walk out of the room and leaned back in the chair. There was so much to plan, decide, he found it exciting, a far cry from his limited life of a few weeks before.

He went to his desk and did a search on his computer for any news relating to the murders. He enjoyed reading what few details the police had released. It served as a prompt for him to remember the events in detail. He smiled as he read a patrolman's comment about the killer being on a power trip.

They thought they had him pegged and they knew nothing. He was little more than a hunter, one that couldn't be tracked down. The thought made him smile. There was no mention of the so-called psychic. He sat at the desk reading, grinning at the police incompetence for a half an hour until he saw a name that made him straighten in the leather seat.

He recognized it instantly as the name on the message. The woman was being interviewed about the children Helen Staples had helped locate. The woman was Helen's aunt. The realization shook him. It was Helen who was trying to warn Gloria. He was sure of it.

"You just put a big target on your head you stupid bitch." Donald said as he closed the laptop.

He got up and paced the room. He'd have to come up with a plan for her. If the cops had proof they would have arrested him already. All they had was some feelings from some damned fortuneteller. He had to stop her, before it was too late.

His blood pressure jumped as the anger built inside him. He'd get pleasure in slicing her throat. It was clear she was still under police protection. He had to find a way to get her away from the cops.

Donald focused on getting through the week. He was glad when he woke Friday morning knowing the worst of it would be over that night. He was expecting everyone who ever met Gloria to attend the memorial service. It was sure to be a long ordeal but one that he knew he wouldn't have to repeat.

By nine o'clock he was dressed and anxious to leave the house. He arrived at the cathedral an hour early and spoke with her friends and extended family. Now he was the man. He got the sense that the people he spoke with had elevated him since Gloria's death. They realized he was no longer marrying into money, he was the money. The thought made him stand taller.

Before the service he called Gloria's house to make sure all of the preparations were made for the gathering at her home following the service. After being reassured by the cook, he shut off his cell phone and took his seat in the front row.

Donald glanced back and was grateful when he saw his aunt and cousin walking down the aisle. He stood and watched as they took their seat in the front row and then sat down, ready to begin.

As the pastor began his opening prayer, Donald closed his eyes thinking about the many high profile attendees. He'd nodded once in the direction of the chief of police and decided he wouldn't look at him again unless the man approached him. He'd kept his expression from revealing his pleasure at seeing Senator Hix seated beside Congressman Lewis two rows behind him.

Gloria's lifelong friend, Genevieve Lawrence, spoke at length about their decades together, stopping to wipe her eyes several times. When she was through she stopped and hugged Donald before taking her seat behind him.

Donald arrived at Gloria's home well before any of the guest and after inspecting the preparations, he went into the den and had several drinks before their arrival. Thoughts of the fortuneteller clouded his mind. He had to fight to focus on being the shocked, grieving widower as the house filled.

He took refuge in a corner of the living room, his cousin beside him, as the guests mingled. The two hours dragged on but slowly the house began to empty. He encouraged his aunt to go home, saying he needed to be alone with his thoughts of Gloria and she was glad to oblige.

Once alone, Donald wandered through the mansion, familiarizing himself with every aspect of his new home. When he was done he was ready to work on a plan to rid himself of the fortuneteller.

CHAPTER 9

▼

Helen shivered and rubbed her upper arms as she walked over to the fireplace. Winter was upon them. She started a fire, sitting by it as it began to roar. She listened to the weather channel and was relieved to hear it wouldn't be a bad storm, just enough to mess up the roads for a day.

She glanced at the clock, anxious for Martin to arrive with dinner. She hadn't seen him in three days and she missed him. The thought brought a smile to her face.

One thing nagged at their time. The case had hit a roadblock. The police ruled Gloria Abington's death an accident and according to Martin, Abington had moved into his wife's house the day after the memorial.

For Helen his motive was simple. He inherited millions from her death. One type of power may have replaced the other. Maybe he wouldn't be so willing to go out and kill again with so much money at stake. Nothing had happened since his return from the cruise and though Helen was grateful no one else had been murdered, she was afraid that the case would go cold.

She'd given Martin everything she knew but it wasn't near enough to charge him. The police needed to find the knife. They needed one piece of solid evidence to be able to put it all together.

Helen jabbed at the embers as she stared into the flames. She jumped when China stood and ran for the door.

"Who is it, girl?" Helen felt better when China started wagging her tail. "I guess it must be him." Helen went into the kitchen to let Martin in.

"Hi. That dog can smell a steak a mile away." Martin laughed, as he walked in and set the bag on the counter. "How are you?" He turned and looked at her.

"Fine. You?"

"I'm good. I've got my other cases clear. Still no luck with the knife."

Helen nodded. "Then let's not talk about it tonight." She felt as though she was in more danger than ever.

"Are you okay? You look worried." Martin touched her arm.

"I'm fine." She managed a smile for him.

"That's much better. So, what do you think about the snow?" He turned to the bag, pulling the cartons from it.

"Looks good." Helen shrugged. "I'm not crazy about the winter. I have a tendency to get cabin fever after the first week of snow and I suffer the rest of the season." Helen explained as she set the table.

"I don't mind the winter...not anymore. I used to hate it when I was a patrolman. I'd get one call after another and for the most part the accidents were from speeding. You can't go even thirty miles an hour when there's ice on the road but year after year they do. I bet you each of the guys out there tonight will get ten accidents before their shift ends."

Martin sat down and smiled at her. "I've missed you."

"And I you."

Martin nodded. "I'm glad to hear that. Let's eat."

After dinner, Helen worked on building a blazing fire while Martin looked through the movie collection.

"I hope I'll be able to stay for this one."

"So do I."

"You'd better be careful." Martin said as he turned on the television. "I might start to think you like me."

"I've never hidden the fact that I enjoy your company."

"I'm just teasing you." Martin laughed. "Now come sit down before you burn me out with that fire."

"Sorry. I've had a chill all evening." Helen said as she joined him on the couch.

"That's why you bought this." Martin pulled the afghan from behind her and put it over her lap.

"I made it."

"You did? Well, I learn a little more about you all the time."

They managed to watch the comedy start to finish before their evening was interrupted by Martin's phone.

"I've got to go." Martin said as he put the phone in his pocket. "I'll call you tomorrow."

"OK." Helen said as she followed him to the door. "Would you like to come for dinner? I'm making beef stew."

"Love to." Martin kissed her on the cheek and bounded out the door.

The smile on his face warmed her as she watched him back out of the driveway. She hated to see him leave. She shut off the lights and lay down on the couch still feeling the chill in her bones.

Helen fell asleep watching the news but flashes of Gloria leaning over the railing troubled her slumber. Helen could feel her helplessness and the cold ocean that engulfed her.

By four o'clock she'd given up on getting any peace and made a pot of coffee. She shook her head as China let out little barks in her sleep.

Normally her restless mood would warrant a walk on the beach and that irritated her further, knowing the murderer was stopping her from enjoying basic freedoms. She made some toast and sipped the hot coffee while she watched the clock. Between the gloomy winter morning and lack of sleep, Helen knew the day could not pass soon enough.

She thought about the effects her gift had thrust upon her in the previous months. Her life was taking a new direction but it left her feeling like a fish flopping around on a wooden dock.

Helen fixed another cup of coffee and walked up the stairs to her parlor. The variety of scented candles lulled her senses and helped her to relax. She sat at the large desk and lit her two favorites. She needed to get focused. She felt it was essential to get deeper into his mind. Helen closed her eyes picturing the killer.

The images came fast. She saw a windowless room. A hidden place. He was moving things around. He was angry and excited. She saw ropes and knives laid out on a marble table in a corner by the thick door.

Helen sat back in the seat, exhausted and cold.

"Helen." Martin called from the bottom of the stairs.

She sat up and looked at the clock and realized she'd fallen asleep. "Yes, I'll be right down. I thought you were coming for dinner."

Helen blew out the candles and went down to see him.

"You had a few messages. One stood out." Martin handed the paper to her as she made the last step.

Helen looked at him and then the paper before reading it aloud. "You had your chance." Helen gave it back to Martin and nodded. "It's from him. He knows I got Madeline to send that message. Now he has set his sites on me."

Martin took a step back. "What else?"

"He's planning to kidnap and kill me. He's setting up a torture chamber."

Martin hit the wall beside him hard enough to make a dent in the plaster. "Shit...shit...I'm sorry." He walked into the kitchen and stopped by the window. "I don't care what you say, I'm staying here until this bastard is caught."

Helen walked to the kitchen and rinsed out her cup before pouring coffee for both of them "I would have told you before but I wasn't-." His wide eyes made her stop.

"You can read my mind."

"More as time goes on."

Martin crossed his arms over his broad chest. "Can I test you?"

"Are you sure you want to?"

"It might help me gauge how you read him."

Helen shrugged and sat across from him, staring into his eyes. "You'd like to take a shower with me." The heat rose to her cheeks.

"I...was thinking that as a test."

"It's not the first time you've thought that." Helen smiled.

Martin put up his hands. "Okay...do you do that to me, you know, and not tell me about it?"

"My senses have been changing, sharpening. Let me give you a for instance." She lit a cigarette, bracing herself to be blatantly honest. "Some people get a ringing in their ears when someone is talking about them. I'm sure you've heard that."

Martin nodded.

"For me, as of late any way, when someone is thinking about me, I know who they are and what they are thinking."

"Can you give me an example?"

Helen took a deep drag and smiled. "Two nights ago, you couldn't get me out of your mind. You were angry and shooting lousy darts." Helen smiled at him. "And finally, you laid down and focused on that morning and how you'd felt sharing a cup of coffee-."

"It's that bad? That strong?"

"Not with everyone, but yes. Remember when little Cathy said she'd been calling for me to help her? That's what allowed me to help her. It's called channeling your thoughts. You do it too but you aren't aware of it. Your mind is still closed off to your other senses." She flicked her ash giving him time to digest her words.

"But I don't want you to be uncomfortable with me because of it. I'm not trying to read you. It just flows into my mind."

"Do you have any books on the subject?"

"I've never needed any." Helen touched his arm.

"So what you're telling me is that he's focused in on you and you can see what he's doing and thinking?"

"Because it is aimed at me. I believe that's what's making things so clear now."

"What's he planning to do? You said torture?"

Helen nodded. "Yes. He has knives and rope." Her green eyes widened. "The knives. Get someone out to a hunting store. These are not steak knives. Somewhere there's a record of what he's bought."

Martin took out his pad and scribbled some notes. "You said it's a windowless room. Do you know where?"

"No. It's not familiar to him. It's…well…I get a sense that he's happy there and that it's a new place."

"Happy?" Martin frowned.

"Yes. He's excited about it. He feels safe there." Helen rubbed her arms.

"Are you afraid?"

"Yes…but in a way, I'm ready."

"Ready?"

"To have this over with. He must be caught, if that means he has to come after me, so be it."

"Oh, God." Martin put down the small notebook and walked over to the counter. He studied her face. "Don't hold anything back from me."

Helen nodded.

"I don't care how crazy something might seem, I want you to tell me about it."

Helen put out the cigarette needing a break from his stare.

"I'm going back to the station to make a few calls and get some boys on the sporting shops. I'll be here for dinner. You call if you need me."

"I will."

Helen put together the stew before starting the housework. China stayed close to her all day, even sitting outside the bathroom door as Helen showered.

"You silly thing. I'm fine." Helen said as she walked into the bedroom. She sat at the vanity brushing out her long hair with China's huge head on her lap.

"You're getting too big for all this. You aren't a lap dog." Helen said as she set down the brush and patted the dog's neck.

Helen threw on a T-shirt and sweat pants and went to the kitchen to stir the bubbling stew. She set the pot to low and set the timer for an hour. Her mood lightening as she thought about Martin's return.

The tap on the door made her jump but the realization that China didn't bark a warning told her it was Martin.

"You're early." Helen smiled at him.

He studied her for a minute making her look down at her attire. "It's nice to see you looking so relaxed."

Helen didn't know if she should change or not as he assessed her.

"You look different with all that red hair flowing down your back." He raised an eyebrow at her and then quickly changed the subject. "I could smell that stew in the driveway." He said as he lifted the cover off of the pot. "Is it ready?"

"Won't be perfect for an hour."

"I don't know if I can wait."

"Sure you can." Helen smiled.

"So how was your day?"

"Productive."

"Anything else?"

"No. Well, I don't…"

"What is it?"

Helen reached for a cigarette. "I think I should warn you not to kill him."

"Please?"

"You're going to want to shoot him at some point, my life may depend on you not killing him."

"Helen, come on." Martin sat at the table.

"You wanted me to tell you what ever came to me and that came through hard."

"He's not going to get to you."

Helen shrugged. She'd seen him busying himself in the room. He had a plan for her. Now Helen had to figure out what it was.

"Are you sure he's going to get to you?"

"Nothing is set in stone."

"What the hell does that mean?"

"It's fluid…it can change." Helen looked at the snow swirling around outside the kitchen window. "Like the weather."

"I don't mind saying you have me freaked out."

"I know."

"Ugh…yes…I prefer saying it out loud." Martin got up and paced the living room for several minutes before returning to the table.

"We have to take it a day at a time." Helen said as she put the rolls into the oven. "For now, let's concentrate on dinner. Do you prefer butter or margarine."

"Butter if you have it."

"Of course." She took the butter out to soften and went to the living room to put another log on the fire.

"It is warm in here."

"I can't seem to get rid of this chill. It goes away for a while but comes back biting at me." Helen stayed by the fireplace until the buzzer on the stove signaled it was time for dinner.

"I haven't smelled food like this since I was a kid." Martin smiled as she took the rolls out of the oven. "My mother was a great cook She always made a big breakfast on the weekend and of course some great dinner every night."

"You had a good childhood?"

"The best. Things changed when I was about thirteen but I always managed to draw on my early years to get through it."

When he didn't expand on the subject Helen felt compelled to share with him. "That's about how things were for me too. When my father was alive we had a real tight family. My mother was very happy and it made us happy. Things went cool after he died. My mother tried but it was a burden for her supporting us. We had some tough times." Helen smiled at Martin. "But I'd always remember the good times and realized early on how lucky I was."

"I've had a few job offers." Helen said as she cleared the dinner plates.

"And?"

"Well, they've been interesting."

"Are you considering any?"

Helen shrugged. "I have to pay my bills. I'm looking forward to putting the bastard behind bars so I can get on with my life."

"Whoa." Martin raised his brows. "I'd hate to be the cause of that look."

"I'm angry…like today…I would have walked two miles or more if it weren't for that creep. I'm a prisoner under guard and he's running around killing people for sport."

"Sport?"

"Sport…at any rate, yes, I'm looking at all of them."

"That's good. I'd feel better if you had a less dangerous job."

"So would I. I'm not enjoying this cat and mouse game at all."

Helen walked out to the living room and put another log on the fire.

"Thanks again for dinner."

"My pleasure."

"So." Martin sat on the couch beside her. "Tell me about these job offers."

"Well, there are two that sounded interesting. Both are working with a private detective finding missing persons. I think I could do that. I'd be using my gifts but in a less hazardous way."

"Are you going to respond to them?"

"I can't do anything until you arrest that bastard."

Martin nodded. "We will." Martin put the afghan over her shoulders. "Maybe you should see a doctor about this chill. It's hot as hell in here."

"No need. It will pass." Helen smiled up at him.

"I think finding missing persons would be a good job for you." Martin stared into her eyes. "We'll still see each other."

Helen wasn't sure if it was a statement or a question. "Of course."

CHAPTER 10

▼

Helen turned on the news at noon and listened to it as she peeled carrots for the pot roast. When she heard the name Katie Johnson the room spun in front of her eyes. She clutched the counter, waiting for it to pass before attempting to sit down. The missing girl's name repeated in her mind as she looked at the photo of her on the screen.

When the segment ended Helen flipped through the channels hoping to hear more details about the case. The news only repeated the same things, ten year old kidnapped as she walked home from school the day before. No witnesses. She was last seen four blocks from her house where she parted company with her friend.

Helen called Martin. "What do you have on Katie Johnson?"

"Not much more than what they're reporting on the news."

"Damn it."

"Why? What is it?"

"I've got a bad feeling…nothing I can put my finger on…but, damn it got cold in here."

"I'm not working the case but I'll talk to the detective who's handling it and see what I can come up with."

"Thanks."

"Are you cooking tonight?"

"Pot roast."

"Enough for two?"

"You know it."

"I'll be there around six."

Helen hung up the phone and turned up the volume on the news. There was something about the girl. Something demanding her attention. Helen played with the fire while she listened for more details.

*   *   *   *

Donald pulled the unconscious girl out of the trunk and flopped her over his shoulder. He carried her around the back of the cabin, dropping her on the ground. His heart pounded as he unlocked the bulkhead that led to the bomb shelter below. He unlocked the inside door and went outside for her. She was starting to come around as he lifted her and carried her inside. She was moving her head as though she could see through the duct tape he'd slapped across her eyes.

It was a shame she had to become such a young victim, Donald thought as he entered the shelter, but it saved her from turning into a bitchy old woman. She'd always be remembered as a sweet little girl. Donald smiled as he laid her down on the bed in the corner. He gave her another shot of the sedative and she went limp in seconds.

Donald walked into the larger adjoining room and smiled as he tapped the knife handles. Before long he'd have the fortuneteller all to himself. He was going to have fun with her.

He checked his watch and headed back to the estate. Dinner with his cousin in one hour, he had just enough time to make it.

All through the meal he thought about the trap. Helen would come to him. His mind went back to the cruise and he knew Helen was going to be a much bigger challenge than Gloria. Killing her had been too easy and he'd been denied the look on her face as she realized her last moment had arrived.

After dinner he returned to his captive who was awake and struggling to free herself.

"Relax."

She jumped when he spoke. "Please let me go. Please. My mom will be worried."

"I will, Katie." Donald walked over to the bed and sat beside her. "If you do as I say I will take you home myself."

"My mom is poor. She can't pay for a kidnapping."

"I'm going to bring you home real soon, for free."

"Can I go now?"

"No. First you have to help me test an old friend."

"Please untie me. My hands hurt."

Donald studied her. "From now on you must obey the rules here. First you don't speak unless I tell you to."

"Please let me go-." Her sentence ended with a cry as his hand came down on her thigh

"I said, don't speak until I tell you to."

"I'm sorry." She nodded, her small body shaking.

"I need you to call my friend."

"Okay."

"In your mind...see...she is the only one who can help you. If you can bring her here, you'll go home."

"In my mind?"

"Haven't you ever wished for something...a toy perhaps...you need to wish for Helen to come and rescue you. Otherwise I'll have to keep you here with me forever."

"Helen. Come in here." The girl cried.

"You'll have to do better than that." Donald laughed. "Keep trying...I have to go now." He said as he laid her on her back. "I'll leave your feet free." He tied her hands to the bed. "I'll be back later."

Donald pulled the syringe out of his pocket and gave her a half dose. "That will help you rest but you must keep on wishing for Helen."

The girl nodded. "I am."

*   *   *   *

Over the next few days Helen was haunted by thoughts of the kidnapped girl but she had no picture, no sense of where she might be. She continued to see the torture chamber associated with the killer but the vision didn't change. The room was still empty. It was Helen that he'd set it up for that was clear. But she felt he was somehow related to the girl's disappearance.

The press had seized upon the statement by the first rescued girl's mother that she said she was calling for Helen, willing her, begging Helen to find her. That fact weighed heavy on her mind. What if he was using the child to lure Helen? The more she thought about it the more likely it seemed.

Helen hadn't seen Martin in days. He'd been slammed with a variety of cases and had used his apartment, which was only two miles from the police station to take the few catnaps he'd found time for.

She called his cell phone and left a message. Within an hour he called her back.

"I want to go to the girl's house."

"I'm sorry, what girl?"

"Katie Johnson. I want to go to her school and walk to her house the way she walked. I'm getting nagged. I know you're busy but I feel I have to go...if you can't take me soon, I'll drive there myself and the patrolman can follow me."

"No. Out of the question...look, I'm tied up for the next, oh, two hours or so...let's plan to go at four, after that we can go for dinner, unless you had other plans."

"Okay. I'll be waiting...maybe you can bring something that belongs to her."

"I'll look into it...hold on sergeant...I'm sorry but I have to go."

"See you at four."

Helen felt better. At least she could do something other than pacing her house thinking about the girl. She was eager for any vision but all she had was the nagging feeling the girl was in danger and it had to do with the killer.

She braided her hair and got ready for Martin then sat at the kitchen table to wait. Martin arrived promptly at four and handed her an old teddy bear.

"The parents gave this to Palmer saying she'd need it when she was found."

Helen held the stuffed animal and got a sense of the girl. She was intelligent and kind. Within a few minutes it all came flooding in.

The terror Katie Johnson felt when she was grabbed from behind caused Helen to cry. Katie didn't see the man's face but she knew it was a man. He'd slapped tape over her eyes as he dragged her to the street. He picked her up and put her in the trunk and then stabbed her leg with a needle to drug her.

"Damn." Helen put the bear down on the table and looked up at Martin who was standing beside her. "We have to find her. He's keeping her drugged."

They headed for the elementary school and though they walked to the house and back twice, all Helen could feel was north. The girl was far north of her home but there wasn't anything clear. It was a mere sense.

"Damn it." Helen said as they returned to his car. "It's just not there."

"Relax. Like you said, you can't force it." Martin glanced at her as he got into the car. "You haven't been eating, have you?"

"No. And you've been living off of fast food." Helen raised a brow at him as she lit a cigarette.

"You got me. I'm ready for a thick steak. We have a reservation at The Hamlet."

"I haven't been there in years."

Helen was pleased to see that the restaurant was the same cozy environment she remembered. It was one of the first places Tim had taken her. She thought about how her life had changed since those innocent, quiet days with Tim.

"Is your drink okay?" Martin leaned toward her as he spoke.

"Yes. Fine. Sorry."

"That's all right. I'm getting used to seeing your wheels spin." He covered her hand with his. "We will find her."

"I have to do it." She stared into his brown eyes. "It's him. He's got her."

"Abington?"

"Yes."

"How do you see them being connected?"

"She's the bait. That's how he plans to get to me."

"Shit." Martin looked up at the waiter as he set the drink in front of him. "Sorry."

"I've heard worse." The young man smiled.

"So what do we do?" Martin asked as he watched him walk away.

"I have to figure out where the girl is."

"And when you do?"

"I'll need your help." Helen knew that it was a statement of fact. The room in her visions haunted her. The knives were like none she'd ever seen. Double edged with odd-looking sides, curves and cuts taken out of the blade.

"You can't let him get you alone. I don't want you to take any chances." Martin leaned closer as he spoke.

"I won't…but I see myself at his mercy."

"Shit."

"You asked me to be honest with you. But I've told you before the visions are fluid."

"Fluid." Martin scowled, leaning back in his chair. "From this point on we are joined at the hip."

"Excuse me?"

"Where I go, you go, until we get this bastard." Martin finished his drink and waved to the waiter for another. "I've been leaving you alone too much."

"You can't call it alone when I've had an officer at my house round the clock."

Martin studied her. "You don't know how he'll try to get to you?"

"Only that it involves the girl as bait. If we find her, we'll find him."

"Are you worried?"

"I'm scared to death." Helen shrugged. "But I'm ready to face him in order to end this."

The waiter brought their salads ending the conversation until the dinner plates were cleared.

"After dinner drink for the lady and I'll have a coffee."

"I've had enough."

"It won't hurt you." Martin smiled at the waiter. "You need to relax."

"Believe me, I am feeling relaxed already. What I really need is a cigarette." Helen said as the waiter served her the drink.

"Drink up and we'll go."

"You're getting kind of pushy." Helen smiled as she reached for the glass.

"Sometimes I can't help myself."

"I'll keep that in mind."

Helen could feel the liquor as she walked out to the car. She'd had that one to many she usually avoided. She melted into the seat as Martin closed the door and listened to the soft music as he drove her home.

"Thanks for dinner." Helen looked up at him as he opened the door for her.

"My pleasure." He said following her inside. Martin put a log on the embers and watched as the flames licked the edges. "I'd like to talk about us." He said with his back to her as she sat on the couch.

"Okay." Helen studied him, feeling what was in his heart.

"I don't know how you feel about me." He turned to face her.

"That's a hard one." Helen patted the seat beside her. "I care about you, as much as I've tried to fight it."

"I love you, Helen." Martin cupped her face in his hands. "I enjoy our time together but I want more. I need to be closer to you."

"There are times that I want to be closer to you, too, but-."

Martin put a finger to her lips. "Let's leave it at that." He put his arms around her and pulled her against his chest. "Let's just sit here together and enjoy the fire."

The last thing Helen remembered was closing her eyes as he stroked her hair. When she awoke she was laying on her bed fully clothed with Martin sleeping beside her. She studied his handsome face needing to absorb the peaceful moment.

Ten minutes later he opened his eyes and smiled at her.

"Good morning." He said, smoothing his hands over his short black hair. "Seven o'clock? That's the most sleep I've had this month. Must be the company."

China walked to the door and looked in at them.

"I can take a hint." Martin said to the dog as he got out of bed. "You relax, I'll let her out and start the coffee."

"You're going to spoil me."

"I'm going to try." He smiled and walked out of the room.

Helen took a shower and joined him in the kitchen as he was pouring the first cup. She asked if they could go for a ride and he agreed. After a quick breakfast they hit the road heading north. They rode around until five o'clock with no results. Helen could feel the girl's panic increasing with the passage of time.

Helen was weighted by the disappointment when they returned home.

She sat at the table studying the map. North of Katie's home was farmland, vacation cabins surrounding a lake and more farmland. Helen split the area in half with a red pen. The girl was below the line and north of her home.

Martin made a few business calls and ordered Chinese food for dinner while she focused on the map.

Helen made a circle, which covered three miles and pointed to the center of it. "She's in this area."

Martin nodded, peering over her shoulder. "We'll get out there in the morning. From now on I want you to keep your gun with you."

Helen got the plates out while Martin set the table. "I plan to."

Helen was haunted by the images of the room. A stark light was reflected off the knives from a bare bulb above. It was cold. The missing girl was near the room. It was all so clearly connected.

"We've got to get your mind off of this for a while."

Martin's voice brought her back from the visions. She looked over at him, rubbing her arms. "I think it's time for me to get closer to the fire." Helen said as she got up and refilled her coffee cup.

"Go ahead. I have a few calls to make." Martin shooed her into the other room.

Helen put the cup on the mantle, struggling with the urgency of the visions. She poked at the embers and laid another log on the flames. Their meeting was approaching and she didn't know how to prepare for it. She had no idea how he would get her alone, but it was clear he would. She'd be at his mercy.

Martin joined her at the fireplace and put his arm around her. "You can talk to me." He said as he wiped the tears from her eyes. "What is it?"

Helen shook her head. "I can't get it out of my mind. The bastard has me scared...for the girl and for us." Helen looked up into his brown eyes. "Is there any chance they'll find the gloves or the knives?"

"They're working on it." He patted his shoulder.

"Can't you bring him in for questioning?"

"Not without cause. We've got nothing on him. Osborne said Abington seemed relaxed when he questioned him. He had an answer for everything and when Osborne brought up Gloria the man sobbed as though he was still grieving." Martin scowled. "He's cagey. Osborne said that if he didn't know any better he would think you were on the wrong track here. When we have something solid we'll nail him."

Helen sat on the couch and China climbed up beside her, putting her head on Helen's lap. "She knows you're upset." Martin smiled as he sat on the chair. "We're going to get through this."

"As soon as we do, I quit."

"I'm looking forward to the day."

Helen tossed and turned all night, finally giving up as the sun rose. When she walked into the kitchen she could hear Martin talking outside. She opened the door to see him standing in a foot of snow.

"Oh, shit, how did this happen?" Helen said as he walked inside.

"Good question. It was supposed to be a dusting but it got stalled over the water and...here's the result. We've got thirteen inches and it's still coming down hard." Martin brushed the snow off his shoulders and arms and stomped his feet before walking inside.

"You're up early."

"The damn phone woke me at four. I couldn't go back to sleep."

"I guess we'll have to put off our ride until this afternoon."

Martin shook his head. "Sorry lady, we'll be lucky to get out by tomorrow afternoon."

"No. We don't have that kind of time."

"The roads are shot. We have to wait." He hung his coat on the hook by the door and sat down to take off his boots. "If we can't move then neither can he.

Come on. Sit down. This stress isn't good for you. Maybe you should bake a cake or something."

"Bake a cake?"

"My mother used to bake up a storm when she was stressed out. She said it was a woman thing."

"I might just do that. Lord knows I've got cabin fever." She went to the cupboard and pulled out a recipe book. "You pick it, I'll bake it."

CHAPTER 11

▼

Martin studied her as she sliced into the Black Forest cake. "You aren't eating enough."

"I can't." Helen said as she cut a slab for him and a sliver for herself. "We've got to get out of here tomorrow morning."

"What if we don't? What if we wait him out?"

"He'll kill her and come up with another plan." Helen sat down across from him. "Try the cake. Tell me if it's as good as your mother's."

"Nothing could be that good, but I'll tell you if you came close." Martin took a bite of the cake and savored the flavor. "Oh, it's real close. Excellent, thank you."

What more could a man ask for, Martin thought as he smiled at her. Everything about her was right for him. They enjoyed each other's company like a comfortable shoe yet there was always the spark, the tension, when they were close enough to touch. He'd endured endless hours of longing to hold her, wanting to stroke her long auburn hair, kiss her, yet he'd held back. He looked forward to the day when he could act on the urges rather than fight them.

He straightened in his seat as her cheeks reddened. "What is it?"

Helen stood and kissed his cheek before going to the sink with her plate.

"Tell me what you are thinking." Martin said as he scraped the last of the frosting from his dish.

"I was thinking about having some wine." Helen smiled.

"Sounds good." Martin stood up and walked over to her. "I'll do the honors."

"Fine. While that's breathing I'm going to shower."

Martin moaned when she disappeared down the hall. He hoped she'd return wearing baggy flannels and a huge terry robe. His thoughts were running away with him and he knew she could sense it. He opened the wine and took out the stemware.

He'd been patient with her. He didn't have a choice. She was the first woman he'd ever wanted to possess. The thought caused him to question himself often. What the hell was it about her that had him so engrossed? His only answer was everything.

He looked out the window at the mounting snow and noticed the officer brushing off his car across the street.

"How is it out there?" Helen asked as she walked over to him.

Martin turned around and was stunned to see her wearing a black silk night-gown covered only by an open black silk robe. The slit on the gown showed her ample cleavage forcing him to turn back to the window as the sight aroused him.

"Damn…yes…it's really piled up but it looks like it's finally starting to slow down."

"The plows have only come by twice."

"Be grateful they've come at all." Martin held onto the curtain.

"Is the wine ready?"

"Sure."

Helen touched his sleeve. "Are you okay, Martin?"

"Yes. Fine." Martin released the curtain and poured the wine. "A shower sounds like a good idea." Martin handed her a glass and hurried off to the bath-room, visions of him laying her on a blanket in front of the fireplace urging him on.

He closed the door and leaned against it, the thought of her looking so sexy was driving him mad. Martin took a cool shower and regained control before joining her in the living room.

"I picked a nineteen fifty's western." Helen smiled up at him as she poked at the flaming logs.

"Do you want a refill?"

"Sure. What were you doing in there?"

"Excuse me?" Martin stared at her.

"You were in there for an hour."

"I was thinking." He walked into the kitchen and retrieved the bottle and his glass. He shut off the living room light as he walked by the switch, hoping it would help if he couldn't see her as clearly.

"Okay." Helen hit the play button as he sat beside her on the couch. "I haven't seen this one in years." She smiled up at him as he refilled the glass. "Do you think we'll be able to get out of here tomorrow?"

"Yes. By the afternoon." Martin finished the first glass quickly and poured another.

"Are you sure you don't want to talk about what ever is bothering you?"

"No…well…no. Watch the movie." He studied her face as her green eyes focused on the screen. He wanted to wake up to that face every day.

"I'll be right back."

"Where are you going?"

"I've got to brush my hair. I'll do it out here."

Martin watched her. He wanted to scoop her up in his arms and carry her to the bed. He shook his head and focused on the television. When she returned she pushed the hassock over by the fireplace and sat down to brush her hair dry. Finally Martin couldn't take it anymore and walked over behind her.

"Let me do it." He held out his hand for the brush.

"One hundred strokes."

Martin knelt down and brushed her long auburn waves. "Do you ever cut it?"

"Trim."

"It's beautiful." He felt like a teenager on his first date as he gave her silky hair one hundred and one strokes.

"Thank you." Helen said as he handed her the brush. She set it on the mantle and returned to the couch.

Martin sat beside her and put his arm around her. "This is a good movie. I've only seen it once." He took a deep breath as she settled against him. "I've been thinking about retiring."

"You have?"

"Yes. I'd draw a decent pension and I'm still young enough to switch gears."

"What will you do?"

"Maybe open a private investigator's office." He smiled when she looked up at him. "Those offers you've been getting have made me think I might be ready for a change."

"I'm glad to hear it." Helen snuggled against him. "You're so warm."

Martin pulled the afghan over them and rubbed her back. "Is that better?"

"Yes."

"You feel warm to me." The truth was she felt like she was on fire as she rested against his chest. He could feel her heart beating in concert with his "Damn it woman." Martin whispered as his body begged to possess her.

"Are you uncomfortable?" Helen straightened beside him.

"No. I'm too comfortable." Martin stared into her green eyes as she moved closer, her gaze flashing between his eyes and his lips. She kissed him and he wrapped his arms around her. "Oh, Helen." Martin kissed her lips, her cheeks and her neck before looking into her eyes once again. "I love you." He said as she wriggled from his grasp.

She stood up and nodded and she had a look in her eyes he'd never seen before. "I think it's time for bed."

Martin felt he'd pushed to hard. His ego deflated, he stood and touched her shoulder. "Can I have a goodnight kiss?"

"You must be tired of sleeping on that couch." Helen said and kissed his cheek.

"You're right. I'm going to try the guest room tonight." Martin shut off the television and the glow from the fire made her appear even more beautiful.

"I'll probably sleep better if you are closer." Helen smiled and held out her hand. "If you don't mind."

Martin took her hand and followed her into the bedroom. "Are you sure?"

"Yes."

"Do you love me?" Martin wrapped his arms around her as they stood by the bed.

"I care for you, Martin." She looked up at him. "I want to share my bed with you."

Martin wanted to demand a statement of love. He knew she loved him, he could feel it. He watched as she took off her robe and climbed into bed. He lay down beside her, his heart pounding with happiness. He leaned on his elbow, staring down at her.

"I want to share a life with you Helen. I want you to be my wife."

"Hold me." She smiled at him, her red hair a wide halo spread over the pillow.

Her beauty silenced Martin as he gathered her into his arms. He lay on top of her and kissed her as the sense of urgency pulsed through him. His passion was elevated by hers, as they loved each other through the night.

By sunrise they lay exhausted and naked. Martin listened to her breathing against his chest as he fell asleep feeling he'd conquered the world.

*   *   *   *

Helen slipped on the robe and tied it as she crept out of the room. She took a last look at the handsome man sleeping in her bed before closing the door. Her mind whirled with thoughts of the passion filled hours they'd shared as she filled the coffeepot.

Martin was in the kitchen wearing only his pajama bottoms before it finished brewing. "Good morning."

"Good morning." Helen said as he wrapped his arms around her.

"You never answered my question last night." Martin smiled and kissed her on the cheek.

"I'm not ready to answer it. Not yet."

Martin frowned. "Reason?"

"I…after we get this case solved…my head will be clearer." Her voice trailed off.

"Fine. I'll wait." Martin tapped her on the bottom and released her. "I won't like it." He looked out the kitchen window. "They did a good job last night."

"Can we take that ride today?"

"Yes. I'll call to see how the roads are up that way later." Martin turned toward her. "How are you feeling this morning?"

"Very good, thank you. If you're worried that I might regret last night, don't be." Helen smiled.

Red flashed across her mind, forcing her to grab the counter for support. The room was bathed in a red glow. He was deciding on a knife.

Helen sat down, shaking. "You'd better get those calls made now."

"What is it?" Martin asked as he knelt down beside her. "You're white."

"He's hurting her. He cut her."

"Is she dead?"

"No…but he's getting angry." Helen went to her room and took a fast shower before dressing for the weather, boots and all. She was glad to see Martin was ready when she returned to the kitchen.

"I'm sorry but route sixteen…" Martin pointed to the road that snaked by the lake on the map. "This road is impassable. They might have it ready by noon."

"She can't wait. Can't we follow a plow up there?" Helen clutched her gloves as she looked out the window.

"They're going to call me when it's clear." Martin pulled out the chair. "Sit, relax. We'll go as soon as we can."

Helen sat down. Her thoughts were with the girl and the panic she was feeling. Acid moved up her throat as she lit a cigarette and looked at the map. She pulled it closer and focused on the lake area.

She finished the cigarette in silenced and began pacing the living room.

"You're driving me crazy. Come here and eat. You need a good breakfast."

Helen looked at the plate of pancakes and eggs as she walked toward the table. "Thank you. Don't you think we can head up there soon?"

"You eat and we'll take a ride. I'd rather be digging my car out of a snow bank than watching you wear out the floor."

Helen picked at the breakfast hoping to satisfy him but all she could think about was getting to the girl. Martin finished eating and leaned forward on his elbows staring at her.

"Are you going to finish?"

"No."

Martin took the plate and scraped it into China's bowl. "At least someone around here appreciates my cooking."

Helen walked to the counter and took the holster out of the drawer by the sink and strapped the gun to her belt. She put the speed loaders into her jacket pocket and picked up the sharp pocketknife she kept by the sink. She turned her back to Martin as she opened her shirt and slid the knife inside of her bra strap under her arm. It wasn't exactly comfortable but she was going to need every advantage.

They headed out into the winter weather in search of the killer. It took hours to reach the area and the roads were as treacherous as Martin had warned.

Helen could feel they were getting closer as they turned onto route sixteen. They'd gone a mile after the turn and the road became more hazardous. The car fishtailed several times before Martin slowed it to a crawl. Helen knew he wanted to turn back but prayed he wouldn't say the words. They were too close to give up now. She felt as though it was their last chance to save the girl from a horrifying death.

A flash of the girl screaming as he sliced her arm made her reach over and blow the horn.

"What the hell are you doing?"

"He's cutting her." Helen cried. "He's tired of waiting. He's tired of hearing her cry." She hit the horn again. "We're so close."

Martin tried to speed up but the car swerved and Martin hit the brakes. "We have to go back."

"We can't. I can't." Helen zipped up her coat and pulled her hat down over her ears. "We'll walk."

"Helen." Martin grabbed her arm. "There's at least a mile between houses out here. Be reasonable."

"I can't." Helen stared into his warm brown eyes.

"Hold on." Martin pulled out his cell phone and called for a plow. "Now sit tight. They'll have someone out here in an hour."

"I can't. We have to go now." Helen got out of the car and started up the road as the girl screamed out in her mind. Her face was frozen by the whipping wind but the rest of her body was sweating out sheer panic.

"Wait up, damn it…this is crazy."

"For you, not for me. She's screaming for help." Helen continued to trudge north as he caught up to her.

"We need a plan."

"He's not expecting us…he's focused on hurting her." Tears flowed down her face as they rounded a bend in the road. Her breath caught in her throat when she noticed the old iron gate. She stopped and looked at Martin.

"She's close." Helen stepped through the shrubs beside the gate and continued to head north ignoring the large log cabin to the east.

"Helen." Martin stopped beside an old pine tree. "Let's try the house first."

"She's not there." Helen pointed to the dense forest ahead of her. "She's up there."

Martin shook his head and followed her for a half an hour.

"Hold up a minute."

"You can catch up with me." Helen headed into the trees, the bile working its way up her throat with each step. She reached under her coat and flipped the safety off of the gun, her eyes searching for a doorway to the girl. All she could see were trees and snow as she forced her aching legs forward. She looked behind her for Martin but couldn't see him though the dense forest and swirling snow.

"Helen." Martin's voice pierced the quiet air.

"I'm-" Helen turned toward the sound of his voice and a sharp pain shot through her head.

The red room swirled before her eyes. A door creaked opened and she could hear whimpering in the distance as heavy footsteps moved toward her. Her hands and feet were bound and she suddenly realized where she was.

"The police are outside, Abington." Helen croaked out the words.

"I know." Donald lunged at her stopping the knife an inch from her right cheek. "You've ruined my fun." He said as he pressed the flat of the knife against her skin. "I guess I have to give you your due…before I slice your throat."

"Let the girl go."

"I can't."

"She hasn't seen you…you can't get away with it."

"I've had time to plan. By the time they-." The gunshot outside silenced him. "You'd better run while you can."

He pushed the tip of the knife into the skin in front of her ear. "I'll go take care of your friend so I can give you a proper, slow, send off." He set the knife on the table next to the narrow bed and ripped open her shirt. "I'm going to enjoy this."

She watched as he picked up her gun off of the table and pulled it from the holster. Helen struggled to free herself as he walked out of the room. She was turning her wrists raw when she heard the girl calling her name.

"Help will be here soon." Helen pulled at the ropes. "Hold on."

"Please...I'm bleeding."

"Hold on." Helen cried. The sound of gunfire in the distance made her fight harder to get free. She thought about telling Martin he shouldn't kill Abington and suddenly realized her mistake. Helen and the girl would surely die if Abington made it back to the bunker.

She finally worked a hand out and quickly pulled the rope off of the other as the room swayed around her. Helen had been drugged but she couldn't remember when it happened. She struggled to keep a level head as she used the jackknife to cut the rope from her ankles.

"Where are you?" Helen called to the girl.

"In here."

Helen followed the sound of her voice, holding the wall for support as the room rolled around her. She found her tied to the bed in the next room, blood covering her right arm. Helen cut her loose and pulled the tape from her eyes. She pulled the blanket up around the girl as she cried.

"I can't see."

"You have to try. He drugged me." Helen staggered back into the doorframe. "You have to run. I'll be right behind you."

"I'm afraid." The girl cried as she wrapped her arms around Helen's waist.

Helen took a step toward the open door, praying for the strength to continue on as the drug slowed her further. "When we get out there you have to run. We'll find you by your tracks. Go. When you come to the road, follow it."

"I can't." The girl whimpered clinging to her.

Helen knew that they couldn't afford to stand there arguing. If the girl didn't have the strength to go alone, Helen would have to help her and pray that she didn't succumb to the effects of the drug before they made it to safety.

"It's going to be fine. We can do this." Helen said as they finally reached the door. She got a read on what she hoped was the setting sun and headed south.

Helen urged the girl along as she fought for balance in the deep snow. She tried to steady her vision but the trees swayed before her. Her freezing feet urged her forward.

"He's going to get us. He's going to kill us." The girl cried as she fell into a snowdrift.

"No." Helen reached for her and pulled her up. "God is watching over us. I feel it. We're going to make it if we just keep moving."

The sound of sirens made her cry as she dragged the girl out of the woods to the road. Helen felt a pain in her leg as it was thrown out from under her and as she hit the ground she heard the gunshot. She slipped in the snow as she tried to get to her feet.

The girl screamed at her to get up. "He's coming." The girl squeezed her arm as she stood.

"Run. Run…I see the police lights…get help." Helen could feel the blood being pumped from her thigh and she reached for her belt but it was gone. She kept moving forward as the little girl got ahead of her. A cruiser rounded the corner and slid to a stop just a few yards from the panicked child.

"Helen." Martin screamed from the woods behind her.

She stopped and as she turned toward the sound of his voice she heard a loud engine in the distance. "He's getting away." She screamed as she dropped to the ground. "You can't let him."

Martin rushed to her side, blood running down his face from a gash on the top of his head. "Where's the girl?"

"They've got her." Helen said as Martin knelt beside her and whipped off his belt.

"This might hurt." He fastened the belt around her thigh and pulled it tight. "Let's get some help over here." Martin waved at the officer. "Get over here."

"The girl is going to be all right."

"We'll find this bastard. I hit him in the arm. I wish you hadn't told me not to kill him."

"I felt it would stop you from finding me. Nothing was clear enough."

"Well, it's over. He'll run until he's caught and I don't think that will take too long. How did you find him?"

"He found me. I've got a major headache." Helen touched the back of her head and saw the blood on her hand. "Guess that's why."

"Damn it." Martin kissed her. "I freaked when I couldn't find you."

"Thanks for listening to me."

"Was she hurt?"

"He cut her arm. I think he might have heard me beeping the horn. I didn't see anything and the next thing I knew I was in that room." Helen tried to focus on his handsome face. "The room in my visions. It was just as I'd seen it."

"We've got him dead to right. It's over." Martin said as the ambulance came around the corner.

"That cut looks bad." Helen looked at the blood oozing down his forehead.

"I'm fine." Martin kissed her again. "And you're out of a job."

"It won't be over until he's caught." Helen watched as the paramedics wheeled over the stretcher. "He drugged me." Helen said as the tall one knelt down beside her. "I don't know what it is."

"Okay." He looked at her leg and back at Martin. "You did a good job. Let's get this lady warmed up."

Martin helped her up onto the stretcher as her teeth chattered. The paramedic covered her with a thin warm blanket before wheeling her to the ambulance. Martin tossed an officer his car keys and climbed in beside her.

"You're going to be fine." Martin said as he held her hand.

"I know." Helen shivered under the blanket. "I just don't think I'll ever be warm again." Helen closed her eyes and gave in to the numbing effects of the drug. "Do you think you'll catch him?"

"I'm sure." Martin touched her cold damp hair. "Relax. Please."

CHAPTER 12

▼

Helen woke in the emergency room as the doctor finished stitching her thigh.

"Hello." He smiled at her. "How are you feeling?"

"My leg."

"It's going to be fine. The bullet chipped the bone but the leg isn't broken. You'll be fine in a few weeks."

"Where's Detective Hamlin?"

"He's right outside. I'll send him in."

"When can I go home?"

"As soon as you're up to it." The doctor smiled and headed out the door.

A few minutes later Martin walked in wearing a grin. "His face is all over the news. It's only a matter of time...how are you feeling?"

"Good. I just woke up a few minutes ago." Helen sat up slowly. "The doctor said I can leave. I need a cigarette."

"Hold on there. You don't look too good."

"Thanks."

"No...I mean...you don't look well enough to leave."

"I want to go home."

A nurse walked into the room carrying metal crutches. "The doctor said you'll need these and if you can sign these forms you're good to go."

"Thank you." Helen smiled in Martin's direction.

"Damn you're stubborn. Nurse, are you sure you should let her go? She looks pale to me."

"She'll be fine. I'm giving her something for the pain. By the time you get her home she'll be ready for bed." The nurse held the metal clipboard as Helen signed the forms. "I'll get you a wheel chair."

"I can walk."

"Would you let the woman help you?"

Helen looked up at him. "What's wrong?"

"I'm worried. Damn you. You just got shot now you're ready to rush out of here like nothing happened. Your body has taken a trauma. This is serious."

"Now all I need is a lift." Helen looked up at him.

"I'll call for a ride. They can get my car to your house."

"I can't believe he hasn't been caught. From what you said he'll need medical attention."

"You need to stop worrying about the case and focus on getting well."

"Yes, sir."

The nurse came in with the wheelchair and pushed her out to the front door. Helen took a deep breath of the snow clean air and smiled as Martin helped her out of the chair and handed her the crutches. A cruiser stopped at the entrance and a tall officer got out to help them.

Helen took it one step at a time as her injured leg throbbed and the crutches shook. Martin held her arm, ready to grab her if she started to fall. "This is going to take some getting used to."

"The doctor said to stay off of it as much as possible. I'm taking a few personal days."

"No. No I don't want you to."

Martin held up his hand. "Closed."

As soon as they arrived at her house, Helen put on the news eager to hear that they'd apprehended the killer.

"I told you I don't want you thinking about the case."

"Right. I'll feel better once he's in custody." Helen grabbed the arm of the couch for support as she lowered herself into the seat. She looked down at her pants, the right leg cut at the top of the thigh.

"I could start a new trend with this. What do you think?" Helen smiled as she reached for the pins on the ace bandage. "They have got this way too tight." She said as she slowly unwrapped it. She took a deep breath as the blood flow increased to her toes.

"You need to put that back on." Martin said, staring at her swollen thigh. "Don't take that other bandage off."

"I won't. I needed to loosen it."

"I'll do that for you." Martin took the bandage and wrapped her leg. "Now. You need to get into bed."

"I'd be more comfortable here. You can have the bed tonight."

"It wouldn't have anything to do with watching the news would it?" Martin touched the bandage on the top of his head. "I'm getting one hell of a headache."

"I'm not the only one who needs to rest."

"We're going to be snowed in again tomorrow."

"Damn. When is this winter going to end?"

"Good question. You get comfortable and I'll call and order Chinese while we still can."

"Thanks." Helen laid down and turned up the television as the weather forecast popped up. Another eight to ten inches was on its way. Helen smiled when she realized her mind was free enough to focus on the weather. She was anxious for the police to catch the killer but the feeling of dread and the horrible images were gone. There was a peace in her mind.

"Are you comfortable?" Martin asked as he walked around the couch. He covered her with the afghan.

"I'm fine. Have you taken anything for that headache?"

"Yes. It should kick in soon." Martin shook his head. "We're quite a pair. Walking or nearly walking wounded. You scared the hell out of me."

"I'm still in shock."

Martin sat down on the chair. "I'll take something out of the freezer for tomorrow's dinner...there's no way we'll get a delivery."

"How do you think he got away? I mean...the cops were all over the place right away."

"They were on the road to the south. He went north through the woods."

"It sounded to loud to be a snow mobile."

"The tracks looked like a snow vehicle. They haven't identified it yet."

"You are sure you shot him."

"Yes. I hit his arm but he kept running."

"Can you get the fire going?"

"Of course, what was I thinking?" Martin laughed. "Relax and watch a pro."

Helen dozed off as Martin started the kindling. She awoke a half-hour later to the sound of Martin talking in the kitchen.

"Hey, dinners here." Martin said as he closed the door. "Any takers?"

"Yes." Helen sat up. "Guess I fell asleep."

"You were snoring so loud I couldn't hear the news."

"I was not." Helen said, rubbing her throbbing leg. "I've got to be due for some pain medication soon."

"Yes. I've got it in my jacket. Hold on a minute."

"You don't have to rush."

Martin brought her dinner on a tray with a pain pill for an appetizer. "Oh, hey, turn it up." Martin pointed to the television.

Helen hit the volume button as she stared at the picture of Donald Abington on the screen.

"Authorities are still searching for-."

Helen lowered the volume. "It's taking too long."

"It hasn't been twenty four hours yet. Relax." Martin looked at the screen and back at Helen. "Don't you want to hear what they are saying about you?"

Helen watched as they showed the scene of her being wheeled into the emergency room. "No. Not especially."

"It's on the national news too. This guy has no where to hide."

"What about Canada?"

"Eat your dinner before it gets cold. Do you want some coffee?"

"Sounds good."

Helen picked at the food and turned the volume up when they went on to the next news story.

"I want you to tell me when you need something so I can get it for you. That's what I'm here for."

"Thank you." Helen looked into his eyes. "You need to get some rest."

"I plan on it."

And hour later Martin put another log on the fire and kissed her good night. "Call if you need me. I'll leave the door open."

"See you in the morning." Helen watched the fire as she wondered about their future. She'd allowed things to escalate between them without a clear vision of what lie ahead.

Helen wanted to be done with murder. If Martin was the connection, she feared it would happen again. The prospect alarmed her.

First thing in the morning Helen began to question him. "When are you going to retire?"

"I hadn't thought of a specific date. Why do you ask?"

"Because I need to know."

Martin shrugged. "Cream cheese and bagels?"

"Yes. You said you were seriously thinking about it."

"And I have."

"Not specifically."

"No you're right. I started thinking about the idea when you started getting those job offers. Like I said, it would be a good fit for you."

"You're having second thoughts about it, aren't you?"

"I help a lot of people in my line of work. I don't know if being a private detective would be as rewarding."

Helen nodded. "I don't want to go through this again. I have to quit…but if you are still doing it, I'll be affected."

Martin's eyes narrowed as he sat down on the chair. "I said I'm looking into it. You aren't having second thoughts about us are you?"

"I only know I want to put all of this behind me."

"I'm not liking the sound of this."

"I was up thinking about it all night, Martin."

"I know you were afraid. This has all been hard on you. You don't know that it will happen again."

"You don't know that it won't…you said you didn't want me in danger again."

"I meant that. You're done."

"But how can I be if you aren't?"

Martin stared at her for a long time before standing up. "I guess this is an issue we are going to have to work out over time. I'll get breakfast."

Helen was glad she'd put it on the table. She knew he'd be there with her for two days but once he returned to work there was no telling what kind of case would come across his desk.

It snowed all day and into the night and still no news about the killer. Helen didn't feel threatened but she didn't think he'd gotten too far. He was waiting them out.

The storm ended early in the morning but Helen took no comfort in the sound of the snowplows driving by. She wouldn't be going anywhere for a week or more. Her leg throbbed whenever she got up, making her spend much of her day lying down.

Martin was sullen all day. After dinner he joined her in the living room to watch a western.

"I'd need an office…there's a lot involved in starting any kind of a business…the process takes time."

"Understand, I am not trying to force you into doing anything. We each have to do what is right. I can't make a habit of working on murder cases. I don't want to. If being a cop is what you have to do. Than do it."

"Change comes hard to me."

"I know." Helen smiled. "It's a big decision."

Martin crossed his arms over his broad chest. "Yes. You know we're going to work this out."

"Yes." Helen didn't know how it would be decided but she knew it would and soon.

The following day she went over the job offers she'd received. Still there were only two that appealed to her. At that, she was in no rush to return to work of any kind. Once her leg was healed she'd need time to recuperate mentally before diving into something new.

Martin closed the phone and sat at the table beside her. "Abington's been spotted in Canada."

"Shit. Can they arrest him up there?"

"Sure, if they can find him. He crossed the border early this morning and was an hour gone before the guards got the flyer on him. He used an alias."

"Figures. He can buy what ever it takes."

"They'll catch up with him. It's only a matter of time. How are you feeling?"

"Better."

"I have to get to the station. Can I do anything for you before I go?"

"No. Thank you."

Helen was saddened by the tension that had developed between them. Martin was torn between a career he was comfortable with and one that would present new challenges.

Madeline came for a visit at noon, carrying a pot of chicken soup and asking a thousand questions. By three the house was quiet and Helen settled in for a nap. China rushed by waking her with a start when Martin returned at six.

"She must have smelled the steak. How are you doing?"

"Good. You?"

"Long day."

Helen made her way to the table. "I could use an appetizer." She smiled up at him.

"Coming right up. Your color is much better."

"I'm getting there."

"The guys gave me a new nickname. You are looking at scar." He said pointing to the row of stitches in his head. "They say it gives me character."

"Your hair will cover it eventually. How does it feel?"

"Sensitive to the touch but I haven't had a headache all day."

"That's good. These crutches take some getting used to."

Martin nodded as he cleared the plates. "I brought you a new gun." Martin tapped the bag on the counter. "And some good news, they found a knife in the storm drain and it matched the ones they found in that bomb shelter."

"A little late."

"It's definite proof that he was responsible for the college murders. It'll help with the case when he's brought back for trial."

"Good."

"The chief asked if you were coming back to work after you healed. I told him it was up in the air."

Helen walked to the living room and sat on the hassock by the fireplace. She pushed another log in and jostled the red embers until flames circled the wood.

Martin knelt down, resting his hand on her shoulder. "I missed you, today." He said as he kissed her neck.

"I missed you, too. My aunt came by and wore me out with her excitement. She's getting some fame by association." Helen smiled. "It makes her happy."

"I want you to be happy."

"I know you do, Martin."

He was gone before she woke up, leaving the newspapers next to the coffeepot for her. Helen had looked forward to a long peaceful stroll once her house arrest was over, yet here she was still recovering from the shot to her leg. Though she was getting around better on the crutches she was eager to be well and reclaim her life.

She left the newspapers untouched and drank down a cup of coffee as she listened to the weather. Clear skies for the next several days was just what she needed to hear. Helen made her way to the slider and opened the heavy drapes for the first time in weeks. The sun shone though and sent Helen was on a mission. She went into every room opening the curtains and felt better when she was done.

Helen spent the morning dusting and managed to vacuum the living room all before lunch. She'd been working with one crutch when she remembered her father's cane, which she kept in the back of her bedroom closet. She took it out and wiped it down and though it didn't relieve the pressure on her leg as much as the crutches, she preferred it. She put the crutches in the corner of the closet and walked out to the living room.

Small steps, she thought as she headed for the fireplace. She was moving forward none the less.

CHAPTER 13

▼

Helen was feeling stronger when Martin arrived in the afternoon. Her house looked better and she'd had a clear head all day.

"Hey look at you." Martin said as she greeted him at the door. "Where did you get the cane?"

"My father's. I never thought I'd use it." Helen smiled as he walked inside.

"I was hoping you'd be up for going out to dinner tonight?"

"You don't have to ask me twice."

"I made reservations for six."

"Great. I'm ready for a change of scenery. Help yourself to the coffee while I go get ready."

"Take your time."

She could feel Martin's eyes on her as she limped down the hallway. Ten minutes later she appeared in the doorway wearing a navy blue skirt and jacket, her long red hair flowing down her back.

"Damn, you look beautiful." Martin smiled.

"Thank you." Helen leaned on the cane and broke into a grin. "You are too much."

"What is it? What did I do?"

Helen couldn't help reading his mind. Martin couldn't take his eyes off of her legs. The skirt covered the wound and the swelling was gone. He wanted to call and order Chinese food and ravage her while they were waiting for it.

"No Chinese. I want steak." Helen laughed.

"You aren't supposed to do that." Martin waved a finger at her.

"I couldn't help it. Let's go." Helen said as she put on her coat. "I'm starving."

"Me too." Martin laughed and opened the door.

Martin talked about the cases he was working on as they dined. At the end of the meal his thoughts turned to their relationship and weighted her mood. Helen could read him more clearly with the passage of time and wondered if it wasn't worth a try to block his thoughts.

They were quiet on the ride home but Helen knew it was only a matter of time before he brought up their future.

"Thanks for taking me out. I needed that. I'm so full."

"I know how you feel."

"I'm going to get comfortable. I'll be back in a few."

"Take your time. I'll play with the fire."

Helen changed into a nightgown and put on her robe and slippers. She walked out to the living room to see Martin sitting by the fire.

"It's a shame you can't see what you want." Martin said as he stirred the embers.

"Sir?"

"I'd like you to look into the future and see me standing beside you."

"Why do you say that?"

"So you'd accept it." Martin turned to face her.

"I see you in my life. It isn't clear, but you are there, somewhere." Helen sat down on the couch.

Martin sat beside her. "So you're unnerved because you can't see our future clearly. Can you see us together like this tomorrow?"

"What?"

"Tomorrow."

"Yes."

"Our future together could be years or days. No one knows when they'll be called home. All we can do is make the best of whatever time we have." Martin touched her cheek. "For me that is being with you."

Helen studied his face, feeling the warmth of his love. "You're making too much sense." Helen smiled. "I'm still trying to deal with all the changes in my life but I'll keep your point in mind."

Martin relaxed and pulled her close. "I can't ask for more than that." He smoothed his large hand over her hair.

The phone rang and Helen started toward it, she froze when she recognized the number. She stared at the receiver as the answering machine picked up.

"Hi Helen, this is Tyler, I got your number from Madeline. I'm in town for a few days." He took a deep breath.

Helen picked up the phone as tears filled her eyes. "Hi, Tyler."

"Hell, woman. How are you?"

"Fine."

"We haven't talked in so long then you make national news. Shit, I've been worried about you."

"No need to worry." Helen pulled out the chair and sat down, wiping her eyes as Martin flashed her a curious scowl.

"I was hoping we could get together."

"Sure. When?"

"How about now?"

"Well, I-."

"I know it's late but I can't wait to see you."

"Sure."

"Great. I'll be there in a half hour."

"See you then."

Helen hung up the phone and looked at Martin. "A friend of mine is coming over. He's Tim's cousin." Helen went to her room and changed into a T-shirt and sweat pants. When she returned to the living room Martin was standing by the fireplace with his coat on.

"What's up?"

"I figured you'd want to have some time alone. I've got some paperwork to take care of. I'll come back in a couple of hours."

"You don't have to leave."

"I know. I'll be back." Martin kissed her cheek and left.

Twenty minutes later Tyler pulled up in the driveway. Helen steeled herself for their visit as she opened the door, holding on to China's collar.

"What is that?"

"My pup. China."

"Your pup? That's no pup." Tyler wrapped his arms around her and bent down to kiss her cheek "You look good."

"So do you." Tears filled her green eyes.

"It's been too long." Tyler said as he closed the door. "I've been worried about you being alone out here."

"I've had China and a detective for company."

"Oh?" Tyler looked into the living room.

"He just left to do some paper work. He'll be back later. Have a seat."

"So, I read somewhere that you and the detective are an item?"

"I don't know."

"You don't know?" Tyler smiled at her.

"It's a long story."

"I've missed you."

"Tell me what you've been up to."

"Keeping busy. I'm moving back here next month. I'm going to run the Boston office."

"Oh?"

"You don't sound too happy."

"I am. That's great if it's what you want."

Tyler nodded and covered her hand with his. "I want to be closer to you."

"What do you mean?" Helen didn't want to be closer to him. Tyler's voice and appearance were too close to his cousins. It would have always been too easy to latch onto Tyler as Tim's replacement but it wouldn't have been fair. Tyler was his own man and no one could ever replace Tim in her heart.

"I…you said you needed time to heal." Tyler's jaw twitched. "I've given you that time. You can't hide in this house forever. You can't be alone. Tim would want you to live your life not endure it."

"I know that." Helen touched his cheek. "You remind me of him in so many ways. Don't you see it couldn't work?"

Tyler threw up his hands and walked to the counter. "This is exactly what I didn't want to do. I'm sorry."

"We've been friends for a long time. Let's keep it that way."

"I've thought about you. Worried about you." Tyler turned to face her, his jaw tightening as he spoke "When it was the three of us, I didn't feel this way about you. Tim was my cousin and my best friend. I considered you a best friend too…after he died, I was glad to help you. I was helping myself as well."

"Oh, Tyler." Helen looked into his pained brown eyes. "I've missed you, too. I've missed joking around with you but when I've thought of you, it's always been as a friend."

"Tim would want us to be together."

"How can you say that?"

"He told me to take care of you. About a week before he died. The three of us were out at the steak house. He asked me when you went to the bathroom. I got an odd feeling when he said it, but I agreed...I haven't done my job. Don't you see that?"

"Will you please sit down?"

"How do you think I've felt these last few months? I've been five hundred miles away while you've been tracking down killers and kidnappers and getting your ass shot up."

"Tyler."

"Damn it woman."

Helen shook her head. "Look. I had no control over the visions or my involvement with the police."

"You're allowing yourself to be put in danger. It needs to stop."

"I didn't ask for this."

"Ah, hell." Tyler pulled out the chair and sat down, glaring at her. "I know I'm coming on strong. Shit. I had it all figured out. I was going to ease you into the conversation with questions and instead I come in here and blast off."

Helen pulled a cigarette out of the pack on the table and he reached over and lit it for her. "So, how have you been?" Helen smiled.

"About the same."

"I can see that."

Tyler took her hand and kissed it. "You light a fire in me woman. It's good to see you."

"You never were a subtle man."

Tyler calmed down and she told him the story about Donald Abington from start to finish before Martin returned.

Tension filled the room as the men shook hands. It didn't take a vision for Helen to see that they both felt threatened. Martin took off his coat and hung it over Tyler's before pouring himself a cup of coffee.

Helen was relieved when minutes later, Tyler announced he had to leave.

"I'm leaving late tomorrow night. I'd like to pick you up for dinner at five. You can finish telling me about your adventures then."

"That will be fine." Helen stood and followed him to the door.

"It was great to see you."

Tyler hugged her and kissed her goodbye. "See you tomorrow."

Helen closed the door and turned to see Martin leaning back in the chair, studying her.

"He looks more like Tim's twin than his cousin." Martin said.

"Yes." Helen took the coffee cups to the sink and rinsed them out. "They passed for twins in school." She dried her hands. "I'm beat. Did you get all of your work done?"

"Yes. Doran signed a confession. He's going to plead guilty to arson and man slaughter."

"I'm glad."

"Are you okay?" Martin leaned forward putting his elbows on the table.

"I haven't seen him in a long time. We were like the three musketeers for years. It's just weird being around him now...hard...brings back memories." Helen shrugged. "I'm going to call it a night." She knew he had questions but they'd have to wait. She patted his shoulder and headed down the hall before he could object.

Helen closed the bedroom door and laid on the bed thinking. It was good to see Tyler but he was still the same hot head he'd always been and just as attractive. Her thoughts bounced from one thing to another until sleep rescued her, giving her mind a much-needed rest.

She woke early the next morning to a note from Martin saying he'd see her the following day in time to bring her in to have her stitches removed. He signed it, love Martin. Helen spent the day puttering around the house. She had mixed feelings about dinner with Tyler but not enough to make her want to back out.

Helen wore a conservative black dress and her lowest pumps and was ready to go by four. She sat at the table smoking as her mind wandered through the trio's time together.

They were always laughing or engaging in a spirited debate. Their time together was easy and fun. They all knew that no matter what was said, they'd remain friends. Helen laughed out loud as she remembered a political debate that had gotten so heated they were asked to leave the restaurant. They left laughing. Tyler on one side and Tim on the other as they escorted her out.

There were so many of those times but it all stopped when Tim died. He left a huge void in the trio that could never be filled.

China ran to the door as Tyler pulled up in the driveway and let out a few barks for effect as he walked inside.

"I think she's grown since last night." Tyler laughed patting the dog on the head.

"She won't be full grown for months so it wouldn't surprise me."

"You look ready, let's not waste any time." Tyler took her coat off of the back of the chair and held it up for her. "I found an apartment in town today."

"Here?"

"Yes."

"That's going to give you a stiff commute."

"I know. I don't mind working in a big city but I'm not crazy about living in one. I'll be looking for a house but that's going to take a little time. At least now I have somewhere to hang my hat." Tyler held the door open for her and followed her out to the car.

"I'm glad everything's working out for you."

"So far so good. You could help things along."

"You know what I meant."

"OK. I'll back off." Tyler smiled. "I'll be a good boy for the evening."

"Thank you. I know it won't be easy."

"How's the leg?"

Helen adjusted her skirt to cover the bandage. "It's getting better. I get the stitches out tomorrow."

"That's great. When I come back in two weeks you should be ready to dance."

"I'll just be happy to walk without the cane." Helen tapped the brass handle.

"What has all this done to your business?"

"I've had to put it on hold. Now I don't know if I want to go back to it."

"Why? Things will die down eventually."

"I know. Things come through more clearly now. It would be too draining, it's hard to explain."

"You're still working with the police department, aren't you?"

"For the time being." Helen shrugged. "I don't know where I'm going right now."

"You're going to dinner with me." Tyler straightened in his seat, smiling. "I need to fatten you up. Maybe we should start with a big, rich dessert."

"Oh please." Helen laughed. "The last time we did that, neither of us ate our dinner."

Tyler glanced at her. "You remember. We laughed a lot that night."

"We sure did." Helen rolled down the window and lit a cigarette. "You know what I'd like to do?"

"What?"

"Go camping. I'd like to go out into the woods, hear a stream, build a fire and totally relax."

"It's a little cold for that."

"Not now. But as soon as the weather breaks."

"Do you still have the camper?"

"Yes. I didn't use it at all last summer. Took it in for a tune up and parked it right back in the garage."

"Let me know when you're going. I could use a nature break."

Tyler kept his promise and didn't bring up even one controversial subject all night. When he asked to come in for a nightcap, Helen was happy to oblige. She was starting to look forward to Tyler moving back.

"My cheeks hurt." Tyler rubbed his face as he handed her a brandy. "I haven't had this feeling in a half a year."

Helen followed him into the living room and sat on the couch. She set down the snifter and rubbed her aching thigh.

"Maybe you won't be up to dancing. Can I get you a Tylenol or something?"

"This brandy should take the edge off." She said as she picked up the glass.

Tyler sat down beside her. "So. What do I need to know about Hamlin?"

"Excuse me?"

"The news said you two were an item."

"I don't know. I care for him. I'm connected to him."

"Are you an item?"

Helen took a few sips of the brandy as she looked past Tyler at the fire. "I guess we are."

"That explains why he was so cold. I wanted to thank him for looking after you but, I guess he had his own reasons for doing it."

"Look, the day I met him was the same day that my senses changed. I started having visions of the kidnapped child. It was a case he was working on. A few months later it started again, with the college murders."

Tyler nodded. "And this means what?"

"I don't know." Helen looked into his chocolate eyes. "It's almost like I've lost control over my life."

Tyler cleared his throat. "Did you sleep with him?"

Helen raised a brow. "Not that it's any of your business…but yes…once."

"Ugh. Then you're in love with him."

"I care for him, Tyler. I've been alone and scared and I turned to him for comfort. He's in love with me. He has been since the first case."

"But you don't know if you have a future with him."

"It's all so complicated. Okay, a few days ago he was working on a house fire. The wife died in the fire, the husband, though injured, made it out alive. Martin was working on the case but he hadn't mentioned it to me. I was standing by the fireplace and saw the whole thing in a vision. It was clear. To make a long story short, Martin used what I told him about the case to get a confession out of the man for starting the fire."

"Just like that."

Helen nodded. "I don't know what it is."

"Looks like your power has been punched up a few notches." Tyler touched her cheek.

"Gift or burden. It's not a power. I don't even want it. I was happy with the way things were going in my life before I met Martin."

"Really?"

"I mean with my work. Doing readings a couple days a week, the rest of the time was my own. Now I get these visions that invade my mind at will." Helen finished the brandy. "I'm still trying to adjust to it."

Tyler refilled their snifters and sat closer to her. "So what are you going to do?"

"That's the thing. I just don't know. I put some pressure on Martin to retire but he isn't ready to do it." Helen shook her head. "I was being selfish. I want the visions to end and since he's connected to them, I thought it would help but I'm not sure. Now that it's happening I don't think there's any way to stop it."

"Maybe you should just take some time off to think it through."

"I have been, but that doesn't stop the visions." Helen lit a cigarette. "Can we change the subject?"

"Sure…well, I'll be back in two weeks. I'll call you when I return but I'll be busy moving in for the first few days."

"So why did you decide to come back?"

"I told you."

"Oh. I thought you were just telling me that to give me a hard time."

"Me? The thought wouldn't cross my mind."

They laughed and talked until ten when Tyler said he had to head to the airport. He stopped and studied her for a moment. "No bad feelings?"

"None at all. Have a safe trip." Helen walked him to the door. "It was good to see you."

Tyler hugged her and kissed her on the lips before heading out into the cold winter night. Helen stood by the door until his car disappeared from view.

CHAPTER 14

▼

Martin stood by the door waiting for her to gather her things. She could feel his dark mood as they rode to the appointment.

"I should be able to drive myself around soon. That will be a grand day." Helen smiled as they pulled up to the doctor's office.

"I'll wait here." Martin said, staring straight ahead.

Helen looked at him for a minute, glad that she could get out of the car and walk away from him. She knew it was Tyler's visit that had him upset but she wasn't ready to talk about it, not yet.

She went into the doctor's and within an hour returned to the car, stitches out and a clean bill of health. Martin's scowl still creased his handsome face as he drove her home in silence. When he pulled up to her house he made no move to shut off the car.

"Are you coming in?"

"I have to get back to the station."

"Do you want to talk?"

"No."

Helen nodded and got out of the car. She fumbled with the keys and finally unlocked the door and went inside. She'd no sooner taken off her coat and the phone rang. It was Madeline.

"How are you, dear?"

"There's a question…fine, I guess."

"I've got a job for you."

"A job?"

"It pays very well."

"What is it, auntie?" Helen asked as she let the dog out the living room slider.

"A man needs help finding his daughter. He's rich and dying. He read some-where that I was your aunt and called me this morning to enlist your help."

"You should tell him to hire a private detective."

"He has, three of them. They haven't found a damn thing except for where the girl's mother is buried."

"How old is the girl?"

"Forty two."

"Oh. And why is he looking for her?"

"Like I said, he's dying. He doesn't have any other heir. He'd like to leave his money to her but he has to locate her first." Madeline took a deep breath. "He's had a fifty thousand dollar reward for finding her and that would be yours if you could do it."

"That's a lot of money...I'd have to meet with him first. I don't know if I can do this." Helen frowned.

"He knows about your injury and offered to send a car for you to go and meet with him at your convenience."

Helen thought about the idea. Maybe she could help. Maybe the strength of her visions was going to remain. "I don't know."

"He lives right in Hyannis. It's not like you'd be traveling the country."

"Hyannis. How did he lose contact with her?"

"His father felt the mother wasn't good enough for him. He threatened her to get out of his son's life when she told him she was pregnant with his grandchild. I guess it was pretty messy. The man's father told him about the pregnancy when he was dying of cancer."

"So he has no leads as to where this woman is?"

"None. He doesn't even know her name."

"Now wait a minute auntie."

"I know. It's a tough one. Come on dear, take a chance, challenge yourself. It will fatten your wallet and make a dying man happy."

"Give me his number."

Helen wrote down the information and ended the call. She stared at the name for a long time but nothing came to her. After puttering around the house for an hour, boredom won out and she picked up the phone.

"Yes, may I speak with Walter Appleton please?"

"Who's calling?"

"Helen Staples."

"Oh, yes, he's been waiting for your call. One moment please."

The line went dead and a moment later a different man answered. "This is Walter Appleton. Thank you for calling."

"My aunt gave me a brief description of your problem."

"Can you help?"

"I'm not sure. I would have to meet with you."

"I'll send a car for you. It can be there in an hour."

"I'll be ready."

"Thank you, Miss Staples. I'll look forward to seeing you."

The limousine pulled up in front of the house exactly one hour later. Helen put on her coat as the driver walked up to the door. She followed him and sat back in the soft leather seat for a comfortable ride to the cape. When they arrived at the stone, castle type mansion Helen's senses were on high alert.

She was led into an enormous library and introduced to Walter Appleton. The tall thin man was clearly in his sixties but didn't appear ill other than being a bit pale. As they shook hands, Helen felt his sadness and released it quickly.

"Please, have a seat. How was your ride?"

"Fine. Thank you."

Mr. Appleton took a file off of the desk and sat in the chair beside her, handing it to her.

"This is all I have. She had a sister, I think that's who raised my daughter."

Helen put her hand on the file, eyeing him. "Your father chased your girlfriend away?"

He nodded. "That's the way things were back then."

"You were an adult."

"Just." He stood and walked to the window staring out at the grounds for a long silent moment. He turned to face her. "My father thought he was doing the right thing. Daisy was from the other side of the tracks." The pain on his face deepened the lines across his forehead and jowls. "Daisy died after giving birth to our daughter."

"How do you know?"

"The detectives researched the newspapers. Daisy was living in the Boston area. Working as a waitress. She worked until the day she went into labor...if I had known I would have stood up to my father. We would have gotten married...but it was like she disappeared off the face of the earth with no explanation. I was home from college and had spent the whole break with her and the day before I went back-."

Helen was hit with a vision. A young woman stood at the door crying before an angry man. She pleaded to see his son, said he couldn't turn her away. She'd just found out she was pregnant and needed to see Walter before he left.

"From what my father said, it was an ugly scene."

Helen nodded, seeing the woman crying against the door as the man closed it. "She was desperate."

"Why do you say that?" He asked as he returned to the seat beside her.

"She hadn't told you about her suspicions because she wanted to be sure. She saw the doctor that morning and came straight here to tell you."

"Can you help me find my daughter?"

"Maybe."

"I'll pay all of your expenses, plus the reward if you find her."

"My gifts, the way they work...well, money doesn't equal results." Helen opened the file and studied the picture of Daisy and Walter on the beach. "She loved you."

"Yes. We loved each other." His blue eyes filled with tears. "I don't have much time left."

Helen saw weeks in his future but nothing more. Helen reached for his hand, holding the photo in the other. She sat focused on the bits and pieces flowing through her mind for more than an hour. "She's not far from here. I'm seeing Chatam. Do you have a map?" Helen opened her eyes and released his hand. "She looks just like her mother. She knows about you."

"She does?" Mr. Appleton walked to the desk and pressed the buzzer beside the phone. The butler arrived at the open door at the other end of the long room.

"Sir?"

"I need a map of Chatam."

Helen watched as the round butler walked over to the ladder and slid it to the end of the bookcase. He climbed up the rungs eyeing the titles and then pulled a thick black book out of its slot.

"Here you go sir." He said as he climbed down. "Anything further?"

"No. But be available."

"I'll be right outside sir."

"Thank you." Mr. Appleton set the book on the desk and searched through the contents as Helen walked over to him. He opened it to the town map and slid the book closer to her. "I'd never believed in psychics until I heard about the cases you've helped the police with. Your abilities are amazing. You changed my mind about such things."

Helen studied the map as he spoke. "She lives over a store, no restaurant, in this area. It's her restaurant." Helen left the book open and returned to the chair. "She's been waiting for you."

"Are you okay, miss? Your face is flush."

Helen nodded. "I could use a drink of water." She watched as he went over and poured her a glass.

"Why do you say she's been waiting?"

"She's heard terrible things about you and your family all of her early life…her aunt Gwen, was horrible to her…Gwen had children of her own and resented having to raise yours. She was too afraid to contact you, instead she got back at you by constantly reminding Alexandra-."

"Alexandra? That's my mother's name."

"And your daughter's…she goes my her middle name, Marie."

Mr. Appleton sat down at the desk and scribbled on the pad. "Could you be right?"

"Sir?"

"I'm not doubting you but-."

"You are doubting me. I understand. I can only tell you what is coming to me."

He stared at her a moment and picked up the book of maps, carrying them to her. Every nerve in her body was setting off sparks as the images became clearer. "I could get a better sense if I went to the area."

Mr. Appleton turned and started for the desk, he staggered and grabbed the edge of the desk for support. Helen rushed to his side, helping him to the chair. He took a few deep breaths, raising his hand. "I'm fine. Thank you." He pressed the buzzer and the butler appeared. "Bring in my wheel chair and have the car ready."

"Yes, sir."

"I hate the damn chair, but there are days when I have to accept that I'm safer in it." He said as the butler returned.

"Souza is ready sir. Is he driving Miss Staples home?"

"No. We are going for a ride."

"Sir? But it's so cold outside." The butler's eyes widened.

"I'll be fine." Mr. Appleton said as the butler wheeled him into the grand foyer. The chauffeur opened the door and helped him into the car.

Helen's excitement increased as she walked outside. When she sat in the back of the limousine beside him, he handed her a paper map.

"It's near the downtown area." Helen said.

"Downtown Chatam."

"Yes sir. The address?"

"We'll let you know where to go from there."

"Yes, sir."

"So she named her Alexandra. How nice of Daisy, she knew how much I loved my mother." He said, staring out the window.

They arrived in Chatam with a formal announcement from the driver. As the downtown area came into view, Helen asked him to pull over.

"I'll have walk."

Mr. Appleton nodded. "We'll follow you."

Helen got out and headed up the street. She'd gone two blocks when she turned into a driveway between two businesses and saw the tall restaurant set back from the street. Her heart pounded as she slowly walked toward the building. She saw a woman sweeping inside the glass enclosed porch and realized at once that it was Alexandra.

She turned and started back to the limousine that now blocked the driveway. Mr. Appleton took her hand as she got into the car.

"It's her. She's sweeping."

His gray eyes widened as they filled with tears. "I...I don't know what to do...what to say."

"You want me to tell her." Helen didn't wait for a response. She got out of the car and walked up to the restaurant. Alexandra opened the door.

"I'm sorry but we're closed." She pointed to the road. "We're just a breakfast place. If you keep heading east, there's a great steak house about a block and a half up."

"Alexandra?"

The woman studied the limousine as she lowered herself onto the caned chair. "How do you know my name?"

"Your father has been searching for you."

"My father."

"Yes. He contacted me to help."

The woman nodded. "What does he want with me?"

"He's dying. He learned about you from his father in a death bed confession. He's tried to find you ever since and finally turned to me out of desperation. And, well...it must be with good reason that I've found you." Helen shivered and sat beside her. "I could tell you recognized me."

"Yes."

"All I can say is I wouldn't have tried to find you if I didn't have a sense that it was for good reason. Does that make sense to you?"

"Yes, in a way."

The woman's eyes widened and Helen turned to see Walter Appleton being wheeled up the driveway. Helen stood and took a few steps back as he got out of the wheel chair and walked up the steps. Mr. Appleton's color faded as he walked onto the sun porch.

"Hello Alexandra."

"Hello."

"I've looked for you for so long." His legs trembled as he lowered himself into the chair. "We have so much to talk about." His eyes filled with tears. "I want to get to know my daughter."

Alexandra burst into tears as she stood and wrapped her arms around him. Helen walked outside, hesitating by the door, before returning to the limousine. Her body was drained by the experience. Her mind was whirling by the speed of information that came to her. She looked at her watch. It was almost six. The day had sped by.

A half-hour later Mr. Appleton and his daughter joined her in the limousine. The trio rode to his house, Mr. Appleton stating his amazement at how quickly she'd accomplished the task. By the look of the pair sitting together, Helen knew it was meant to be. She accepted his compliments with a nod and a smile.

When they arrived at the mansion Mr. Appleton wrote out a check for Helen and asked the driver to take her home. He thanked her repeatedly before allowing her to leave. Helen folded the check and put it in her pocket as she walked out to the limousine.

When she arrived home Martin was waiting in the driveway. He walked over to the limousine as the chauffeur opened the door.

"Where the hell have you been?" Martin asked through clenched teeth.

"I was on a case." Helen smiled. The phrase sounded good. "I made a pocket full of money and I'm ready to get off of the city's payroll."

"Just like that?" Martin followed her to the house.

"Just like that…I enjoyed what I was doing today and it came so easy. Like a snowball getting larger as it rolled down the mountain." Helen opened the door and walked inside to open the slider for China.

"You're excited." Martin smiled as he walked toward her.

Helen took the check out of her pocket and blinked when she saw it was double the reward. "Oh, my, word."

"What is it?"

Helen showed him the check and sat at the table staring at it. "One hundred thousand dollars. I don't need to work for the rest of the year."

Helen made a pot of coffee as she explained the day's events.

"That's incredible."

"I'll call the chief in the morning…" Helen poured the coffee and sat down beside him. "I've been pushy with you, about the retirement…I'm sorry for that." She took a deep breath. "You need to do what you are comfortable with. I need to do the same."

"Are you saying this because of what happened to you today?"

"Yes. I realized that my name is out there. I don't expect to have a day like this again, but I think I could get reasonable fees. Enough to get by on."

"And I don't have…you don't want me to quit the force?"

"Not until you are ready to do it. For yourself." Helen smiled.

"Where does that leave us?"

"I don't know."

Martin lit a cigarette and leaned back in the chair staring at her.

"See what happens."

"Have you eaten today?"

"Not since breakfast."

"Let's go out for dinner…where's your cane?" Martin looked around the room.

"Shit. I left it in the limousine. I'll call Mr. Appleton in the morning. I can do without it. I'll freshen up and be ready in a few minutes."

They enjoyed a delicious baked shrimp dinner tucked away in a corner booth. Helen was still excited about the way her gifts were accelerating. She was glad Martin had dropped the subject about their future because she didn't know what to say. She enjoyed his company, she cared about him, she was connected to him but she didn't know where it would go. She couldn't see their future as a couple. It didn't mean they wouldn't have one, she just couldn't see it one way or another.

It struck her how she could walk in and see a family's past and present but she couldn't understand herself or her life. She smiled as the waiter cleared the plates.

"I don't think I've ever seen you eat that much. There wasn't enough to take home for China." Martin laughed.

"I feel good today. Better than I have in weeks."

"I'm glad to see it. I still can't get over the size of that check."

"Tell me about it. Even what it should have been was overwhelming." Helen smiled. "It gives me the financial freedom to see if I can do what I want to do. Thinking about Mr. Appleton getting some kind of closure before he died, it was such a special thing."

"The chief isn't going to be happy."

"I'll let him know I'll still be available if I can help but I feel it's a conflict, drawing a salary from the city and the private sector."

"I understand…it's for the best. As long as it doesn't change things between us."

Helen wanted to talk to him about the way Tyler's visit had upset him but she didn't want to sour his mood. She was sure it would come up at some point.

CHAPTER 15

▼

The next morning her cane arrived by special delivery along with a touching thank you note from Walter Appleton.

A week later Helen had mixed emotions when she read his lengthy obituary. She was studying his photo when her aunt called saying she was on the way over.

"How are you dear?" Madeline asked as Helen opened the kitchen door for her.

"I'm fine. How are you?"

"Good. Good. I read about Mister Appleton."

"He was a good man. At least he had closure before he died. Would you like some coffee?"

"I was hoping you'd ask." Madeline laid her coat over the back of the chair and sat at the table, watching her pour the coffee.

"So what brings you out here this morning?"

"You need to talk."

"I do?"

"Yes. I want you to tell me how you are doing. I heard Tyler is moving back to town."

Helen rolled her eyes. "Yes. I saw him. He's got a job in Boston."

"I see. And how is Detective Hamlin?"

Helen took a deep breath. She decided to be patient with her aunt. It had been a long time since the woman had given her a good grilling. "He's fine. Busy."

"Are you seeing him, dating him?"

"I don't know what we are doing. I really don't."

"You slept with him." Madeline stared into her eyes.

"Once. Weeks ago."

"And?"

"And it was probably a mistake. I was vulnerable, I wasn't myself." Helen scowled. "He's a good man and I care about him."

"You quit your job with the police department."

"Yes. After the Appleton case I felt I had to and I'm glad I did."

"Have they tracked down that murderer?"

Helen lit a cigarette. "Last they knew he was in Canada." Helen shrugged.

"No more visions of him?"

"No." Helen looked up at the ceiling. "Thank God. You don't know what it was doing to me, auntie."

"I have a good idea. I thought about what you said about avoiding reading people with a bad aura. I can't imagine how seeing such vile brutality would feel." Madeline touched her hand. "You've been very brave."

"Thank you. I didn't feel brave. I guess that's how I crossed the line with Martin. I do wish it hadn't happened. I wasn't ready for everything that came with it."

"We all make mistakes, dear. And we just have to deal with them and go on. If he isn't right for you...well."

"It's not that, auntie. I don't know if he is or isn't. That is the real problem."

"And Tyler? I remember what happened before he moved away."

Helen shook her head. "He came on like gangbusters...You know Tyler. But he calmed down."

"This ought to be interesting." Madeline leaned back in her chair.

"I need some peace in my life." Helen said. "It's funny. When I was doing readings and living a quiet life, I didn't appreciate it. Since these visions began my life has changed drastically. I've decided to accept what's happened and earn what I can with my gifts...Mister Appleton's generosity has made it possible for me to relax and chose what cases I'll work on. I prefer finding missing persons to helping track down murderers."

"I can understand that." Madeline checked her watch. "I have to go. I've got a reading at eleven." Madeline stood and put on her coat.

After her aunt left, Helen took the stack of mail upstairs. She lit a few candles and sat at the small cherry desk to sift through the letters. She pulled the rubbish basket over to the desk and one by one tossed the absurd requests. She laughed out loud at one letter requesting the lottery numbers for the first of January as she threw it away.

But her mood quickly darkened when she opened the next letter. It was a plea from a mother living in Ohio. Her sixteen-year-old had run away with a man almost twice her age three months before. The woman felt her daughter was in danger and asked for Helen's help.

Helen set the letter and photo of the girl in the corner of her desk before opening the next. Three more foolish letters and then another plea for help of a missing child, this time it was a thirteen year old girl. By the time Helen was through, she had six serious requests for help.

She leaned back staring at the letters for several minutes before going back to the first. She looked at the picture of the girl as she reached for the phone.

"Yes, may I speak to Mildred Wiler?"

"This is she."

"I'm Helen Staples. I received your letter."

"Can you help me?"

"I get a sense that your daughter isn't far from home...she is with that man, David...do you have a phone book handy?"

"Hold on."

Helen took a deep breath as the image of the girl dancing, neon lights flashing around her, came into her mind.

"I've got it."

"I'm sorry to have to tell you this but he has her stripping...and since she started...her disgrace has kept her from returning home."

"Oh, my God."

"Please read the names of the strip clubs." Helen said as the woman cried on the other end of the line. "I am sorry."

The woman began reading the list and Helen stopped her when she heard the name. "It's Sweet Sensations...don't go there alone."

"I won't. I'll bring my husband...can you tell me anything else?"

"Just that she does want to go home. She's seen some...upsetting things. She's ready to be your little girl again."

"Thank you Miss Staples."

"Good luck." Helen hung up the phone and set the letter and photo aside.

She looked at her watch and decided to go out to dinner.

When she arrived at the restaurant she noticed Martin sitting by the windows in the dining room. He spotted her at the same time and waved her over.

"This is a surprise. Were you looking for me?"

"Just out for a bite to eat."

"Will you join me?"

"Sure. It's nice to see you. Are you working late?"

"Of course. I had a few small cases to clear. I have to go back after dinner." Martin studied her. "So how are you? We haven't seen each other for a few days."

"I'm fine. Has there been any word on Abington?"

"Nothing new. He hasn't crossed the border. We have a flag on his fake I.D."

Helen nodded. "I hope they catch the bastard soon."

"You haven't seen anything?"

"Not where he's concerned." Helen smiled. "I'll feel better once he's locked up though. It's always in the back of my mind. I guess it will be until it's over."

"Taken any new cases?"

"No. I'm in no hurry either."

Martin's phone rang and Helen leaned back in the seat and looked out the window while he answered.

"Sorry about that." Martin said as he put the phone in his pocket. "While I'm thinking about it, I've got a stack of mail for you. I can bring it over later tonight if you like." He said as the waiter served their dinner.

"That would be fine…I've missed your company."

"And I yours. I've been trying to give you some space."

"I appreciate that." Helen studied his handsome face, seeing the sadness in his brown eyes. "Would you like to come for dinner tomorrow? You can bring me my mail then, save you a trip."

"I'd love to. What time?"

"Five, six, what ever is good for you. I'll make lasagna."

"I'll be there at five."

Helen was up early and checked her messages from the night before as the coffeepot gurgled out its last few drops. She stared at the machine as the voice turned her cold.

"I'm not through with you yet, bitch…I don't want you to think it's over."

China barked at the machine, the hair on her back bristling. Helen patted her as the beep signaled the next message.

"Thank you so much. We found our daughter…" The woman cried. "She was right where you said and she'd been drugged…she's safe…she's in the hospital. Thank you again for helping us."

Helen nodded. She reset the machine and put in a new tape, leaving the other on the table for Martin. She knew she'd be in danger until Abington was caught but she had to focus on the fact that she was safe for the moment, knowing that he was hundreds of miles away in Canada.

She layered the lasagna and put it in the refrigerator to set, all the while reliving the terrifying day she'd come face to face with the murderer. His call clouded her day. It wasn't until Martin arrived that evening that she felt any sort of relief.

Martin played the message several times before putting it in an envelope. "I can't hear any background noise but they might be able to do it with the computer. Are you okay?"

"Yes. So long as the creep stays away." Helen lit a cigarette. "I have to admit it threw me hearing the bastard's voice again."

"I'm sure it did." Martin sat at the table. "I'm going to get an extra patrol over this way."

"No. It's OK. I'll be fine." Helen touched his shoulder. "Really." She checked the lasagna in the oven and turned the temperature down for the last fifteen minutes.

"You tell me if you change your mind."

"I will."

After dinner Helen stoked the fire and then sat on the couch with Martin.

"They've been keeping me busy. This is my first night off this week." Martin smiled at her. "I've missed being here with you."

"I've missed you, too."

Martin rubbed his stomach. "I ate way too much."

"I'll send some home with you."

"So, can we talk about us?"

"I'm not ready to make a commitment, Martin."

"Where does that leave us?"

"I want to see you. I enjoy our time together. Can't we leave things as they are for now?"

"Does it have anything to do with Tim's cousin?"

"No." Helen took a sip of wine as she gauged her words. "I don't regret our night together...but I realized later that it had different meanings for us...I was weak...I needed your love that night but it was wrong of me not to explain that before hand."

Martin studied her.

She could see the pain in his eyes. "I'm sorry."

"Did I disappoint you?"

"Not at all." She covered his hand with hers. "It was a night I'll always remember. I just wasn't emotionally ready for it."

Martin's smile caught her off guard. "So, if I understand you correctly, you aren't letting me down easy, you just want to take it a day at a time."

"Yes. I understand if that's not what you want."

"You're worth waiting for…but I have to ask you point blank if you are planning on dating Tyler."

Helen smiled. "No. We are old friends. It is going to stay that way."

"I noticed how he looked at you."

"He made a promise to Tim to look after me and he took it too seriously." Helen shrugged. "I value his friendship and that is all there is to it." Helen could see the tension leave his face as she spoke. "I'll see him, go out to dinner here and there. Romance doesn't enter into it."

"Good."

"I hope you understand. I hope I'm making myself clear." Helen shook her head. "I wish I could give you more…"

Martin put up his hand. "Enough. I understand. I love you. I don't want either of us to rush into anything. We enjoy each other's company. We'll keep it at that…for now." Martin put his arm around her and pulled her close, stroking her soft red hair. "You've been on a wild ride the last few months. I know your head is spinning from all of it."

"Oh, Martin. You are just too good."

"Yes, well, don't tell anyone, it will tarnish my image as a hard ass cop." Martin laughed and squeezed her tight. "Just do me a favor…if you are going to take a job and be out of town, call and let me know. That Appleton business…I bit my nails to the quick not knowing where you were."

Helen laughed and looked up at him. "I will definitely call you."

✳   ✳   ✳   ✳

Donald Abington woke up in a cold sweat. He threw the blankets off and went to the bathroom to shower as the anger bubbled up from his gut. He'd realized quickly that Canada was a bad choice. He stood out in the French dominated province. It was time to move again.

He scowled when he looked in the mirror. He'd died his hair and eyebrows black and hated the way it changed his appearance. After his shower he packed his bags and checked out.

He drove to the bank and cashed a large check before leaving the area. As he headed down the two-lane highway he thought about the fortuneteller. He planned to torture her with messages and phone calls until the day they would finally meet and he would give her her due.

Donald noticed a young hitchhiker and stopped to pick her up. "Hey, where are you headed?" Donald popped open the passenger door for her.

"West. I'm on my way back to Oregon." The girl smiled as she took off her bulky pack and set it on the back seat.

"You're a long way from home."

"How far are you going?"

"Straight through to British Columbia." Donald smiled.

"That's incredible." The girl gushed as she pulled off her hat, exposing a short crown of bright red curls.

Donald froze when he saw her hair. He swallowed hard, clutching the wheel.

"How long do you think it will take to get there?" She held out her hand. "My name is Ann...and you are?"

"Don. Nice to meet you. I figure we'll be there by tomorrow night."

"This is great. I told my parents I'd be home Friday. I'll be able to surprise them."

Donald kept his eyes on the road as she chatted about college and her parents. He couldn't resist having some fun with the redhead and planned it as he drove the long snaking highway. They stopped to refuel and continued on until seven that night when Donald stopped for something to eat.

Ann sat across from him in the booth, totally at ease as she ordered a burger and coke. Donald ordered the same and sat back staring at her.

"I can't believe my luck." Ann smiled. "So you didn't say what you were going to BC for."

"My mother lives there. I haven't been to see her in over a year. She's not getting any younger and I had vacation time coming."

"Oh, by the fancy car I thought you were independently wealthy." Ann laughed.

"I wish." Donald looked up at the waitress as she set down their drinks. "Thank you."

Donald unfolded the map on the table and found the perfect spot. It looked to be one hundred and twenty miles away.

"You don't need to worry about that. This highway goes all the way there. Doesn't even change numbers between provinces."

"That's great." Donald set the map on the seat. "How simple is that?"

They finished their dinner and Donald went into the convenience store to pick up a few things. Ann stood outside the door smoking, as he collected the items on his list. Scissors, duck tape, disposable camera, manila envelopes and postage stamps. For effect he grabbed some snack foods and soft drinks. When he walked outside Ann followed him to the car. He put the bag of food in the back seat and put the other in the trunk.

"Help yourself to the junk food." Donald said as they headed back onto the highway.

"I couldn't eat another thing right now, thank you." Ann relaxed in the leather seat looking out the window.

An hour and a half out, Ann fell asleep only to wake a short while later when he pulled off into a picnic area.

"What's wrong?"

"Nothing. I just need to rest my eyes for a few minutes. I hope you don't mind."

"Not at all."

"Nature calls, I'll be back." Donald said as he pulled out the keys. He grabbed the knife wedged between the door and the seat and slipped it into his coat pocket as he got out of the car.

He walked into the woods and found a small clearing thirty feet in and returned to the car with the knife in his hand. She smiled at him as he walked toward her and opened her door. The smile turned to horror when he stuck the knife to her throat and ordered her out of the car.

Donald popped open the trunk with his remote and dragged her backwards to retrieve the bag.

"What are you going to do? Please let me go." Ann cried as he pressed the knife against her throat. "Please, I have a family. Please let me go."

"Don't fight and everything will be fine."

"Please let me go." She sobbed as he dragged her into the woods.

CHAPTER 16

▼

"Martin." Helen cried into the phone as she stared at the yellow envelope.

"Calm down. What is it?"

"He killed again…he sent me a letter with red hair in it and a young woman's license." Helen was shaking, as she spoke.

"I'll be right over."

Helen hung up the phone and walked out to the living room. She paced in front of the roaring fire, her muscles tight, her body cold, as she waited for Martin. China ran to the door as he pulled into the driveway. Helen rushed to him and cried against his chest as he embraced her.

"I'm here."

"It's been three weeks since I got a message from him and now this." Helen released him and stepped back, pointing at the table. She wiped the tears from her eyes as he walked over and picked up the envelope.

"It was sent from Canada."

"He's back in the U.S." Helen sat down. "West coast."

Martin took a plastic bag from the cupboard and sealed the envelope inside. "He's a savage." Martin spat through clenched teeth. "Damn him."

"He's not going to stop until he's caught." Helen covered her face with her hands, leaning her elbows on the table.

"They're going to catch him." Martin patted her shoulder.

Helen looked up at him, wiping the tears from her eyes. "I'm sorry. It was just such a shock." Helen rubbed her upper arms and walked over to the fireplace.

"Look, I'm going to take this to the station so we can forward it to the FBI. How about I pick up take out and come back here for dinner?"

"That would be wonderful. I don't feel like being alone." Helen couldn't control the sobs that wracked her body as she grabbed for the mantle.

Martin rushed over to embrace her. "It's okay. The guy is too far away to hurt you."

"I'm sorry." Helen looked up at him. "Go do your job."

"I'll be back in an hour." Martin said as he released her. China stood beside them head down. Martin patted the dog's back. "You look after her until I get back."

Martin swooped up the plastic bag of evidence and rushed outside. He returned forty minutes later with dinner in a paper sack. "How are you?"

"Better." Helen moved the stack of mail to the counter and set the table.

"Did you go through the rest of this?"

"Not yet."

"May I?"

Helen nodded.

"Shit." Martin held up another envelope. He opened it carefully and dropped the contents onto the counter. A note was attached to a disposable camera. It read: Pictures of my vacation. Enjoy.

"Shit." Martin took out another plastic bag. "This guy is too cocky to hide much longer."

"Do you have to leave?"

"No. I'll bring this to the photo lab in the morning." He said as he set the bag on the counter.

"Didn't they freeze his assets?"

"In the U.S. But they have no jurisdiction over accounts in other countries. I'm sure he's got a few of those. We just have to be patient."

"That's hard to do with him sending me this shit." Helen walked to her bedroom and grabbed a thick sweater. When she returned Martin was doling out large portions of the food.

"I can't eat all that."

"You are going to try." Martin smiled. "Come sit down."

*   *   *   *

The following morning Martin brought in the film and waited for the photos. The technician came out of the room shaking his head.

"These are disgusting." He handed the stack of pictures to Martin. "Where did you get the camera?"

"Donald Abington sent it to Helen Staples. He also sent another little package with the woman's hair and license."

"Gees. Any leads on the his location?"

"No, the camera was mailed from Canada." Martin flipped through the gory pictures.

The first few photos showed the victim with her mouth and hands taped, the next she was naked and they only got worse from there, the last being her naked bloody body duct taped to a tree.

"Forward these and the camera to the FBI." Martin said as he handed them back to the technician.

"Sure."

Martin returned to his office weighted by a feeling of dread. He called Helen and explained what had been on the photos, leaving out the details. He was glad to accept when she invited him to dinner. It didn't hurt that she was baking a cake for dessert.

He felt better after the call but still worried that the bastard would come back for her if given the chance. He put in a call to Agent Parker only to be disappointed by the lack of developments in the case.

Martin signed off on two case files and headed for his apartment. He packed up a bag, hoping Helen wouldn't object to him staying with her again. The West Coast was only a few hours away by plane and the idea of Helen being alone was out of the question.

"Hey. Dinner won't be ready for another two hours." Helen looked down at his leather bag.

"Yes, well…" Martin set the bag by the door. "I've decided to bunk with you for a few days."

"Why?"

"Why? The guy could hop on a plane and be here." Martin snapped his fingers. He took off his coat and hung it on the hook. "I don't want to risk you being here alone any more than is necessary. I'll take the guest room." He picked up the bag and walked down the hall.

He set the bag on the bed and closed the curtains then went room to room until they were all closed.

"Oh, Martin."

"Hey. We can't take any chances."

"Did you hear something?"

"No." He said as he pulled the slider drapes closed. Martin wished he'd killed him when he looked at Helen, her face pale, her eyes filled with fear. "Hey, the FBI wants him and now the Canadians are looking for him as well. It won't be much longer."

Helen nodded and checked the temperature on the roast. Martin watched her as she pulled the chocolate cake out of the upper oven.

"That smells great."

"You can bring half of it to work with you or it'll go stale. I only know how to make it in one size." Helen smiled.

"The guys will be amazed...hey...I don't think I want them to know what a good cook you are. I don't need the competition."

"You couldn't have competition." Helen laughed.

Martin studied her. Maybe it was going to work out between them. He had to believe it. Martin wished he could find Abington and put an end to Helen's fears. The job was out of his reach so long as the bastard didn't return to the area. Martin would be ready for such an event and no warning from Helen would spare his life this time.

"What dark thoughts you're having." Helen scowled. "That won't help my mood. You and I both know you would never kill unless you had no choice."

Martin leaned back and crossed his arms over his chest. "You aren't supposed to be doing that."

"You set it out there."

"Damn."

"Damn nothing." Helen smiled. "I am flattered by your intensity." She shrugged and the buzzer on the lower oven went off. "Can you put a log on the fire while I mash the potatoes?"

"You must go through a shit load of wood. I've never seen anything like it."

"It's one of my few luxuries. I burn all winter long. I love the smell as well as the heat." Helen smiled.

She was clearing the table when the phone rang. Martin watched as Helen answered and wasn't happy when he heard it was Tyler. The guy was a ringer for her deceased boyfriend and he wanted back into Helen's life in a big way.

Martin walked over to the mantle and looked at the picture of the trio as Helen spoke to Tyler.

"No. I'm not up to company tonight. I'm going to turn in early...sure...yes...okay. I'll talk to you then. Take care."

Martin was glad she couldn't see his smile but he felt smug when she quickly turned down Tyler's request to visit.

Martin was there not only to protect her but also to be near her. He knew the odds of Abington being stupid enough to come back were a million to one, but that one stabbed at his mind.

He studied Helen as she sat on the couch. Martin couldn't help wondering when she would be his. He longed for the day when he could be on solid ground with her. No doubts, no tension, just closeness.

"You out did yourself with that dinner tonight."

"Thanks."

"How are you holding up?" He asked as he sat beside her.

"I'm all right…but I won't feel safe until Abington is put away."

"I should have killed him when I had the chance."

"If you had and I didn't get free, the girl and I would have died down there. We got lucky, he got sloppy." Helen shook her head. "I don't understand how someone could be so evil. Plenty of people a have harsh childhood, unhappiness, they don't grow up to be mass murderers."

"It's a power trip."

"But the guy's an asshole."

Martin grinned at her choice of words.

"He has money. He can simply disappear and live quietly somewhere. Instead he chooses not only to kill but to brag about it to me."

"He's connected with you."

"Don't say that."

"Not in that way…I mean, he probably blames you for the situation he's in. He wants revenge. Right now he's focused on you but he can't get to you…so he'll torment you from a distance until he can."

"That's a comforting thought."

"I'm trying to help you understand. He isn't like most people…thank God. Everything about his thought process is warped." Martin thought about the pictures of the murdered redhead. "Change of subject. Do you mind if I put on the news?"

"Go right ahead."

"The body of a missing Oregon woman was found by police in Canada this morning. Her murder is being linked to the college murders in this area." The young newscaster spoke standing outside the yellow tape that cordoned off the crime scene. "We have information that Donald Abington…" His photo was posted in the corner of the screen. "Has been spotted in several provinces in Canada and was last seen in British Columbia. We will keep you updated on the story and the FBI as well as Canadian authorities asks that anyone with any information about Donald Abington call the police immediately. They caution not to approach him as he is armed..." the reporter glanced over her shoulder at the crime scene. "And dangerous."

"So much for changing the subject." Helen said, shaking her head.

*   *   *   *

It took three days for Helene to decide to go through the mail she'd let gather on her desk. Boredom engulfed her when Martin was at work. Though she no longer had an officer posted outside, Martin insisted on keeping the shades drawn. She was beginning to feel cooped up in her cottage. She hoped the mail would offer her some relief.

The third letter she opened contained a missing poster with the photo of a young woman. By the dates on the flyer she'd disappeared from her home almost a year before. Helen read the letter, sent by the woman's mother. In it she begged for Helen's help. She wanted to put her daughter to rest if she'd met with foul play. Helen set down the letter and stared at the woman's photo.

After a few minutes she dialed the number on the letter.

"Yes, could I speak with Tina Jarvis?"

"This is she."

"Hello, Mrs. Jarvis, this is Helen Staples." Helen lit a cigarette. "I've just read your letter."

"Can you help?"

"I'm willing to try. I want to meet with you."

"It's about an hour drive...I can be there by two o'clock."

"I'd rather come to you, if you don't mind." Helen had the feeling she could help, but nothing else came to her. "Is her house near yours?"

"Yes."

"Is anyone living there?"

"Yes. Her husband, Andrew."

"I'd like to meet with him." Helen studied the woman in the photo. "How long were they married?"

"Four months...to the day." The woman cried.

"I'll be there at two-thirty."

Mrs. Jarvis gave directions to Helen and she jotted them down on the back of the letter. She let China out and packed an overnight bag. She was about to walk out the door when Martin called.

"Oh, hi. I'm just on my way out. I've taken a case in Rhode Island. I think I might stay over night." Helen said as China leaned against her.

"Would you like me to come by and let the dog out tonight?"

"You can stay here if you like. I should be back by tomorrow night."

"I have some things to take care of at my apartment, but I'll let her out tonight and before I go to work in the morning."

"Thank you, Martin. I really appreciate it."

"Good luck. Call me if you need anything."

"Thanks. I will. Talk to you tomorrow."

Helen was excited about getting out. She patted China and gave her instructions to behave before she left. She needed a change of scenery. More so, she needed something to focus on other than Donald Abington.

She enjoyed the long drive. Helen arrived at the Jarvis home and was greeted by Tina Jarvis and Andrew Torris, the young woman's husband.

When Helen walked in the house she could feel the warmth and love. There were several photos of young people including Wendy, the missing woman. Helen turned to Mrs. Jarvis.

"Can you tell me about the last time you spoke with her?" Helen asked.

"Please have a seat." The woman said with tears pooling in her blue eyes. "I talked to Wendy the night before she disappeared…she was excited about her trip to Boston the next morning."

Helen turned to Andrew. She had a sense he didn't approve of her being involved. "When was the last time you spoke to her?"

"The night before. I was working the night shift at the plant. I went in at ten. When I left the house she was there. When I came home in the morning she was gone."

"Was her purse there?"

"Everything was." He stood and walked to the window. "Her car was in the driveway, keys on the counter where she always left them."

"I'd like to go your house." Helen said as she walked toward him. Helen was getting a deep sense that he was hiding something but it confused her because she felt Wendy was still alive.

"I told Tina I'd cooperate with you, but I don't believe in psychics." Andrew stared down at her.

"I know. I appreciate your indulgence." Helen smiled.

"I'll come too." Tina said.

"I'll follow you." Helen walked out to her car and looked back at Andrew in the rear view mirror as he spoke to Mrs. Jarvis by her car door. He appeared nervous which made Helen even more anxious to see his house.

They drove the six blocks and Helen parked on the street in front of the brick front cape as Andrew pulled into the drive. It was quite a spectacular home, which puzzled Helen given Andrew worked at a plant and Wendy had worked as a secretary.

She walked up the stone path to the front door and as soon as she stepped inside, she was hit by a vision.

Andrew and Wendy were fighting. Wendy ran out into their yard and Andrew tackled her. Her head struck the corner of the outdoor brick fireplace as she was knocked to the ground. Andrew got up, stunned.

Helen opened her eyes and looked at Andrew and then at Mrs. Jarvis. "She's confused...but she isn't dead."

Andrew rocked on his feet and quickly sat down. "What do you mean?"

Helen studied him as she sat on the chair by the door, the vision looping in her mind's eye like a re-run. "Why was she going to go to Boston?"

"She was going with my other daughter, Brenda. They did it every year. They'd spend the weekend shopping and going to shows and concerts. It was a tradition."

Helen looked around the living room at the built in shelves holding family photos and the seascape paintings. And then turned her attention back to Andrew who was sitting rigid on the chair, staring down at the floor.

"You didn't mean to hurt her. She's still alive."

Mrs. Jarvis jumped off the seat. "What do you mean?"

"Do you want to tell her, or should I?"

"I can't. I love my wife...I didn't mean for it to happen."

"For what to happen?" Mrs. Jarvis screamed at him.

"Please sit down." Helen said, touching the woman's arm.

"What is it?" She cried as she lowered herself onto the chair.

"They had a fight that night. Wendy ran outside."

Andrew looked up at her.

"She fell and hit her head on the fireplace out there."

Mrs. Jarvis turned toward her son-in-law. "Why didn't you call an ambulance?"

"I thought she was dead." Andrew cried. "I chased her outside...we were fighting about the weekend...I didn't want her to go. She hit her head..." He said as he stood and walked to the door. "I thought she was dead. I tried to wake her." He shook his head.

"What did you do with her?"

"Nothing." Andrew turned to face her. "After a few minutes of trying to wake her up, I came inside to get a towel for her head...when I went outside, she was gone."

"Why didn't you tell the police?" Mrs. Jarvis asked.

"I thought no one would believe me."

Helen could see Wendy stumbling up a hill in the darkness. Boston. She had gone to Boston. Damn, Helen thought, why did Wendy have to pick such a big place to get lost in.

"I need your most recent photos of her."

Andrew walked over to the small desk in the corner and pulled out an envelope containing photos. He set two aside and handed them to Helen. "Do you really think she's alive?"

"I'm sure of it."

Andrew sat down on the chair and covered his face with his hands. Helen looked at the pair knowing they were going to have a lot to talk about.

"I'm going to leave."

"But you only just got here." Mrs. Jarvis said.

"I'm going to look for her. May I keep these pictures?"

"Yes." Andrew said, wiping his red face.

CHAPTER 17

▼

Helen left and headed north to Boston. She was sure Wendy was there. How to find her was another thing entirely.

It was early evening when she checked into the hotel. After bringing her bag up to the room she went down to get something to eat. The elevator door opened and Tyler was walking through the main entrance. He stopped and his mouth dropped open when he saw her.

"What are you doing here?" Tyler asked as he rushed over and hugged her.

"I'm working on a missing person's case."

"Gees, woman, haven't you had enough trouble?"

"This is different."

"Tell me about it over dinner." Tyler said smiling down at her.

"What are you doing here?"

"I work right across the street. I've had dinner here twice this week. You know I don't cook…come on, you can tell me all about the case."

"Sure."

Tyler hooked her arm and walked her into the dining room. "Tyler Jones, I have a reservation for one, it's now two."

"No problem. We'll have that ready for you in a moment." The elderly host said as he waved a waiter over.

"It's good to see you." Tyler smiled. "I'm almost to the point where I can take a few days off. We need to plan something."

They were escorted to a table with a grand view of the budding garden. Tyler pointed to the window. "Beside the food, it's got a nice view. I'd rather look at that than skyscrapers." Tyler smiled.

"I'm so glad winter is almost over, though I'm not putting my heavy coat away just yet."

"You still planning a camping trip?"

"Yes. For now, I'm working." Helen smiled at him. "I enjoy helping people. It's so different from how I felt about readings." She put up her hand. "Don't get me wrong, it paid the bills for several years…but this…it's so different."

"I guess."

"It's like…watching a movie rather than seeing a frame here and there."

"Is it really? Like watching a movie, I mean?"

Helen nodded. "Take today. I talked to this woman in Rhode Island. I have a feeling I should go there so I go." Helen held her thought while Tyler ordered their martinis. "So anyway…the case is cold. Police have no leads. When I meet the husband, I know he's holding something back. Nothing specific. We go to the missing woman's house and as soon as I walk in, it hits me. I can see the woman and her husband fighting…she falls and hits her head…he panics. He didn't mean for her to get hurt but she is."

"You've got to be kidding me."

"No. It was like I was there watching it when it happened." Helen took a sip of the drink as Tyler ordered a special dish for the two of them. "After I told the pair what I saw, the husband admitted it."

"Case closed?"

"Not at all. The woman is still alive."

"How do you know?" Tyler waved off the last statement. "Sorry. I still haven't adjusted to your powers."

"Gift. My mother was right. I may not feel grateful for it, but gift is the best description."

"Do you think you can find her?"

Helen shrugged. "I will if it's meant to be. She's been gone for a year. She could have started a new life or she could be wandering the streets. I know she's confused."

"You're amazing." Tyler smiled. "So you came here to find the woman. But she's from Rhode Island."

"She's here. I'm going to start with the hospitals first thing in the morning."

"You're excited about this, aren't you?"

"I am. Right now I can pick and choose the cases I work on. Funny thing is, it isn't work. It's like I'm pushed in this direction or led in that direction. I'm just following my gift."

"I noticed it last time I saw you…" Tyler leaned back in his seat and crossed his arms over his wide chest. "You've changed."

"How could I not with what has happened?"

"It's like you're stronger now."

Helen smiled. "I am. I feel good." She studied his handsome face. "How's the transition been for you, at work?"

"No complaints. They had to adjust to me as well as I to them. Normal stuff." Tyler grinned. "I'm seriously thinking about buying a house. I was hoping you could help me with that."

"Me? I don't know anything about real estate."

"You know what you like. I was thinking I could give you a rough idea of what I want and you could narrow down the field for me."

"I'll do what I can. What exactly are you looking for?"

"Three bedrooms, large kitchen-."

"You don't cook." Helen laughed. "What's the three bedrooms for?"

Tyler shrugged. "The future. I don't want to have to look for a bigger place in five years. I'd rather get what I need the first time."

Helen didn't bite. "Anything else? Garage?"

"I've made out a list."

"Well, I'm happy to help you when I'm free. I don't imagine this case will take me too long. I'll call you and we can sit down and go over the list."

"How about next weekend?"

"Right now it looks good but I'll call you say, Thursday."

Tyler raised his glass. "To friends."

"To friends." Helen touched her glass to his and finished the last of the drink as the waiter served their dinners.

Over the next two hours they talked about their work and the changes in their lives.

As soon as Helen was alone in the hotel room she went to the window and stared out over the city. She looked at the high rises and wondered how many people lived in those buildings and why anyone would chose to live in such an impersonal environment.

Tomorrow she'd hit the hospitals with the photos and prayed she'd find a lead that would narrow down the search. She tried not to dwell on the enormity of the task. Boston was a huge city but Helen was sure that Wendy was still there.

Sunrise brought the bustle back to the city as people rushed to the subway and hailed taxis on the street. Helen felt renewed by the good nights sleep and ready to start her search in earnest.

She got a taxi and spent all morning going hospital to hospital, showing the photos of Wendy. Helen describe the situation each time she hit an emergency room but no one could remember any such woman being there.

Just after noon Helen decided to take a break. She walked into the lobby of the hospital and looked for the cafeteria. She bought a sandwich and juice and took her tray to the dining area. Helen was surprised to see it was packed. She walked to a table where a nurse was sitting and asked if she could join her.

The blond nurse smiled up at her. "Feel free. I'm about done anyway."

"Thank you." Helen sat down and took a deep breath.

"Are you visiting family here?" The nurse asked.

"No. I'm looking for someone."

"Maybe I can help. Does this person work here?"

"No. Well, at least I don't think so. Her name is Wendy Torres. She's twenty-three. She's been missing for a year, she's from Rhode Island but I believe she might be in Boston." Helen took the picture out of her purse and showed it to the woman. "She sustained a head injury right before she went missing. I think she's confused or maybe has amnesia-." Helen stopped talking as the nurse studied the photo.

"She looks a lot better in this photo…if it's the same woman."

"What do you mean?"

"I work in emergency. About a year ago a man brought her in. He'd found her in the subway. She had a bad gash on her head and…" the nurse looked up at her. "She had amnesia."

"Do you know where she is now?" Helen's heart sped.

"No. Like I said, I work emergency. She was transferred to a ward once we fixed her up. I believe she came in for a few visits with Dr. Brahn."

"She didn't know who she was?"

"No idea. The doctor nicknamed her June and from the grapevine I understood she kept the name after she was released." The nurse took another look at the photo and handed it back to her.

"Her family is desperate to find her…this is such a big city…" Helen looked out the window.

"I'll take you to Dr. Brahn. I have to caution you, we are very strict about patient confidentiality."

Helen nodded. "I just need to be pointed in the right direction."

"Wait a minute…aren't you that psychic?"

Helen smiled as the heat rose to her cheeks. "Yes. But I'd rather not advertise the fact." Helen lowered her voice as she spoke.

The nurse nodded and checked her watch. "I've got to get back to my station." She stood and picked up her tray. "You can find me in the emergency room when you are done with your lunch."

"No. That's okay. I'm not really hungry. Could you take me to Dr. Brahn?" Helen picked up the tray and followed the nurse to the disposal area. "I really appreciate your help."

"The first week she was here I visited with her a few times. She was one lost soul."

"She still is."

They walked to the elevator and went to the third floor. The nurse held the door open.

"They're paging me. I've got to get back downstairs. Just go straight down this hall, Dr. Brahn's is the last door on the right."

"Thank you so much for everything."

"I hope you find her."

Helen waved and walked down the hall, the smell of disinfectant irritating her nose. She hated the smell of hospitals from as far back as she could remember.

The doctor's door opened and a tall man with stark white hair walked into the hall.

"Dr. Brahn?"

"Yes?" His hazel eyes narrowed at her.

"My name is Helen Staples." She said as she opened her bag. She pulled out the photo and showed it to him. "I was hoping you could help me find this woman. Her name is Wendy Torres. I believe she was a patient of yours about a year ago."

The doctor glanced at the photo and looked into her eyes. "Patient confidentiality." He shook his head. "I can't talk about her."

"If, if I could tell you a story, maybe we could think of a way to help her."

He stood silent for a moment and then walked into his office, leaving the door open behind him. Helen walked inside and sat at his desk facing him, still holding the photo in her hands.

"Are you a private detective?"

"Of sorts."

"Do you have a business card?"

Helen wished he'd had a thousand but she didn't have one. She shook her head.

"The story?"

"A year ago, Wendy…" Helen held up the photo. "Had an argument with her husband. She ran outside and to make a long story short, fell and struck her head. Her husband couldn't wake her, he went inside to get something to put on her wound and when he came back she was gone. Her family lives in Rhode Island."

"So how did she get here with such an injury, as you've described it?"

"That part I don't know. What I do know is that every year, Wendy and her sister came to Boston for a weekend. Their trip was planned for the following day. I feel…" Helen knew what questions were to follow but continued anyway. "When she woke, she was focused on Boston but didn't know why. She came here for answers."

"How do you know?"

"I just know."

He leaned back in his chair and studied her for several minutes. "That isn't much of an answer." He shook his head. "Like I told you to begin with, patient confidentiality. I can't help you."

"She may have adjusted to her knew life, but I can assure you, she's very sad and confused. She'll stay that way until she finds out who she really is. You can't want that for her."

"What are you? What's your job title?"

"I locate missing persons."

"You're a private investigator."

"Along those lines." Helen could tell she was losing him. "About three months ago I helped find a little boy who was missing from Boston. He was trying to find an elderly neighbor and made it all the way to Cape Cod."

The doctor crossed his arms over his chest. "I see."

"I found him. Now I'm going to find Wendy. If that means I walk every street of this city, so be it. But it would be a lot easier if you'd give me even a north, south, east or west."

He checked his watch again. "I must go. Good luck finding her." The doctor got up and walked to the door. "Please. I have an appointment."

Helen walked over to him and touched his hand. When she did, she saw what she was looking for. "Where is Henry's Place?"

He shook her hand off of his as if it were burning him and took a step back. "Leave now." He growled.

Helen walked into the hallway and he closed the door behind her. Dr. Brahn had a personal interest in Wendy. He'd fallen in love with the young woman. He'd taken her under his wing and the more she depended on him, the more he loved her.

Helen went to the nurse's station and borrowed the phone book. She jotted down the address and ran to the elevator. When she got downstairs she rushed out to a yellow cab, her heart was banging in her ears as she rattled off the address to the driver.

She shook her head when he drove two blocks and pulled over. With the traffic she could have walked there faster. She paid the driver and went inside. The lounge was dark and it took her a few minutes to focus.

"Have a seat. I'll be right with you." A brunette said as she rushed by carrying a full tray. "It's kind of busy. We have a big party going on in the back."

Helen nodded and walked directly into the noisy back room. She spotted Wendy in the corner clearing glasses off of a large round table.

Helen walked over to her. "Excuse me."

"Excuse me. This is a private party. I know you aren't on the guest list." Wendy eyed her.

"I came here to see you." Helen smiled.

"I don't know you."

"Your mother sent me."

Wendy swayed and grabbed the table. "My mother?"

"Yes…" Helen looked around the room. "Can we go somewhere and talk?"

"I…" Her face had gone white. She held up a finger to the tall waitress. "I'll be back in a minute."

"It had better be a minute." The tall one hissed.

"What do you know about my mother?" Wendy asked as she walked out the side door.

"She's been looking for you for almost a year."

Tears welled in her eyes when Helen showed her the photo. "Where did you get that?" Wendy asked as she lowered herself onto the old wooden bench.

"Your husband gave it to me. Your mother asked me to help find you."

The tall waitress popped open the side door. "You got a call."

"Take a message, please."

The woman scowled and walked inside.

"I'm married?"

"Yes. Your family is very worried about you. Maybe it would help if we go to them."

"I have to work…" Wendy cried "I don't remember them."

"I know. It might help if you meet with them. What time do you get off?"

"I just started. I'm on until nine, maybe ten, depends on when things die down."

"How would you feel if I arrange for them to come here?" Helen asked as the tall waitress opened the door again.

"What? I…I don't know."

"I'll call them. Tell them to come here…you're an adult, you can end the conversation any time you want."

Wendy nodded as she stood. "I…will you be with them?"

"I'll be here." Helen didn't want to tell her that she couldn't get rid of her if she tried. She watched Wendy walk inside before calling Mrs. Jarvis on her cell phone. "Hi, this is Helen Staples. I've found your daughter." The woman screamed in her ear and quickly apologized.

"When can we see her? How did you find her? Where is she?"

"She was brought to a Boston hospital. She has amnesia."

"How is she?"

"She looks fine. She's working as a waitress near the hospital. She's agreed to see you when she is done working tonight. By the look in her eyes I'd say she's afraid but she's desperate to know who she is."

Helen gave her directions and promised to keep an eye on Wendy until they arrived. Helen walked around the building and in through the front door. The same waitress that greeted her the first time did a double take when she walked in. Helen smiled at her and took a seat by the window to wait. She decided to stay another night since the meeting wouldn't take place for hours.

She ordered a soft drink and looked over the menu. She felt someone staring in at her and looked up to see Tyler with his hands on his hips. He laughed and walked inside.

"What are you doing?" He asked as he walked to the table.

"Working. I told you about it last night."

"Did you have any luck?" Tyler glanced around the room.

"See the waitress with the short brown hair?"

"Yes. She looks ill."

"That's her. I just talked to her. Her family is coming up." Helen slid the menu over to him. "Did you eat?"

"About an hour ago. I was just walking back from a lunch meeting when I saw you. Are you sure you have the right woman?"

Helen's eyes widened when Dr. Brahn walked through the door. Wendy saw him and ran into his arms, crying. He helped her to a table in the corner where he tried to comfort her. "He's going to complicate things."

"Who is he?"

"Her doctor...and lover."

"Man." Tyler shook his head and then looked at her. "How do you do it?"

"I don't know. I just hope her mother and husband come straight here."

"Chalk another one up for Helen." Tyler checked his watch. "I have to get going. I'm working late tonight...care to meet me for dinner?"

"Sure. I'll be tied up here for at least a few hours."

Tyler opened his briefcase on the table and pulled out a real estate book. "I got this in the morning mail. Maybe you could look through it for me while you wait." Tyler set the book in front of her. "And here's a rough list of requirements." Tyler stood and kissed her forehead. "Thanks. You've got my cell number, call me when you're ready. And take a cab. You can't walk around out here after dark."

"Yes, sir." Helen laughed. "I'll call you."

She glanced over at the doctor and Wendy as Tyler walked out the door. The doctor was looking at her as Wendy spoke. Helen opened the book and flipped through the photos. She was half way though when Dr. Brahn walked over to the table and sat down.

"I'm sorry. You caught me off guard...we tried to find out who she was in the beginning...shit. She told me you said she has a husband."

"Yes."

"Is he involved with anyone? It has been a year."

"Not that I know of. I'm not sure." Helen could see the fear in his eyes.

"We're a couple. Of course our relationship began long after I stopped being her doctor."

"I understand you are both in shock...I'm sure everything will work out."

"When will they be here?"

"Probably close to three."

"Thank you." Dr. Brahn stood and returned to Wendy. They held hands and he quietly convinced her to take the rest of the shift off. When she agreed he walked over to the bartender to explain.

Helen flipped through the real estate book and made a serious effort to concentrate but ended up reading every description without really registering the details. She'd eaten a sandwich and finished two soft drinks and a glass of water before she saw Mrs. Travis rushing toward the door.

Helen stood to greet her.

"Where is she? Oh, God, I can't believe this." She cried.

"Please try to calm yourself." Helen pointed to where the couple was sitting and saw Wendy's mother's knees buckle. She grabbed for her arm as she burst into tears. "Please. She's very upset. She's had quite a shock."

"Wendy."

Wendy's eyes were wide as the woman rushed toward her. "Mama?" She stood and embraced her. "Mama, I've been…I know you…I know you, Mama."

Helen stood back, crying. Poor Dr. Brahn looked like he'd been stricken as he watched the reunion. But Helen had a feeling he didn't have anything to worry about. She returned to her table as the three sat together and watched from a distance as they hugged and cried.

An hour later Mrs. Jarvis walked over and sat opposite her. She opened her purse and handed Helen an envelope. "You are a miracle worker. I can't thank you enough for finding my baby."

"I'm glad I could help…may I ask why her husband didn't come?"

"I couldn't get a hold of him and I didn't want to wait."

Helen smiled. "It's probably better this way."

Mrs. Jarvis glanced over at her daughter. "She…it seems she's involved with that doctor…He's older than I am."

"And he loves her. He's taken excellent care of her for a year, you might want to focus on that when you relate to him."

"Of course. Of course. I don't care if he's ninety. He's kept her safe. Oh, Lord what a great day." Mrs. Jarvis stood. "You'll always be in my prayers."

"Thank you." Helen followed her over to Wendy's table. "I'm going to be leaving. Take care, and take it slow."

"Thank you so much." Wendy cried as she took her hand.

"I'll follow you out. I need to give these ladies a few minutes alone." Dr. Brahn said.

"Don't go to far." Wendy said.

"I won't. I'll be right outside." The doctor smiled.

Helen walked of the lounge and looked up the road for the cab.

"You found her because you touched me, didn't you?"

Helen looked into his hazel eyes. "Yes." Helen smiled. "That's when it all became clear."

"I don't understand it."

"Neither do I. You two are going to be fine."

"Excuse me?" He looked through the lounge window. "You said she is married."

"When I said she fell and hit her head, well, her husband, a young, hot headed man was chasing her. When he tackled her, that's when she hit her head. He didn't tell the police what happened and he's spent the last year thinking she was dead because of the injury." Helen shook her head. "She never had with him what she has with you. Don't be pushy, she's going to need a lot of time."

The doctor reached for her hand and thought better of it, quickly putting the hand in his pocket. Helen couldn't resist smiling.

"Thank you, Miss Staples."

"You're very welcome." Helen waved at the approaching cab and it squealed to a stop. "Take care."

CHAPTER 18

▼

Helen got into the cab and took a long deep breath. She was exhausted from the emotional day. Helen returned to the hotel and enjoyed a long steaming bubble bath before calling Tyler.

"I was wondering if you were a missing person." Tyler laughed.

"I needed an hour to shake off the day."

"Congratulations on a job well done."

"Thanks. I was just about to fix myself a drink." Helen said as she walked to the bar in the corner of the room.

"I'll join you."

"Where are you?"

"Just getting out of the elevator." Tyler knocked on the door.

Helen closed the phone and tied the sash on her bathrobe. She opened the door and Tyler stood there smiling, holding a glass vase filled with white roses. "What are you doing here?"

"I saw you get out of the cab. I told you I work across the street." He handed her the flowers.

"Thank you." Helen walked over and set them on the corner of the bar. "What can I get for you?"

"Martini." Tyler said as he loosened his tie. "How'd it go? Shit I was thinking about that woman during my last meeting. What a shock. Anyway, how did it work out?"

"Good." Helen smiled. "It's all going to work out fine."

"Do you think they'll press charges against the husband?"

"No. But the marriage ended the night she disappeared. They'll both figure that out quickly."

"Damn." Tyler sat on the barstool staring at her.

Helen poured their drinks and raised her glass. "To the lost, may they be found." She smiled.

"That's a good one. Here's another. To Helen, an extraordinary human being."

"Thank you."

It had been a good couple of days for Helen and she felt stronger because of it. They shared a drink and Helen got ready for dinner. She wore a short black dress with a sheer jacket and brushed out her hair, leaving it down for the evening. Helen had just picked up her purse to head out the door when her cell phone buzzed.

"Hey. How are you doing?" Martin asked. "Are you still in Rhode Island."

"Actually, I'm in Boston. I found her."

"Damn, you are something. Congratulations. Are you going to be home tonight?"

"No. I took the room for another night. I'll be back tomorrow morning."

"OK. I'll feed China for you."

Helen felt a pang of guilt for forgetting her loyal companion. "Thank you. I appreciate you looking after her."

"I'm happy to do it for you, Helen."

"I'll come by the station and see you tomorrow."

"Great. See you then."

When Helen hung up she felt Tyler's dark eyes burning into her. She returned the intense gaze with a smile and walked out the door.

"So, I take it he's got the keys to your place." Tyler said as he followed her to the elevator. "Do you think that's a good idea?"

"China does." Helen smiled and hit the lobby button.

"Look, Helen, you are still trying to figure out where you are going with your life. Don't you think this is going to complicate things?"

"This? This what?"

Tyler groaned and then was silent until they were seated in the corner of the restaurant.

"The guy is obviously interested in you. Do you think it's right to use him as a dog sitter."

"We are friends. Friends do things like that for each other."

Tyler slapped the table. "Don't tell me that's all you are."

"Tyler I don't think this is a…let's drop this okay?"

"I'm concerned. I don't think you should get involved with anyone, least of all the man who got you involved in a crime, got your damn leg shot."

Helen rolled her eyes. "My gifts got me involved. I went to him."

"Either way, you said your gifts changed when you met him."

"True. And look at me now. I've been able to help several people in dire need."

Tyler touched her hand. "Sure, but I worry about you. I've seen the news Helen." He scowled staring into her green eyes. "The bastard is still out there murdering woman. He's taken to murdering redheads. Don't tell me that has nothing to do with you."

"Red, blond, brunette, the man is a murderer."

"And he's holding a grudge against you."

Helen took in a long breath wishing she could light a cigarette. "You are right." She narrowed her eyes as she lowered her voice. "But I'm not going to live my life in fear. I know he'd like nothing better than to slice me up. I came face to face with the disturbed son-of-a-bitch. I know what he's capable of. I also know he's on the West Coast somewhere. I'm not in danger so long as he's not around here."

"And how will you know if he gets on a plane and comes after you?"

"I'll know."

They focused on their dinner, leaving the sprinkling of dialog to their food and surroundings.

"So, did you have a chance to look through the real estate book?" Tyler said as he stirred the cream into his after dinner coffee.

"I looked at it, but I couldn't concentrate on it." Helen smiled. "I will though. I plan to take a few days off so I'll have time to really focus on it."

"I'd appreciate it if you could set up appointments if you find something."

"I was thinking about it, why not find something closer to the city. You've got an hours commute each way."

"The way I drive it's about forty-five minutes." Tyler grinned.

"You should at least get closer to a T station."

"My mind's made up."

"Okay. Your choice." Helen smiled. "I did notice a house that might be perfect for me. A little bigger than mine but it has a fireplace in the living room, master bedroom and an attached studio or in-law apartment with a separate entrance that would make a perfect office."

"I didn't know you were thinking of moving. What brought this on?"

"The ad. I never planned on staying at my place forever. I bought it because it was a fixer upper on the water. It's worth three times what I paid for it...plus..." Her eyes filled with tears. "I shared many good times there with Tim and it would probably be good to start fresh in a new place. I'll still have my memories but not constant reminders."

"You never stop surprising me. Well, we should go see it this weekend." Tyler smiled.

"How about Saturday noon?"

"Try to set it up...but don't forget, we are supposed to be house hunting for me."

"I know. I'll dedicate my afternoon to your search."

Tyler walked her back to her room and asked to see the ad. "Oh, this is nice." They spent a few minutes going through the book before Tyler took his leave.

Mrs. Jarvis called Helen at eight in the morning to thank her again. The upbeat call started Helen's day on a high note. She was packed and driving out of the city by ten o'clock. She hated driving in the city but it was a straight shot from the hotel to the highway.

She went to see Martin before going home and was greeted by him scowling and rushing her into his office.

"You had a few notes from Abington. I turned them over to the FBI."

"You look horrible." Helen sat across from him at the wide desk.

"I'm worried...you're not?"

"I'm concerned. I'll know if he gets close. Then I'll worry. I can't let him control my life."

Martin leaned back in the chair and studied her. "Fine."

"I'm going to be moving. That should help."

"Moving where?"

Helen explained what she was planning.

"That should help. Damn, your house was on the news for weeks. That's a good idea."

"Like I said, it's not why I'm moving but a definite benefit if it works out."

Helen spent a half-hour with him and once he seemed to relax she headed home. China was happy to see her and Helen played on the beach with her in an attempt to make up for her time away.

After lunch she sat at the table and studied the description of the house that had caught her eye. She noted the name of the realtor and decided to call to set up a viewing for Saturday.

"I am showing it to a perspective buyer for the second time at four this afternoon. We do have several other fine homes in the area."

"Has he signed anything on the property?"

"Well, no, but he does seem quite interested. I'm sure-"

"I'm going to be selling my house if I can find the right home. I would need a realtor." Helen smiled.

"What is your address?"

"211 Beachwood."

"That's on the ocean side."

"Yes. Now I'm free all day."

"I have an appointment near the home in a half hour. I guess I could show it to you then, but like I said, the gentleman will probably sign on it this afternoon."

"I'll meet you there in an hour."

"The price is reasonable and firm." The realtor warned.

"That isn't a problem."

Helen was excited and went to the desk for her checkbook. If the home was even close to the way it appeared in the photos, she was ready to buy it. She walked around the house for a few minutes before deciding to head out to the property to wait.

It was only a mile and a half from her house. There was a stone wall separating the property from the neighbors on each side with a wrought iron fence across the front. The perfect set up for her dog. Helen pulled up in front and walked up the driveway. She peeked into the two-car garage and was surprised at how deep it was.

She heard a car behind her and turned to see an elderly woman waving at her as she shut off the car.

"Miss Staples. It's a pleasure to meet you. My name is Eleanor Turner…now as I said on the phone, I do have a serious buyer looking at it in an hour. But the house is vacant so we can have a look. I did pull up a few other houses along this beach that may be appropriate. If anything interests you we can set up a viewing. I am booked for the rest of the day." She said as she walked toward the front door.

Helen was sure it was the right place when she saw the inside. The kitchen and living room were open and huge. The stone fireplace reached to the vaulted ceiling as it did in the master bedroom. French doors that led to a deck and gave a dramatic view of the ocean and the lighthouse accented the living room.

The basement was finished complete with a bathroom but the kicker was the studio apartment. It had a full bath and a kitchenette behind a sliding wood curtain, a large brick fireplace in the corner and the same fantastic view as the living room. By the end of the tour, Helen was in love with the place. She could picture her office furniture in the studio and aside from adding color to the white walls throughout, it was perfect.

"I'll take it." Helen said as she followed the realtor through the glass-enclosed breezeway that connected the studio to the main house.

The realtor turned and looked at her, her round cheeks flush. "Well I…Mr. Hunter will be here soon."

"You said he hasn't signed anything. I've got my checkbook and I'm ready to sign a binder."

"Don't you need time to think about it?" She checked her watch.

"I know what I want."

"You haven't' been pre-qualified."

Helen thought about the check for twenty-five thousand that she'd deposited that morning on the way to Martin's. The amount in her checking account was mind boggling. She pulled out her cell phone and called the bank, smiling at the realtor all the while. Helen requested her balance and held the phone out so that Mrs. Turner could hear. She thanked the teller and hung up the phone.

"Will that do? Or should I call back and get you a balance on my savings account too?" Helen asked smiling.

The woman shook her head no and pulled the cell phone out of her purse. "One moment please."

Helen walked into the master bedroom for another look as the realtor called and gave the bad news to the man.

"He wasn't happy." She scowled.

Helen shrugged. "I am. This place is wonderful. And of course I'll sign you as the realtor for my house." Helen saw her mood change with the idea. "Maybe your client would be interested in it."

"Maybe. But first things first."

They sat at the kitchen island and worked out the details.

Helen put down a fifty-percent deposit and took the papers to the bank to get the mortgage going. She dropped everything off at the realtor's office at six o'clock that night.

"I've crunched the numbers on your old house and it works out to be a pretty even trade." The realtor slid the paper work over to her. "When would you like to close?"

"As soon as possible. I have a lot of painting to do before I can move in and I'd rather move out of my house before you start showing it. I have a large dog who wouldn't take to strangers coming and going without me being there."

"I see. Well, I'll make a call to the owners and see what we can do. They moved out of state a few weeks ago." She said picking up the phone.

Helen walked out to the waiting room and paced in front of the bay window while Mrs. Turner called the owners. When the realtor opened the door she was holding the keys to the house.

"They don't want you to move in before the closing date, but with the cash deposit, they don't have a problem with you doing your painting in the interim. We can speed things up and perhaps close in as early as two weeks."

"Two weeks." Helen beamed.

"Of course, you'll have to change over the utilities."

"I can do that tomorrow." Helen said taking the keys. Her mind raced with all she had ahead of her.

"You do work fast." The woman touched her white hair. "I've never had a sale like this."

"I appreciate all you've done and I look forward to working with you on my old house." Helen's words brought a grin to the woman's face.

"As do I."

Helen walked outside clutching the paperwork and called Martin with the news.

"Where are you?"

"North Main Street. I just left the realtor's office and I have the keys in my hand."

"You're kidding."

"Not at all. I can't believe I did it. I'm so excited." Helen said as she got into her car.

"I'm almost done here. Let's meet for dinner."

"Sure."

"Damn, woman, I can hear you smiling."

Helen met Martin for dinner and told him every detail she could remember while she showed him the photos in the book. When they finished eating she invited him to follow her over. She wanted to have a nice long look around.

Martin was happy to join her. Helen gave him a grand tour and he laughed when she saw all of the fireplaces. He joked about the amount of wood she'd have to buy to keep them all going. Martin bounced on the thickly padded carpeting as they walk through the breezeway to the studio.

"The place needs color."

"Once you get pictures up and such it will look better."

"I have to paint it."

"Maybe the realtor can turn you on to some reputable workers. Make sure they have a license."

"No. I'll do it myself. I've got two weeks before we close. I can do it."

"This is a big place. Shit, the studio is as big as my apartment."

"I'll enjoy it. I painted my house, plastered holes in the walls, I'm a regular handyman." Helen laughed.

"I'm still learning new things about you." Martin walked over to her and put his arm over her shoulder as she looked out at the lighthouse.

"It's perfect. Or it will be once I'm finished." Helen looked up at him. "I like the idea that China will have the whole yard to roam."

"I'm sure the neighbors will be thrilled to see her." Martin laughed.

"They'll adjust."

"It's great to see you so happy."

"If I had a bucket of paint I'd start right now."

"I'm sure you would."

Helen was back at the new house first thing in the morning taking notes on the carpet colors that thankfully were all muted earth tones. She made a list of the color directions for each room before heading to the home center for supplies. It was the beginning of a huge project. One that Helen was glad to have.

Martin offered to help her in his off time and brought over white coveralls for both of them. By Thursday night they'd finished half of the studio. Helen was rinsing the brushes when her cell phone rang.

"Can you get that for me?" Helen called to him.

"Sure. Hello...yes you have the right number, her hands are wet, can I ask who's calling?" Martin put his hand over the phone. "It's Tyler."

"Oh, shit." Helen rolled her eyes. She'd been so caught up in her own house that she'd forgotten about searching for his. She dried her hands and took the phone.

"Was that the cop?" Tyler asked, his voice loud enough for Martin to hear.

"Yes, it was Martin." Helen smiled as she noticed a smear of pale peach paint on his cheek and pointed to it. "He's helping me paint my new place."

"New place?"

"I'm in the process of buying the house I told you I wanted. It's great. Wait till you see it."

"I don't understand. You're painting your house?"

"My new house." Helen laughed.

"I don't get it."

"That house I showed you the picture of, I am buying it. I put a down payment on it and they gave me the keys so I could start painting. We close in two weeks."

"I don't believe it."

"Well you'd better."

"Have you had any luck finding something for me?"

"I am going to look over that book and take notes tonight. I'm sure I can have a few things lined up for Saturday. I can bring you by here, you won't believe this place. It's perfect for me."

"You bought a house and you are painting it."

Helen laughed. "Meet me at my old house at say nine on Saturday and I'll bring you over before we go looking for yours."

"Okay. I'll see you Saturday."

Helen hung up the phone and laughed even harder. "I can't believe I forgot to look for him. I got so caught up in this place…I've got some work to do when I get home."

"So is he looking to buy in this area?" Martin asked as he dried the brushes on the rag.

"Yes. He gave me a list of things he wanted and I haven't given it a thought. I told him I'd help him over the weekend. I know, I'll give my realtor a call and read her a list, she can come up with something for Saturday." Helen looked around making sure they'd put everything away.

"How about going out for dinner? I'm starving."

"I say we go back to my place, clean up and order in. We both smell like paint and Lysol."

"Sounds good. Let's get."

CHAPTER 19

▼

Martin followed her back to her house and felt good when she showered and came out wearing nothing but a small T-shirt and sweats. The woman looked good in anything and though he wanted to say the words he could tell by the way she was smiling at him that she was reading his mind. He tried not to think about how inviting her breasts looked covered by the thin fabric as he phoned in their dinner order.

He couldn't take his eyes off of her as she poked and prodded the last of the embers breathing life into the dying fire. "You aren't going to have to many more fires. Winter is over. Spring is springing."

"It's cold enough tonight for a grand one." Helen flashed him a smile. "And didn't you notice the nice fire pit down by the beach. I'll be having year round fires in and out at the new place. Isn't it great?"

"Year round fires?"

"My new house." Helen shook her head. "It's going to be great for China. I think I'll bring her with me tomorrow. She can get used to her new yard." Helen reached over and patted the dog.

"You aren't like most women...they take an hour to decide what shoes to wear, you see a house in a magazine take one look at it and write out a check."

"I wanted it."

There was a gleam in her green eyes that he'd seen only once before. The night she invited him to bed she had a look like that. He was waiting as long as it took to have her feel that way again.

"I've thought about it." Helen said as she looked down at the flames. "I...just don't want you...I know."

"You can stop babbling. I was thinking. Not speaking." Martin spotted the headlights in the driveway and went to the door.

"I'm sorry, Martin." Helen said as she walked past him. "My treat tonight." She said as she grabbed her purse off of the counter. She pulled out a wad of cash and walked outside to get the food.

"What did you order?" Helen asked as she came back into the kitchen carrying two big bags.

"Everything. I told you I was hungry." Martin laughed, taking a bag from her. He needed to satisfy one of his appetites.

Everything tasted wonderful and he ate until he was full, knowing he'd be heating more up in a matter of hours. As much as Helen reading his mind could unnerve him, it did have it's advantages. She knew how much he loved her, how he desired her, without him having to say it out loud.

"You ate well." He smiled over at her.

"I'm stuffed."

"A nice smooth brandy would top off this meal. I'll pour." Martin said as she cleared the plates.

"Sounds good." Helen walked out to the living room and sat on the couch.

Martin brought the brandy out and sat right beside her without giving it a second thought. Her cologne swirled around him as he sipped the brandy attempting to keep his thoughts of her pure.

He took a deep breath and relaxed. "I do like this couch. It's probably going to look small in your new living room."

"I have a matching loveseat upstairs. I'm going to use that and that chair. I have a rocker I'm going to put in there to."

"So much for me making suggestions." He smiled and lit her cigarette.

"Oh, no, please do. I appreciate you helping me with the painting."

"I enjoy it. Can't you tell?"

"Yes." She smiled up at him. "We've been having a good time."

"I'll make myself scarce this weekend."

"You don't have to do that."

"I have my own things to take care of." He smiled at her. He was going to give her all the space she needed because he knew in the end that she would be his. He knew it as sure as he was going to refill their glasses. It was meant to be. "Maybe you can get Tyler to pick up a brush for a few hours."

Helen laughed so hard she started to cough. After a few minutes she got herself under control and took a deep breath.

"The man needs help picking out a house. He's good at his job, papers, figures, and such but when it comes to home repairs, it's out of his league. When I was painting up in my office, Tim and Tyler came to help me. It was a disaster. I ended up putting the paint away until they left." She shook her head. "I'll spend the days with him and work over there in the evening after our house hunting."

Martin was glad to hear it. He enjoyed helping her. It was clean time, no crime conversations, just joking and painting. His right arm was feeling the hours of brush strokes because of it.

"This is good." He smiled. "Funny thing is, I think my feet hurt more than my arm."

"Take your shoes off and put your feet up." Helen said as she put a pillow on her lap. "Go ahead."

"I'll get us a refill first." His heart pounded as he got up and grabbed her glass. Just the idea of laying on the couch looking up at her got the blood racing through his body. He poured the brandy and stayed in the kitchen for an extra few moments, getting his thoughts under control.

"Here you go." Martin handed her the glass as she flipped on the television.

"Thank you." She set down the remote, put out the cigarette and patted the pillow. "Come relax."

He took off his shoes and stretch out on the couch but he'd no sooner looked up at her as he knew he had to get up. Helen grabbed his shoulders and he gave in, closing his eyes. He took a slow breath and turned his head toward the television before feeling it was safe to open them again. She stroked his hair with her small fingers as the old western began. It was going to be a good life with her, he thought, a good life.

✳   ✳   ✳   ✳

Helen spent the morning checking out houses with Tyler and the realtor. The first stop was nice and though it had everything on his list they both knew he could do better. When they headed southeast Helen began to wonder how close to her new neighborhood they were going to get. The second stop was one mile from her new home and the third house was two blocks away and better than the first two.

Helen's question about where the fourth house on the list could be was quickly answered when Tyler followed Mrs. Turner onto her very road. Helen looked at her new home as they drove past it. As they stopped five houses away from hers, Helen decided not to say a word about it unless Tyler liked the house. Then she would have to try to talk him out of it.

Unfortunately for Helen, the house was fantastic. From the spacious rooms to the décor, to fitting every specification on his list and then there was the view.

"Now I'd say this is as close as I'm going to come to perfect." Tyler said as he walked through the house for the second time. "The den will be my office. I like the huge tub in the master bath."

Helen stood by the door watching him. "How many do you have lined up for us tomorrow?" Helen asked Mrs. Turner.

"Just two. I'm still looking. Your friend gave me an extensive list of require-ments. Really narrowed things down for me."

"This one will stay at the top of the list. The other three don't compare." Tyler said as he tapped the granite counter top. He walked over and shook Mrs. Turner's hand. "Thank you. I'll see you tomorrow at nine. Shall we meet at your office again?"

"It would be as easy to meet at Miss Staples new home. And by the way, we have the closing set up for Wednesday." The realtor turned to Helen.

"Excellent." Helen said but she couldn't help feeling apprehensive about the idea that Tyler might be a neighbor.

"So nine o'clock at Miss Staples."

"We'll be there." Tyler smiled as they walked out to his car. "So, where do we go from here?" He asked as he opened the passenger door for her.

"I'm five doors up."

"No…damn…imagine that." He said as he walked around the car.

"The one with the black iron fence."

"Great. Are you going to give me the grand tour now?"

"Sure."

They spent an hour at her house before going out to dinner. The evening con-versation centered around the houses they'd seen that day and over coffee Tyler asked her point blank what she thought of the house near hers.

"It's nice. You still have others to see."

"This coming from a woman who picked a house out of a book?"

"That was different. I'm different." She smiled.

"You sure are…so you've got the cop painting for you."

"Martin is painting with me. He's doing a great job too. Well, you saw." Helen wasn't comfortable with either of the men in her life bringing up the other.

"You are too close to him." Tyler frowned.

"I enjoy being with him. He's been a great help to me."

"I don't like it."

"Tyler, you know you're friendship will always be important to me, but I'll chose who I get close to." She took a deep breath as his scowl deepened. "I'm not rushing into anything with Martin. I'm comfortable with him. He's been a good friend."

"We both know it's a lot more than that."

Helen nodded. "Yes. But I don't know how much more…we're taking it one day at a time."

Tyler shook his head and leaned closer. "I don't want to see you get hurt."

Helen wanted to lash out at him for keeping his own desires out of the conversation but she held her tongue. "Martin loves me. If anything he'll be the one getting hurt by this." Helen leaned back in the seat, putting more distance between them.

"Do you love him?"

Her blood pressure was on the rise. "I care for him. Now let's change the subject."

"Fine. I like the last house I saw."

Helen rolled her eyes. "I don't think it's a good idea for us to be neighbors."

"Damn it, Helen." Tyler finished his drink and ordered another round.

Helen took the opportunity to turn the tables on him. "Okay. Let's talk about that.What is going to happen if you move in there? Once you meet someone and start dating, I'll be driving by your house. I'll know who's there and when."

"In other words that will be the same for me. I'll know when your cop is at your house."

"Or anyone else I chose to see. For what ever reason." Helen stared at him.

"I've angered you."

"That's an understatement…look, I love you Tyler. My relationship with Martin can't change that because I love you as a friend. I don't think of you in any other way." Helen reached over and touched his hand. "I've had a hell of a year…you've been there for me. I treasure our friendship."

"As do I."

Helen could see the pain in his brown eyes as he spoke.

"It's good having you back, Tyler."

"Good. Can I at least tell you that I would like to be living near you. I'd like to be able to keep an eye on you. I think about that nut running around loose…you need looking after."

"You're going to buy the house."

"If I don't like one of the two we'll see tomorrow better. Yes. I'm going to buy it."

They met Mrs. Turner at nine o'clock the next morning and toured the homes she'd line up. When they were through Tyler asked to see the one near Helen's again. They followed her there and Tyler walked around the house, basement to attic. When he was through he questioned the realtor about any other homes that fit his list. There were none though she said she was constantly getting new properties and could let him know once something came in.

Tyler took a last look at the bedrooms and den and returned shaking his head. "It's just what I need. I'll take it." He smiled at Mrs. Turner.

"I can draw up the purchase and sales for you this afternoon. I have a showing at two, I could meet you at my office at four. How would that be?"

"Great. We'll see you then." Tyler walked outside and stood in the front yard as Helen and Mrs. Turner spoke about the closing.

When they were through Helen walked over to Tyler and waved goodbye to the realtor as she drove away.

"I'm glad to see you are in a better mood than you were last night. I didn't know if you would be angry about my decision." Tyler said as he put his arm over her shoulder.

"I knew you were going to do it the first time I saw the place." Helen smiled up at him.

"Now I know I'll be able to borrow a cup of sugar from my neighbor without feeling like a smuck." Tyler laughed. "Thanks for helping me. Hey, we have a few hours to kill, do you want me to help you do a little painting?"

"No way." Helen laughed as she turned to face him. "I remember the last time. Forget it."

"So, we have a couple of hours to kill, what do you want to do?"

"You could help me pack the books in my office. I want to be packed by Wednesday and I still have a hell of a lot to do."

"Let's get to work." He said as they walked to his car. "I don't suppose you'll want to help me pick out the furniture for my new house." He smiled opening the door for her.

"I'll be happy to."

*   *   *   *

Donald headed across the border in his new jeep. The I.D. was cheap enough to buy and he'd wired money into a new account in Mexico. Though he hated his black hair and eyebrows, it helped him fit in as he drove down to La Paz. He was fluent in Spanish though he'd never quite mastered the accent.

He took a room in the small but clean hotel and rested for the evening. He was tired of running but La Paz didn't suit him as much as he thought Mexico City would. He had some decisions to make. He could run and he could live, but the bitch would nag at him until he settled the score.

The following morning Donald thought about going after her as he headed north and then south to Mexico City. He would have been free if it wasn't for her. Free and living the life he deserved in Gloria's mansion.

He remembered the hot surge of excitement he felt as he dragged the fortune-teller's limp body back through the doors of the bomb shelter. He thought he had her but she'd slipped away. All she had to show for the encounter was a bullet in the leg, he on the other hand had to endure a life on the run.

He wondered if she was tracking him at that moment, giving the cops her freaky tips. The police he could outsmart but she had proven to be another story. He decided to continue to Mexico City for a week or so while he formulated a plan. He didn't want to hire someone to do the job. He had to figure out how to get to her himself and now, after all he'd been through, he would be happy to make it a quick kill.

Once she was out of the way he'd decide where to settle. He had his mind on Europe. With all of his refinement he could easily blend in with the upper class and they'd be none the wiser. Donald was keenly aware of all the press he'd received in the U.S. and Canada but he doubted that word of the killings had reached Europe. With his Mexican papers he'd be able to fly there without a problem and begin anew.

CHAPTER 20

▼

Monday morning Helen woke with a start. For the first time in weeks the thought of Donald Abington turned her cold. The phone rang and she walked over to answer it but it hit her. It was him. She stepped back and listened as the recording came on.

"I'm thinking about you." Abington growled into the phone.

He hung up and Helen called Martin.

"I think he's coming back here for me. He's getting closer." She said as she sat at the table.

"OK. I have to go to the station for a few minutes and then I'll be over."

"I don't think he's here. But he is coming back...soon." A shiver ran down her body. "I'm going to take China over to the new place with me. The movers are coming on Thursday and I still have three rooms to paint."

"Good idea. I'll be there soon."

Helen could hear the worry in his voice. "Thank you."

She made a thermos of coffee and loaded China into the back of the car. She felt better when she arrived at the new house. She let the dog loose in the yard and dove into her work. Helen had half of the living room painted by the time Martin arrived.

Helen put down the brush and greeted him at the door. "Good timing. I'm ready for a cup of coffee."

Martin wrapped his arms around her. "I'm sorry about this lady."

"It's not your fault." Helen smiled up at him as he released her.

"I've arranged to take the week off. They owe me a few weeks worth of personal days and things have been slow lately…" Martin smiled at her. "I'm at your disposal for the next seven days."

"I hate to admit it, but I'm glad. Thank you. I'll certainly feel better with you around. Damn I hate feeling vulnerable."

"I know. But this guy is too dangerous. I won't take any chances. And this time I will shoot to kill."

Helen nodded. "So will I." She fought hard to hold back the tears as she walked to the counter to pour their coffee. "I close on Wednesday. The movers come on Thursday. I finished packing what I could last night. I'm down to the bare bones in the kitchen."

"You've done a great job in here." Martin said as he walked over and touched her shoulder. "I won't let anything happen to you. You know that."

"Yes."

Martin looked out the window as China raced by. "She likes it here."

"Yes. She spends more time in the front yard than the back." Helen smiled as China ran by again. "I wish I had her energy."

By Thursday night Helen was all moved in, each room with its proper furnishings and boxes lining the walls. She was pleased with the smooth transition and ready to celebrate the change.

Martin had been with her round the clock since Monday helping her in any way he could.

"All right then. I say we should clean up and go out to dinner. My treat."

"I could go for that. Casual or dress."

"I feel like dressing up."

Martin nodded. "Let's do it."

Helen took a long hot shower and unzipped the garment bags she'd hung in her closet that morning. She chose a short cream colored dress and opted for high heels for the first time in months. She dug her make up bag out of the box and stood in front of the mirror to decide whether to wear her hair up or down. She felt free at that moment. Free and happy.

"What's taking you so long?" Martin knocked on her bedroom door.

"I'm trying to figure out how to wear my hair." Helen giggled. "I'll be out in a minute." She could hear Martin tapping his foot in the hallway. She twisted her hair into a French bun and slid a gold hairpin through it to hold it in place. "I'm ready."

She popped the door open and Martin stepped back to look at her.

"Oh, baby, you look delicious." Martin smiled as his eyes went from her heels to her hair.

"You look great." Helen touched the lapel of his black suit. "I'm starving."

"Were are you taking me?"

"Alberto's."

"Are you kidding?"

"I told you it's my treat." Helen smiled as she walked past him. "I'll call and make the reservation."

"How are you going to get a reservation there on such short notice?"

"Madeline has a thing going with the host. I'm sure it won't be a problem." Helen made the call and was assured a romantic booth by the gas fireplace. "We're all set. Our table is waiting."

When the forty-year-old host greeted them it gave Martin something to think about. The handsome man had been going out with Helen's sixty-year-old aunt for close to two years.

"Were you kidding me?" Martin whispered after the host walked away.

"Not for a minute. He went to her for a reading and asked her out before he left. They've been hot and heavy ever since." Helen smiled.

"Wow. I'm impressed." Martin laughed.

"So am I. He's a very nice man and he is just crazy about Madeline. She told me he makes her feel like she's young again."

"How about that. So, what are you planning for tomorrow?"

"Tomorrow?"

"All week we've been scrambling around trying to get things ready for today so what are we doing tomorrow?"

"I hadn't given it a thought. I guess we should take a day off. I'll putter around and open some boxes."

"They call that unpacking and that is work." Martin smiled as the waitress brought the wine to their table.

"You got me. We could go shopping for furniture."

"Work."

"I take it you have something in mind." Helen smiled at him. He looked so handsome and happy at that moment.

"I'd like to get down to the shipyard and have a good look at my boat before they put it in the water. The hull might need some scraping and painting."

"Now that sounds like work." Helen laughed.

"Not at all. You like being near the water and I love being on it."

"Well, how is this for a coincidence?" Tyler said as he walked over to their table.

"What are you doing here?" Helen asked as Martin stood to shake his hand.

"Out for a bite. I didn't expect to see you here. How'd the move go?" Tyler asked standing over her.

"Smooth sailing. Of course the house is filled with boxes but I'll peck away at them."

"Would you like to join us?" Martin asked, pulling out a chair.

"Well, I don't want to intrude...I was planning on eating alone." Tyler nodded and sat down. "Thanks Martin." He turned his attention to Helen. "You look great tonight."

"Thank you."

"Hey, did Helen tell you we're going to be neighbors?"

Martin's eyes widened. "Why no."

"We've been so busy." Helen squirmed. She'd been waiting for the right moment to tell him knowing that he wouldn't be thrilled by the idea.

"Sure. I bought a place up the street from her. It is fantastic. Hell, I'll be moving in three weeks. Helen offered to help me pick out the furniture. The place I'm in came furnished. I need everything. Worst part is, I hate to shop for that kind of stuff."

The waiter rushed over and set a place for Tyler. The trio ordered the house specialty, lobster casserole. It wasn't the dinner Helen had in mind with Tyler in the mix but the food and service was excellent as usual.

"So when were you going to tell me?" Martin asked as he set his coat on the hook by the door.

"I don't really know...Look...Fact of the matter is, that house is just what he was looking for."

"It's awkward."

"What is?"

"Having him a few houses away. I know what his intentions are."

"Damn you. You two act like cavemen." Helen took the pin out of her hair and it fell over her shoulders like an auburn wave. She clutched a handful of hair, glaring at him. "Next thing you'll be dragging me down the hall by my hair."

He leaned back and looked at her, his eyes wide. "I was surprised."

"You knew he was looking for a house. It just so happened it was up the street. Neither of us knew ahead of time where any of the houses were. Damn it, Martin. The man is my friend. We've been through this before. Shit. He whines about you…" She slipped off her shoes and started for the hall. "Now I have to listen to the same thing from you. It's foolish."

Helen went into her room and closed the door. She wanted a quiet evening of celebration and ended up with these two bulls blowing smoke at each other. She paced the room for several minutes before changing into her sweats.

When she walked out of the room Martin was standing in the hallway.

"Fine. You're right. I do feel threatened by him."

"Well, you don't have to." Helen walked past him into the living room as China gave her a curious look from her bed in the corner. "He knows where he stands with me."

"Maybe that's the problem." Martin walked up behind her and turned her around to face him. "I don't."

Helen looked up at him. "I care for you, Martin. You're the only man in my life…in a romantic sense." He smoothed her hair from her face as she spoke.

"Okay. I'm sorry."

"Why the hell did you invite him to join us anyway?" Helen raised a brow at him.

"I don't know. It seemed like the thing to do." Martin said as he wrapped his arms around her. "I love you. I guess being in limbo is getting to me. I can be close but only so close. I can be with you but I can't possess you."

"You said you could be patient."

"And I have been. I said I'm sorry."

If only she could see their future. She wanted to give him what he wanted but she felt like him, she was on cracking ice and it could go either way. Helen nodded and walked over to the couch and sat down. She looked out the glass doors at the lighthouse flashing it's steady light like a slow dependable heart beat.

"I shouldn't have asked you to marry me. It scared you." Martin said as he sat down beside her. "That's what put the breaks on things."

"I was flattered to think you love me enough to ask but I'm…I'm not there. I care for you. I enjoy you."

"I know. It shows, Helen." He moved the red curl from her eye. "You wanted to wade into the water and I dove into the sea."

Helen looked at him and smiled. "I don't know what I'm going to do with you." She said as he put his arm around her and pulled her close. When she felt his arms around him she thought about what he'd said about making the most of each day they're given. She wanted to be released from questions about their future.

She loved Martin but the fear of having him and losing him made her keep her feelings inside. She thought about how good she felt whenever he called or knocked on the door. Time with him was special, she thought as she studied his full lips.

Helen woke as the sun peeked through the curtains.

Martin smiled over at her. "Good morning."

Helen's face flushed as she thought about the night before.

"I really like this new bedroom. Though I've got a feeling my view might change once winter comes and you burn me out with that fireplace." He grinned as he smoothed his large hand over her face. "Thank you for last night."

Helen tapped his bare chest. "You don't have to thank me." She said smiling at him. She didn't know how it had happened. First they'd argued over Tyler, then they apologized for getting upset, then he carried her into her bedroom.

"You look great for having two hours of sleep." Martin squeezed her and kissed her forehead. "I love you."

"I love you, too, Martin."

"You…" Martin's brown eyes widened. "Oh, damn, this must be my lucky day." China barked from the doorway and Martin got up. "You stay put. I'll let her out and get the coffee started."

"I'm going to hop in the shower." Helen waited until he left the room before she got up. She indulged in a long steaming shower and threw on her robe and slippers before joining him in the kitchen.

"You've made me very happy." Martin said as he poured the coffee wearing just his black sweat pants. The smile on his face said it all. "Can you say it again?"

Helen shook her head and laughed. "I love you."

"Good. Okay."

China barked at the door and Helen walked over and let her inside. "Oh, wow, it's pretty warm this morning."

"Spring has sprung. So how do you feel about going to the boatyard?"

"Sounds good."

After a quick breakfast spent smiling at each other they were off to inspect Martin's boat. He pointed out the cabin cruiser as they drove into the yard. A man waved to him as they parked by the boat.

"Hey Martin. Good to see you."

"Sculey."

"We just unwrapped her. She's going to need some scraping."

The men shook hands and Martin introduced Helen. Sculey nodded and Helen walked around the boat as Martin inspected the hull. It was much larger than the twenty-one footer her father owned. The name painted across the back of the boat made her stop and stare. Martin joined her a few minutes later.

"The Mystic Winds. Now tell me where did you come up with that name."

"Strange huh? The previous owners named it. I was going to get around to changing it but it had a little more meaning after we met."

"I like it."

"Somehow I knew you would."

They climbed up the ladder and Martin gave her the grand tour of the cabin below. "It's no yacht but it's paid for." Martin inspected the cupboards, pulling out scrapers and wire brushes. "I'm going to need some paint."

"This looks like work."

"I don't plan on getting started today. I only want to check things out. See what I need."

Helen smiled and shook her head. "We're dressed for it. At least we can get the scraping out of the way today."

"Are you sure?" Martin hugged her and kissed her cheek.

"I'm happy to do it with you. I'm getting used to physical labor after all the work I've done on that house."

Martin kissed her lips and released her. He handed her a scraper. "Let's get to it then."

$$* \qquad * \qquad * \qquad *$$

Donald smiled at the tall pretty waitress as she set down his coffee.

"So, what brings you to Richmond?" She asked holding her pad and pencil.

"How do you know I don't live here?"

"The accent."

Donald laughed. "Well, can't argue with that. I'm passing through..." he glanced down at the menu. "I'll have the number six."

"Very good. White or wheat?"

"Wheat."

"I'll be right back with it." She winked at him and walked away.

Donald studied her slender figure as she walked to the cook's window. When she returned a few minutes later with his breakfast he turned on the charm. "So, what do the locals do for excitement?"

"I thought you were just passing through?"

"I took a room up the road for the night." He eyed her for a moment. "Any good night clubs around?"

"Plenty. Depends on what style of music."

"I like them all." He checked her out slowly from her face to her white work shoes. "I'd bet you are quite the dancer."

"I try."

"I don't see a ring on your finger. Are you married?"

"No."

"Adele." The cook yelled and rang the bell.

"That's me. I'll be back to check on you in a few minutes." She smiled and rushed off.

"I'll be here."

Donald had finished his breakfast by the time she returned to freshen his coffee. "So. What time do you get off?"

"I don't usually date customers." She smiled.

"Come on, Adele. You'd make my day."

"I am kinda' seein' someone."

"I'm only asking to take you out dancing." Donald smiled. "I haven't danced since my wife's accident."

"You're wife?"

"She died last year." He shook his head and looked down at the coffee cup. "I haven't thought about dancing since then, until I saw you."

"Oh, I'm so sorry."

"Adele." The cook banged on the bell again.

"I'll be right back." She ripped his check off of the pad and set it on the table before rushing off.

Donald leaned back in the booth knowing he had her. He laid a twenty over the bill and set the cup on both.

"I get off at four." Adele said as he returned to his table.

"Great. We can go out to dinner and then dancing." Donald smiled. "I went to a great restaurant the last time I was in Richmond. It's about twenty miles north of here. I can't think of the name but I past it on my way into the city."

"I just live a couple blocks from here. I could be changed and back by five."

"Sure. I'll meet you here at five."

CHAPTER 21

▼

Helen sat down with the mail in her new office. She'd let the letters pile up for more than a week and with Martin returning to work, it was time to get back down to business. She'd only read through the first three letters when the doorbell rang.

Helen thought it was Martin because China didn't bark but when she went to the door Tyler was standing there grinning at her, waving a set of keys.

"It's mine."

"What are you doing here? And how did you get past her?" Helen looked down at China.

"She likes me."

Helen nodded and China walked inside with him. "Would you like some coffee?"

"Of course." Tyler smiled. "It's another beautiful day out there."

"Yes. Why aren't you at work?

"I told you. We had the closing this morning. I was hoping you could go furniture shopping with me today."

"Do you know what you want?" Helen set down the cup of coffee on the kitchen island.

"Not exactly. I want the place to look neutral. Not male or female if that makes any sense. Except the bedroom. I want big, manly type furniture for that." Tyler said, flexing his muscles.

Helen laughed. "Manly, huh?"

"Yes. You know, this is exciting." Tyler fiddled with the keys. "Hey where's the cop?" Tyler looked around the living room.

"Working."

"Does that mean you're free today?"

"Sure. I'll go. Give me a few minutes to get dressed." She tugged at her T-shirt and finished her coffee. "It'll be fun to spend someone else's money for a change."

"Let's not get carried away." Tyler laughed.

"Do you have the room measurements?" Helen asked, rinsing out the cup.

"I do."

"Fine. Let's go by your place for another look before we head to the stores. I want to refresh my memory." Helen headed toward her bedroom. "I've got a home decor magazine on the coffee table. Flip through it for ideas while I get ready."

Her mood changed quickly as she walked to her room. A sense of foreboding made her suddenly cold. It was Abington. He was getting closer. Red flashed before her eyes and then she saw the long drapes in her old living room being slashed.

"Oh, shit." She said as she pulled on her jeans. She threw on a thin, short sleeved sweater and picked up the phone.

"Martin…" Helen worked hard to control the panic in her voice. "He's back. I can see him in my old house." Helen left out the part about the long sharp blade slicing her old drapes as it replayed in her mind.

"Stay put."

"No."

"No?"

"I won't be a prisoner to this guy." She said as she opened the nightstand drawer and took out the snub-nose .38. She clipped the holster in place at the small of her back and took a deep breath. "Tyler closed on his house this morning and he wants to go furniture shopping. Abington isn't going to come after me in broad daylight."

"Are you talking to me?" Tyler asked as he tapped on the door.

"No. I'm on the phone with Martin. I'll be right out."

"Let me talk to him."

"Martin."

"I'm serious Helen. Put him on the phone."

"I'll tell him."

"You'd better."

"Maybe you should have someone keep an eye on my old house."

"I will. Now hang up and tell Tyler what's going on."

"Yes, sir."

"If you leave that house you'd better be armed."

"I am."

"Okay. I love you. I'll be over there about six."

"I love you, too." Helen hung up the phone and opened the door to see Tyler scowling down at her.

"What's going on?" Tyler asked as she walked past him. "Hey, what's that bulge in your back?"

Helen lifted her sweater and showed him the gun.

"You're expecting trouble?"

Helen nodded. "Abington is close. He's coming back to the area."

"Damn it. Have your boyfriend get some cops out here."

"I'm sure he will." Helen said as she reached into the cupboard and took out a standard thirty-eight. She grabbed the speed loaders and put them in her large purse.

"What are you doing?" Tyler gawked at her. "We aren't going anywhere."

"If you're afraid to be out in public with me, I understand. But I'm not going to let that son-of-a-bitch keep me prisoner in this house." Helen shook her head and grabbed the windbreaker off the coat rack.

The slight wrinkles in his forehead deepened. "I don't like it."

"I'm not too happy about it either. There's nothing I can do but be ready." She picked up the purse.

"You can go into hiding until they catch the freak."

"How long have they been looking? Come on Tyler. He could disappear again. I can't live that way." Helen managed a smile for him. "He doesn't know I moved. Not yet anyway. Now let's get going."

Tyler paced the living room while Helen walked through his empty house.

She smiled as she emerged from the hallway. "I've got some good ideas."

"I still don't like it."

"You're bringing me down. It's much better for me to be busy than to sit home and worry. Please."

"Damn you're one stubborn woman."

"That's me, stubborn and armed to the teeth." Helen said as she picked up the heavy purse off the counter.

"Maybe I should just hire an interior decorator."

"Let's go, Tyler." Helen walked out the door.

"Damn." He followed her to the car. "You're putting on a good show." Tyler said as he got in beside her. "But you're pale as a ghost."

"Of course I'm scared. The bastard already shot me once...but I'm not going to give in to the fear. I refuse." Helen lit a cigarette and rolled down the window.

"Fine. Make sure you tell your cop that I tried."

"His name is Martin."

"Keeps slipping out of my mind." Tyler smiled as he started the car.

"Right."

They spent the morning shopping for Tyler's house and after lunch Helen happened on the perfect furniture for her office, which at the moment was furnished only with her dark cherry desk and two black leather chairs.

Martin was waiting at her house when she returned. Tyler rushed over to him.

"Find out anything?" Tyler asked as Helen followed him into the yard.

"Nothing yet." Martin said as he walked toward Helen. He wrapped his arms around her and kissed her forehead. "How are you doing?"

"Good." Helen smiled up at him. "We made a good dent in Tyler's list and I bought what I wanted for my office. All in all it was a very productive day." Helen said as he released her and walked to the front door. "Oh, let me grab the mail."

"I'll get it." Martin turned and walked across the yard as Tyler and Helen went into the house.

"You shouldn't be standing outside like a sitting duck." Tyler grunted as he closed the door behind her.

"Yes, sir." Helen smiled, knowing he was right. "How about some coffee?"

"I'd rather have a good stiff drink. I felt like I was holding my breath all damn day."

"I'm sorry, Tyler."

"Don't worry about it. I feel better now that you're home."

Martin walked into the house scowling. He held out a letter as he moved toward her. "It's postmarked New York City."

Helen sat down at the table and took the letter from him. She was instantly hit with flashes of Abington.

Tyler walked over to the wet bar in the corner of the living room. "I'm making martinis, any takers."

"We'll both have one." Martin said as he sat down beside her.

"He's died his hair black and he has a mustache…he's driving a black jeep…it's been painted twice already." Helen said as she set down the envelope.

"You're white as a ghost." Martin touched her arm.

"He's here." Helen looked up at him as she rubbed her arms.

"Where?"

"In the state. In the area."

"Would he be that nuts?" Tyler asked as he served them their drinks.

"Believe it." Helen nodded.

Martin pulled out his cell phone and called the station with the details. "I already had them put an extra patrol out here." He said as he hung up.

Helen sipped the drink as Tyler sat at the table.

"At least we know what we are looking for."

"You guys have to get this bastard." Tyler growled. "Do you want to lay down Helen?"

"No. I'm okay."

"You don't look it." Tyler slammed his fist on the table. "Damn it this isn't right." He glared at Martin.

"We're doing everything we can. The FBI has been tracking him. We're going to get him."

"I think she should leave town." Tyler said, taking his empty glass to the bar.

"Do you want to, Helen?" Martin asked.

"Come on. You've been talking about going camping. It's warm enough to take that camper out. Go up to New Hampshire for a few days. Give yourself a damn break from all of this bullshit." Tyler turned to Martin. "A little help here."

"It does sound like a good idea." Martin smiled at her. "I could use the break."

"You've used up so many days already, Martin. I wouldn't want to go alone."

"You can't go alone. I meant with him. Shit. Come on. You'd be doing everyone a big favor." Tyler smiled at her. "Please Helen. It would be a few days that I wouldn't have to worry. You could have that thing loaded in a half-hour. It would give the cops time to find him."

"I can't believe you're trying to get rid of me." Helen smiled at Tyler.

"You know…well, I guess I am. I'd go with you but I've taken too much time off as it is. Especially since I just started there. I'm still working out some bugs. Come on, lady. Fresh air, pine trees, big, no, huge bonfires in the wilderness. Don't tell me this doesn't sound great."

"He's right. I can arrange it."

"Are you sure, Martin?"

"Yes." He smiled at her. "There isn't anything we can do. Everyone from the locals to the FBI is searching for him. We should take off and try to relax. By the time we come back it should be over. I'm going to run out and grab a few things, I'll be back soon."

"Now tell me this wasn't a great idea." Tyler smiled.

They went out to the garage and Helen opened the camper. It was only the second time she'd been in it that year. The first time being when she'd driven it over to her new house.

"This is great. Reminds me of the time the three of us went for a week." Tyler smiled as he walked to the back of the long camper. "We had some laughs that trip, didn't we?"

"Oh, yes." Helen smiled as she thought of the three musketeers. Tim, Tyler and Helen trooping through the woods, telling jokes about Robin Hood, building a lean-to. "Yes. That was a great time."

"Last time you used this thing?"

Helen nodded.

"Then it's time to build some new memories." Tyler took the small block of wood out of the refrigerator and closed it. He sat down at the small table and smiled at her. "I want you to be happy, lady."

"I know you do. You're a good friend."

"I sure am." Tyler laughed as he reached over and flipped open the cupboard. "You've got plenty of paper goods. I think you'll need a few extra blankets."

"I should have some over here." Helen looked in the storage under the couch. "Yes, there are three here." Helen pulled out the plastic bag with the flattened quilts. "Okay, I'll need coffee and filters."

"Food. Real food."

"I can get that on the way. Thank you, Tyler. This was a good idea."

"What are friends for?" Tyler said, standing up. "I wish I could go, too. Next time we'll plan something. For now, I'm glad to get you out of the area. You can't keep going on like this without a break. It's not good for your health."

"You're right. A few days of fresh air and bonfires will do me good."

Helen went in and packed a small bag of jeans and T-shirts and by the time Martin returned she was ready to leave.

"Do you want me to take care of China?" Tyler asked.

"Oh, no. She's going." Helen smiled.

"Great. I'll see you in a few days then." Tyler kissed her cheek and hugged her. "Enjoy yourself."

Helen felt she was doing all she could do. At least her movements on a camping trip wouldn't be as constricted as if she stayed home. As much as she loved her new house, Abington was too close for her to risk him spotting her. Helen realized the urge to continue life as normal in spite of the killer was too dangerous. A couple of days in the woods just might give the police time to catch him.

Helen had everything ready when Martin returned. "Well, I've got three days off. We have two detectives going on vacation so that's all the time I could get."

"It sounds fine. The campground isn't that far away."

Helen and Martin put away their bags and China took a seat on the couch at the rear of the camper. When they pulled onto the highway, Helen took a deep breath and smiled at Martin.

"This was a good idea. I feel better already." Helen said.

"You drive this like a car."

"I've had a lot of experience. We...I used to take this out three or four times a year."

"And you drove?"

"Always." Helen smiled. "I enjoy it."

"Then I'll just sit back and enjoy the ride. Cigarette?"

"Sure."

Martin lit two and put his feet up on the dash. "Do you realize I haven't had a real vacation in two, maybe three years?"

They drove for two hours and pulled up to Helen's favorite campground.

"You're smiling again." Martin said. "You look so beautiful when you smile."

"So do you." Helen laughed.

"I think your friend is warming up to me."

"I think you're right."

They walked into the little store and Helen picked out a site and filled out the paper work. They grabbed their groceries and headed down the winding dirt road.

"Did I read that warning right?" Martin asked as she backed the camper into the spot.

"You mean about the bears?" Helen laughed.

"Yes."

"They don't bother you if you don't bother them." Helen got out of the camper and went to the back to unhook the lawn chairs. "Come on. We don't have too much time before the sun goes down. We need to get some wood if we're going to have a fire."

"The bears?"

"They won't attack the camper. We just have to be sure to gather any left over food and put all of our rubbish in a trash can off site." Helen laughed as Martin leaned out of the camper and looked around. "I'll gather the wood. You get the charcoals started."

Helen set the chairs beside the stone circle and headed into the woods with China at her side. She returned with an armload of wood and then went around the site collecting kindling. By the time she was done, Martin had the hot dogs cooking and the picnic table set for dinner.

After they ate, Helen built a fire and Martin fixed a pitcher of martinis.

"Now this is camping." He smiled as the flames rose, lighting the site. "Come here and give me a hug."

Helen walked over and embraced him. They watched the fire and listened to the sounds of the night. Helen was glad they'd come early in the season. The four surrounding sites were empty giving them plenty of privacy.

They enjoyed three days and nights of serenity. On their last night in the woods Martin turned serious.

"What about kids?" Martin asked, poking the embers with his marshmallow stick.

"What about them?"

"Do you want some?"

"Well...I've thought about it."

"And?" Martin looked into her eyes.

"Some day."

"You aren't getting any younger."

"I don't believe you said that." Helen tapped his shoulder.

"I mean, neither of us are."

"Where is this coming from?"

"I could see us sitting here in a few years, screaming kids running through the woods. You know."

"You said kids, plural."

"I know. I'd like to have six."

"Six?"

"Sure. That way they won't be lonely."

Helen nodded. "Two would have each other."

"We can start with that."

"We? Start?"

Martin leaned back in his seat and looked up at the stars. "This life doesn't last forever. I'd like to leave a kid on the planet. A part of myself."

"You're sounding pretty serious." Helen studied him.

"I've been thinking about it a lot lately."

"You should probably get married first." Helen smiled.

"Just say the word."

Helen was silent.

After several minutes of listening to the crackling campfire, Martin kissed her cheek. "We can talk about it some other time." He said staring into her eyes. "Let's turn in."

Helen woke with the chirping birds feeling invigorated from their night of passion. Martin was sound asleep as she crept out of the bed and made the coffee. She heard Martin yawn as she poured the first cup.

"Where's my woman?" He growled.

China moaned in his direction and they both laughed.

"Good morning." He walked up behind her and kissed her neck. "I wish we didn't have to go back."

"But we do. You told the chief you'd be in by noon today. That gives us time to have breakfast and hit the highway."

"Kill joy." He nibbled her neck. "Hey, I could have you for breakfast."

"I've created a monster."

"You don't know the half of it, you sweet thing."

"Enough. Drink your coffee. It's back to the real world." Helen turned toward him and kissed his cheek. "It's been a wonderful vacation. Thank you."

"Oh, thank you." Martin took his cup and scowled. "I wish it had been a week."

Helen wished they never had to go back. Her senses were clear. She felt better than she had in weeks. She knew it would change when they returned home but she had to face her fears.

They were packed and on the road by nine. Helen drove the speed limit and Martin was quieter than he'd been on the way up. They arrived at her house giving Martin just enough time to change his cloths and rush out the door.

CHAPTER 22

▼

Home for just a half a day and she was once again plagued by the vision of Abington being in her old house. She was glad when Tyler showed up at four, giving her a distraction from her thoughts. Tyler chatted about his house asking about curtain ideas and sea paintings he wanted to buy. He finally got around to asking about her vacation.

"I take it the trip didn't go so well."

"It went very well. I'm just bugged by Abington."

"Still no leads?"

"None. He's close though."

"You're wearing that gun...It's unnerving." Tyler scowled.

"May well be but I have to be ready."

"I thought a few days off would take your mind off of him."

"It did. Really. I don't think I thought about him once." Helen shrugged. "Of course since I've been back I have the feeling that he's closing in on me."

"Damn. Where's your cop?"

"Martin is working. They've got extra patrols in the neighborhood. There isn't anything else they can do until they get a solid lead."

"I'm ready for a drink. Would you like one?"

"Sure. Let's change the subject. How's work going?"

"Good. I'm whipping them into shape." Tyler laughed. "No, really, I've got a crack team working for me. It's going very well."

"I'm glad."

"How about you? Are you taking any new cases?"

"I'm kind of in limbo here. I will, I just don't know when."

"You should to keep your mind off of that creep."

"I can't help what I feel."

China ran for the door her tail wagging, signaling Martin's return. He tapped on the door and walked inside.

"Hi Tyler. How are you doing?"

"Playing bartender. Are you up for one?"

"Sure. A short one." Martin said as he walked over and kissed Helen on the cheek. "Figured I'd have dinner with you then I have to get back and do some paperwork."

"Your favorite." Helen smiled up at him.

"Any more, feelings?"

"The same, over and over. He's close."

"She's wearing that little gun." Tyler said as he poured the drinks.

"Good."

Tyler rolled his eyes as he served them and went back for his.

Helen grew cold, her mood darkening as she pictured him slashing her old drapes again. She started to get up and another vision hit her, sending her back into the seat.

"No." Her chest tightened as she saw Mrs. Turner's terrified expression in her mind's eye. "Get someone over to my old house." Helen squealed. "Oh, God."

"What is it?" Martin asked as he dialed the station. "What are you seeing?"

"He's attacked the realtor."

"This is too freaky." Tyler stopped with the full martini, drank it in one gulp and turned back to make another.

"She's dead…that poor woman." Helen started to shake.

Martin pulled out his cell phone and called the station. He rattled the address off to the dispatcher and headed for the door. "You stay here with her. I'll be back soon." Martin said.

Helen looked up at him, wiping away her tears. "I didn't know she'd be there."

"It's okay. I'll be right back. Look after her for me, please. Get these blinds closed. All of them."

Martin ran out to the car and screeched up the street. Tyler rushed around closing the blinds and curtains in every room before returning to her side.

"Maybe it was just a premonition." He said patting her shoulder.

"I wish it was." Helen pulled the gun out of her purse and set it in the middle of the table. She lined up the speed loaders and then unclipped the small revolver from her belt and set it beside them.

✳   ✳   ✳   ✳

Martin raced to her old house and pulled into the driveway behind a navy blue sedan. As he got out of the car he heard sirens in the distance. He pulled out his gun and held it shoulder high as he approached the open kitchen door.

He kicked the door open all the way and swallowed hard, adrenaline coursing through his body. A woman in her thirties lay in a puddle of blood, multiple stab wounds covered her chest, abdomen and there were several defensive wounds on both of her forearms. The living room slider was wide open, the drapes in tatters blowing in the wind. An older woman lay spread eagle, in the middle of the living room, her throat had been slashed.

He searched every room, closet and even the vanity cabinets in the bathrooms before returning to the living room.

"Detective Hamlin?"

Martin turned to the young officer. "Get Detective Miller down here now."

"He's not on tonight."

"Get him." Martin growled. "Then get this whole area taped off. I don't want anyone coming in here without my permission." Martin walked out to his car and got evidence bags out of the trunk.

He bagged both women's hands even though it didn't look like the elder woman had put up much of a fight. His heart was pumping when he thought about Helen. It could easily have been her laying on the bloody kitchen tiles.

A few minutes later Detective Miller walked into the kitchen. "Son-of-a-bitch." He gawked at the carnage. "Who reported this?"

"Helen saw it."

"Your psychic?"

Martin nodded. "It was Abington."

"I don't doubt that but I thought the last line they had on him was in California." Miller said as he walked over to the younger victim. He undid the tape around the outside of the bag and inspected her broken nails. "I'd say this one did some damage." He put the bag back in place and walked over to the woman in the living room. "This is Eleanor Turner."

"You know her?"

"She was the agent on my house. Nice woman. Shit. This is going to really piss some people off. The chief's wife was her best friend." Miller shook his head. "Shit."

Martin walked outside and sent the first officer he saw down to the station. He wanted two photos of Abington and a black magic marker.

The officer shrugged and went back to his car. He raced off sirens blaring as the Channel Seven News crew arrived. Martin turned to another patrolman and told him to let the press know he'd be making a statement soon.

"Don't give them any details. Tell them to hold on and I'll give them the whole story." Martin said. He headed back inside, his eyes drawn to the victim in the kitchen.

A few minutes later the officer returned with the photos and marker. Martin stood by the counter and altered one photo to reflect the black hair, eye brows and mustache that Helen had seen in her vision. The forensic team arrived and Detective Miller barked out orders as they snapped photos of the victims and began dusting for prints.

Martin walked outside and took a deep breath before going over to the crime scene tape where the reporters waited like piranhas for their first bite about the murders.

"We have two women murdered inside this vacant house. We are not releasing the names of the victims until their families are notified."

"Isn't this Helen Staple's house?" One reporter yelled from the back of the pack.

"I'm not taking questions at this time. Please let me make the statement without interruption." Martin snapped.

"We can nail this monster with the public's help. His name is Donald Abington. Our sources tell us he's driving a black jeep and he's dyed his hair black or dark brown. He may have a mustache. Abington is well known in this area and the department is going to be putting photos of him everywhere." Martin held up two pictures of the man.

"If you even suspect you've seen this man, we urge you to call and report it. We need the public's help before he kills again."

Martin turned to walk away as the reporters yelled out questions.

"Was Helen Staples one of the victims?"

Martin hesitated mid-stride as the question hit him, then continued into the house. Helen could have easily been a victim if Abington had returned just a few days earlier. The thought twisted his gut.

"I think Abington is a good call for this one." Detective Miller said as Martin walked inside. "I called the chief, he's getting the state police and sheriff's departments to set up road block check points."

"Any I.D. on the other victim?"

"Yes Tawny Brooke. She was lying on a small purse. She was thirty-four."

"The bastard could have fled when they came in."

"I think he was pissed when he found the place empty. The slashes on the curtains are clean. He did that before they came in." Miller said. "So the psychic told you it happened...I hate to ask but, you don't think she could have seen it, I mean been here at the time?"

"She was with me." Martin understood his skepticism, he'd felt the same at one time. "It's crazy how it happens. She looks like she's watching something and to everyone else there's nothing there but for her it's as if she's seeing a movie. She saw him attacking the realtor, she didn't say anything about the other victim. I called it in, raced over here and found this."

"You understand it's too weird for some of us?"

"Hell, yes. But I've seen her work. A few weeks ago she found a Rhode Island woman who'd been missing for a year and her family had presumed she was dead." Martin shrugged. "It's one of those things that even she doesn't understand."

"And you?"

"I accept that it's real because I've seen her pull this shit out of thin air but I don't understand it."

Detective Miller nodded. "I hear you two are seeing each other."

Martin scowled as he stared down at the women's bodies. "Yes."

"You putting a man at her house?"

"You're looking at him."

"I don't know if I could be involved with a woman like that...all that mystical shit."

"She's special. The psychic end is just a part of who she is."

"Detective Hamlin." An officer waved to him from the door.

Martin walked over. "What's up?"

"The press wants to ask some questions."

"I made a statement. Tell them that's it for the night. Tell them to get Abington's picture on the air."

*   *   *   *

Helen turned down the volume on the television and looked at Tyler. "He's not leaving."

"What do you think he's going to do?"

"He knows I've moved. He's going to try to find me."

"That's stupid with everyone on the alert now."

"Him coming back was stupid. He thinks he can out smart the police." Helen studied his worried face and dropped the subject. She knew Abington would be madder than ever after such a huge screw up.

Martin returned an hour later, the horror he'd seen tightening his jaw. "How are you?" He asked as he walked over to Helen.

"Fine."

Martin sat beside her on the couch. "The guy's an animal...he was over there hacking up your curtains when the realtor arrived with a buyer." Martin shook his head. "He killed both of them."

"Are you going to get a cruiser out front?" Tyler asked.

"No. I'll stay here and we have an extra patrol in the area. I think it would just bring attention to the place to have one parked here. We don't want to tip him off." Martin scowled. "You're going to have to stay put." He raised his hand. "Don't argue."

Helen reached for a cigarette. "I won't."

"The chief ordered round the clock protection for you, I volunteered for the job." Martin said. "We're both staying here until he's caught." He studied her. "Or leaves the area." Martin looked at Tyler. "I'm going to order Chinese, you're welcome to join us."

"Thanks. I think I'd feel better if I hang around."

"The more the merrier." Martin said as he took out his phone. He made the call and turned up the volume on the news. "Can you see anything else, Helen? Anything at all?"

"No. He's furious. He feels trapped and he's very close." Helen shrugged and picked up the empty glass.

Tyler took it from her. "Let me at least play bartender."

"I could try to find him." Both men turned to her.

"Oh, no. Don't even think about it. You're staying right here."

"He's right." Tyler said as he poured the vodka into the shaker. "Relax."

"That's a good one, Tyler." Helen scowled. "Make it a double."

They ate dinner listening to the news and waiting. Tyler stayed until midnight, promising to call and check on her in the morning.

"You weren't serious when you said you should try to find him, were you?" Martin asked as he locked the door behind Tyler.

"Yes. It would be scary but I think I could do it."

"There is no way in hell you are going after that guy. It's out of the question."

"Someone had better find him soon. He's going to keep on killing. You know that."

"Yes." Martin sat beside her and pulled her close. "They'll nail him. He screwed up coming back here. And anyway, I get to spend a few more days with you and get paid for doing it." He smiled down at her.

"I appreciate it." Helen smiled. She snuggled against him for warmth and he pulled the afghan down over her shoulders.

"Just rest, lady. Everything is going to be fine." Martin said, stroking her hair.

Helen woke on the couch beside him as China nudged her arm. "Okay, pup."

"She's like a clock." Martin said, stretching his arms and legs.

"Sure is." Helen turned up the TV and opened the back door for the dog. "Looks like rain."

"They said we were supposed to have thunderstorms later today. Maybe you should bake a cake." Martin grinned.

"That seems to be a reoccurring idea."

"Can't help it." He shrugged. "You do make the most delicious cakes."

"I'm frustrated. They should have caught him by now." Helen pointed to the television as they flashed Abington's photos again.

"You've given us a lot to go on."

"But it isn't enough."

After two days of empty news reports Helen still felt Abington's presence. He wouldn't leave until he'd gotten his revenge. She was sure of it. Helen walked into her office and spread the area map out on her desk. She lit several candles and sat in the leather chair to study it.

If the police couldn't find him, she'd have to try. She stared at the area around her old house and then focused on the outlying areas, one map square at a time. Her body tensed as she moved east toward her new neighborhood. He was there, in the four block area.

"Martin." She split the block in fours with faint pencil lines as he walked to the door.

"What's up?"

"He's closer than we thought." Helen nodded, staring at the four smaller squares. "You need to have your men check the vacant homes in this area."

Martin walked over to the desk. "You can't be serious."

"I'm telling you, he's in this area."

China barked and they both jumped. "What the hell?" Martin started out of the room.

"Shit. My furniture's here. I'd forgotten." Helen said as she rushed out behind him. She grabbed China's collar and led her into her bedroom. "You stay put. It's okay."

The dog didn't seem to mind. She looked over at Helen's bed and back at Helen as she closed the door.

Martin was outside checking the men's identification when she walked into the kitchen. He opened the door and walked over to her. "You deal with them I'll make the call."

Helen nodded as the men walked inside with the leather sofa. They followed her to the office and she directed them on its placement. The movers made three more trips and the room was done.

Martin escorted the movers out before joining her in the office. "That wraps up the house nicely."

"Thanks." Helen sat at the desk and lit a few more candles.

"What do the candles do?"

"Smell good." Helen flashed him a smile.

"I just remembered I never gave you your housewarming gift. "I'll be right back." Martin returned a few minutes later carrying a large box and a huge square of corkboard.

"What is all this?"

"A dart board."

Helen set down the pencil and joined him by the couch. "A dart board?"

"It beats pacing." Martin smiled.

"I don't know how to shoot."

"I'm going to get this all set up and give you a few lessons."

"We have to find this guy. This is crazy."

Martin embraced her. "No, baby. It's called living. We can't do anything more. They are going to thoroughly check every vacant house. They still have checkpoints set up and they are canvassing the area showing his pictures."

Helen went back to the map and studied the area hoping for any hint of where he was. Martin busied himself with getting the board set up and when he was though he walked over and took the pencil out of her hand.

"Come on. It's time for lesson one."

They threw several rounds with most of Helen's darts going into the outer edges of the corkboard and Martin's on the mark every time.

"It's going to take a while to get the hang of this."

"I shoot almost every day. It helps clear my mind."

"You do have to focus."

"That's the whole point. You have to let go of your problems and think the dart and the board. Believe me, it works much better than pacing." Martin smiled. "Now, how about lunch?"

CHAPTER 23

▼

Donald trained the gun on the maid from the closet behind the front door. He'd seen the officer stop in front of the house and planned to kill both of them if the woman screwed up.

"I'm sorry but the Carltons are in Bali until the end of the month." The maid said with a thick Spanish accent.

"We are looking for this man. Have you seen him?"

"No. No, sir."

The officer stepped inside and looked around. "You're here alone?"

"Yes sir."

Donald could see her hands trembling at her sides as she spoke.

"Make sure you keep the doors locked even during the day." He turned and walked outside. "Thank you for your time, ma'am."

"You're welcome." The maid took a step toward him. "Officer?"

Donald tensed, his finger tightening on the trigger.

"Do you really think he's around here?"

"Yes. We believe he's responsible for a double homicide two days ago."

"Oh." Her voice was two octaves higher.

"You have a good day."

Donald stayed in the closet until she'd closed the front door. He put his finger to his lips as he stepped out. "You did well." Donald whispered, grabbing her arm. He led her to the kitchen. "Fix me something nice."

"You should leave." She whispered.

"I will when I'm ready. Now fix me something to eat."

"Are you going to kill me?"

"I said fix me something." Donald waved the gun toward the refrigerator and sat at the table to watch.

He'd stayed in his jeep for two days eating snack food before deciding to get something real to eat. The murders were all over the news and the radio did a good job of describing the many roadblocks the local and state police had set up. It was a stroke of luck that the maid opened the back door just as he was about to break the glass. No signs of forced entry meant he could stay there as long as he needed.

"I don't know what you want."

"Dinner." Donald growled.

The maid grabbed several things out of the refrigerator.

"Turn on that TV. I want to see the news."

Within moments his face was on the screen. They showed the two body bags being taken out of Helen's house as the reporter described the scene. The maid was shaking and crying as though seeing the report for the first time.

"You don't watch TV?"

"No." She cried as she sliced a chicken breast.

When the reporter began to talk about the background on the initial search for Donald Abington, a photo of Helen Staples appeared in the corner and the maid grunted when she saw it.

"Do you know her?" Donald asked.

The maid shook her head too quickly and Donald rushed toward her, waving the gun. "You know her. Tell me the truth." He put the gun to the back of her head.

"I don't know her."

"You've seen her. Where?"

"Across the street." The woman whimpered.

"Does she live there?"

"No. She was there with the man who bought it. I think they are friends."

"Who is he?"

"I don't know." The tears fell from her old brown eyes as he pushed her toward the window.

"Which house?"

"That one. He...he hasn't moved in yet." Her shoulders slumped as though she'd just given away her best friend to the murderer.

"What do you know?"

"Nothing. I told you. A man just bought the house. I haven't seen him over there in days. Really."

"And the woman. When was the last time you saw her there? Be specific." His pulse raced as he waited for her answer.

"I…I think it was last week. I'm not sure. I know I saw them but I didn't pay that much attention."

"Finish cooking my dinner." Donald said, pushing her back toward the kitchen.

Once she'd served him he tied her to a kitchen chair and took his plate to the living room to think. It was a smart move letting the maid live. The old lady knew how to cook and she'd kept the cops at bay. He thought about what to do with Helen. He could easily shoot her from a distance. End it quickly. Though he wouldn't get as much pleasure out of it as he would a hands-on attack, his anger had waned to the point where he would be satisfied to get it over with.

He looked out the window, watching the house across the street. Who ever had bought it was the key to locating her. Donald was sure of that. He finished his dinner and went to the bathroom to put more of the antibiotic on the scratches on his cheek and neck. As he inspected himself in the mirror he was glad to see that the redness around his wounds was clearing.

He grinned at his reflection. "I'm coming for you bitch."

✳   ✳   ✳   ✳

Helen rubbed her arms wishing it was cold enough to make a fire. She grabbed a sweater out of her closet and went out to the living room.

"Any news?" She asked Martin.

"No. No sign of him."

"He can't get away again." Helen sat down on the couch and turned on the news. "If he does, you'll never catch him." She rubbed her hands together and reached for a cigarette.

"What is it?" Martin asked as he sat down beside her.

"I'm not sure. He's so close…I feel if I could get out there, I could find him."

"I told you before that's out of the question." Martin scowled and put his arm around her. "Maybe you should bake a cake."

"We have half a cake in there."

"Make some cookies then."

"Enough." Helen walked over to the door and eased the curtain aside. "He's here. Damn it." The pressure was building. She wanted to get outside and walk until she found him. She wanted the fear to end. Even with the bulky sweater, she was bone cold.

"Would you please come away from the window."

Helen turned to him and was about to say something when China rushed to the door, her whip of a tail swinging. "Must be Tyler." Helen said as she went to answer it.

"Hey." Tyler smiled as he walked inside. "How are you?"

"I'm here." Helen grumbled. "Would you like some coffee?"

"Why are you looking at me that way?" Tyler asked.

"I don't know." She stared at him. There was something there, something dark. "Why aren't you working?"

"My furniture is going to be delivered at noon. I figured I'd stop by here for a little while...what is it?"

"I don't know." Tears filled her green eyes. "It could just be the stress I'm under."

Tyler walked over and hugged her. "It's going to be okay, Helen. You can get through this."

"I know." She patted his back. "It's all gotten to me." She stepped back as he released her. "Sorry." She turned to the counter and fixed the coffee as the dark feeling threatened to engulf her.

"Helen?" Martin walked over to her. "You'd better sit down. You're pale."

Helen looked at him and then Tyler. "Cancel the movers."

"Why?"

"Cancel. You can't go over there." Helen trembled as she walked to the table and sat down. "Call them."

"They're on their way."

Helen spun around, her tear filled eyes wide with fear. "I said you can't go there." She screamed.

"OK...but they're going to be there in twenty minutes."

"What is it?" Martin sat beside her and put his hand on her shoulder.

"He's waiting for Tyler...he's watching his house." Helen cried. "Believe me, Tyler." The feeling she had threatened to send her to the floor. She put her hands on the table as the dread filled her chest.

How much more loss could she be expected to bear? The danger was right there. Clear. It was close enough to cut her. Helen could see him staring at Tyler's house. She could fee the raw deliberation as Abington waited.

"I do I believe you." Tyler pulled out a chair and sat down. "Calm down. I won't go."

"Thank you."

"I'll go." Martin said. "Can you see where he is watching the house from?"

"The front…he's waiting…he has someone with him."

Martin nodded. "Make the call and cancel the delivery. To be safe, put it off for a week or so."

Tyler made the call and Martin called the station to order another house to house search for Abington.

"Are there any houses for sale across the street from yours?" Martin asked.

"No. There's one on the same side, eight or ten houses up."

"He's in one of the houses across the street. It isn't vacant…he's with an elderly woman." Her hands trembled as she lit a cigarette.

"Is she alive?"

"Yes. She knows who he is…and she's terrified." Helen took a deep drag. "He'll kill her if you don't find him in time. He's not planning on leaving her alive when he decides to move on."

"Can you see a house number?"

"No." Helen looked at him. "He has a clear view of Tyler's house."

"But you don't think he's in Tyler's house."

"No. He's waiting for him though. Somehow he's made the connection." Helen was exhausted. She prayed for it to be over with soon. She felt like she'd snap under the pressure if he weren't caught.

Martin scowled. "Tyler, stay with her. Lock the door after me. I'm going to do the house to house with them."

Before Helen could object he raised his hand. "I'm a cop. Now you relax here with Tyler and I'll be back in an hour or so."

Helen followed him to the door and locked it behind him. She peeked out the curtain and watched him walk up the road as the first cruiser pulled up in front of Tyler's house.

"You shouldn't be near the window." Tyler put his hands on her shoulders.

"He's a sitting duck out there. Abington will recognize him." Helen shuddered as she sat at the table.

Tyler sat across from her. "You were thinking about Tim when you asked me to cancel the delivery. I could see that Tim look in your eyes." Tyler shook his head. "I can only imagine how different our lives would be if he was here." Tyler smiled. "I miss my best friends. Both of you."

"Oh, Tyler. I'm still here."

"You are and your not, lady…maybe that is my fault. You've been on guard with me and I know I brought it on. All of this has freaked me out. Damn it woman. Tim and I used to talk about it. Speculate at how you made your living. Was it lucky guesses? The full moon? It wasn't until he died that I knew." Tears filled his brown eyes. "When he called to complain about how…how silly you'd been, well, it gave me the creeps. I really knew at that moment, that you were for real…damn it woman."

Helen tilted her head as she stared at him. "You never told me he called you."

Tyler nodded. "I couldn't. I didn't know how to react to the whole thing…" Tyler stopped as he watched her light the cigarette. "I told him not to go…he laughed and said I was getting as weird as you were." Tyler rubbed his face. "I should have stood up for your…feeling. He'd still be here if I had."

"No he wouldn't." Helen touched his hand. "He would have had even more determination to get on the plane just to have the satisfaction of proving us wrong. I'm sure of it."

Tyler took a deep breath. "Sorry." He stood and walked to the door, peeking out of the curtain. "So you're really serious about Martin."

"I am. We're good together."

"Even though all of this started when you met him?"

"I've thought about that a lot Tyler." Helen tapped the back of the chair. "The first vision I had was of the plane crash. I saw it as it happened." She took a deep breath as he sat down.

"I thought you said your feeling wasn't clear."

"It wasn't…I knew something bad was going to happen. I could feel it but I couldn't see it. The moment the plane crashed I saw the whole thing." Tears filled her eyes as she spoke. "I thought I'd gone crazy. I didn't know how I could imagine something so horrifying. I tried to block it out."

"So all this…it has nothing to do with Martin?"

"Yes and no. He's made it easier for me to accept the visions. He helped me to see the good in it." Helen took a deep breath. "It all seems so clear now."

"It does?"

"I pushed Martin away for a long time because I thought he somehow brought the changes on. I'd managed to put the vision of the crash out of my mind." Helen was floored when she put all of the pieces together.

Madeline's call interrupted their conversation.

"How are you holding up dear?"

"Fine. I'm staying in the house until they catch him. I don't want you to worry."

"Is Detective Hamlin with you?"

"Tyler's here, Martin went out to talk to the officers up the street."

"Is he staying with you?"

"Yes. I have all the protection I need." Helen looked over at the guns and ammunition in the middle of the table.

"You'll call if you need to talk?"

"Yes, auntie."

"Take care now."

"I'll call as soon as I have any news."

"Thank you, dear."

CHAPTER 24

▼

Martin got to the first cruiser as the second pulled up behind it. He waved the two officers out of the second car.

"Abington could be inside one of these houses." Martin nodded toward the other side of the street. "We're going to stay together. As we approach each house I want you to stay with me." Martin pointed at the blond officer. "I want the two of you to circle around, check the garages, back yards and be alert."

Martin surveyed the situation and started with the closest house with a view of Tyler's. He knocked on the door with Abington's photo in his hand and one officer behind him.

A woman in her mid thirties answered and shook her head before he could speak. "I already told the other officer that I haven't seen him."

"Could I come inside for a moment?" Martin asked looking past her.

"Well, yes." She backed up allowing him into the foyer.

"I'd like you to think for a moment."

"I haven't seen him. Believe me I'll call if I do."

Martin nodded "Yes, ma'am, I understand. We have reason to believe he is right in this area. Now, if you could think for a moment." He glanced into the living room. "Have any of your neighbors been acting strange the last few days? Maybe staying in their house when they'd normally be going to work. Anything at all."

The woman scowled and studied him. "I did notice that my...it's probably nothing."

"Anything. What did you see?"

"When I came home last night I noticed that my neighbors hadn't taken their papers out of the box. Now normally their housekeeper would get the paper every morning, before I even go outside. But the housekeeper is probably just taking it easy since the neighbors are on vacation." The woman shrugged.

"When was the last time you saw the housekeeper?"

"Two, maybe three days ago. There's nothing strange about it though. Sometimes I don't see her in a week. I just notice that their paper box is empty by the time I take my morning walk."

"Which house is it?"

"This house." She pointed to the house directly across from Tyler's.

"Can you think of anything else?"

"No. I'm sorry I couldn't be of more help."

"I thank you for your time. I'd appreciate it if you'd stay inside with your doors locked until we leave the area." Martin pointed to the cruisers across the street.

"Yes. Sir."

Martin walked outside and signaled the two officers in the back yard to join him. The adrenaline was coursing through his veins as he tried to devise a plan. The four of them stood on the woman's lawn. For a moment Martin thought about how young the three in uniform were but quickly forced it out of his mind and focused on the job.

He knew there was a housekeeper inside. From what Helen had told him it made perfect sense that Abington was in that house. He couldn't rush in there and risk the hostage being shot so he'd knock on the door with the same routine he'd used on the last house. Two men around the back, check the garage, the yard, he'd ask a few questions and assess the situation, pull back and regroup. Chances were, Abington had been watching them, so if they repeated their moves he'd think it was routine.

"Keep your heads." Martin said.

"Aren't we going to call for more backup?" The youngest of the men asked.

"Once we scope it out. I don't want to come down on the place until we are sure he's in there...let's do it."

Martin walked up to the front door as the officers took their positions. He rang the bell and a minute later a small elderly woman cracked the door open.

"Good morning ma'am. I was wondering if I could come in and ask you a few questions." He said as he studied the woman. He saw tape marks on her wrist as she undid the chain on the door and stark fear in her bloodshot eyes as she opened it a few more inches.

"What can I do for you?" She asked her eyes wide.

Martin held up the two photos of Abington. "May I come inside?"

"I'm here alone." Her brown eyes darted to her left several times. "I'd rather you didn't, sir. I'm really quite busy."

Martin nodded. "Have you seen this man?"

Again her eyes shifted to her left. "No sir."

"We have a tip that he's in this area." Martin took a step closer and the woman tensed.

"I haven't seen him. Sorry I can't help." Tears filled the old woman's eyes as she looked to her left once again.

Martin nodded. "Your neighbor was concerned that you hadn't retrieved your newspapers." Martin took a step back. "You really shouldn't leave them there." His heart pounded.

If he left the woman there and they surrounded the house she was as good as dead. He had to make a move. His mind raced with possible moves as he studied her.

"I've...I've been afraid to go outside...a policeman was here and said that man..." She pointed at the picture of Abington with darkened hair. "Was wanted for killing someone."

Martin smiled. "I understand. However." He saw movement through the crack in the open door. "That is a signal to criminals that no one is home."

"Yes, sir." The woman began to shake as tears rolled down her face.

Martin knew he was running out of time. "Why don't you get them now...while we are here." Martin put the photos in his pocket, still smiling at the woman. "We'll, wait until you are back inside before we leave." He grabbed the small woman by the arm and yanked her out of the door, flinging her onto the lawn as the door slammed behind her.

"Get her across the street and call for back up." He yelled to the officer a few feet behind him.

Shots rang out behind the house and Martin rushed around the right side, acid rising in his throat. Two more shots and then dead quiet as Martin reached the edge of the house. He saw one of the officers sprawled out on the lawn but couldn't see the other.

"Halbert. Halbert." He didn't know if Abington was still inside so he doubled back around as the taste of bile hit his mouth. "Halbert." The only sound came from the sobbing woman across the street.

Martin heard sirens in the distance and yelled to the officer with the woman. "Have them block off the area. Get some man power down here." Martin yelled as he rushed to the garage side of the building.

The sweat was dripping down his face as he peered into the garage window. There were two cars and no sign of movement. He moved along the side of the building, hugging the outer wall, his heart was racing so fast he thought he'd pass out.

He came around the corner and saw the other officer laying dead across a patio chair. "Shit." He scanned the yard and the tree line that separated the property from the neighbor behind it and he moved back toward the street.

He made his way to the officer by the cruiser, sweat dripping from every pore. Police cars from the state, city and county converged on him and he screamed out directions for them to fan out. Abington was there, somewhere.

Martin ran to the cruiser the housekeeper was in. He opened the door and looked at the woman laying on the back seat crying in her hands.

"Stay down." He crouched beside the door. "Did he arrive in a car? How did he get to your house?"

She looked up at him. "God bless you. God bless you. You saved me." She started to sit up but he pushed her back down.

"Please, stay low. We don't know where he is." Martin glanced up at the house as the officers surrounded it. "Did you see how he got here?"

"No. I heard a noise outside and when I went to the door he was standing there." She clutched his hand. "God bless you."

"How many weapons did he have?"

"One big gun. That's all I saw."

"Can you think of anything he said...anything at all?" Martin patted her shoulder.

"A woman. There was a woman on the TV...oh, God, I'm sorry. He knew that I recognized her."

"What woman?"

"He put a gun to my head...I had to tell him. I'm so sorry."

"It's all right. Please. Tell me the conversation. As much detail as you can remember."

"The woman on TV. I had seen her." She pointed to Tyler's house. "She was there with the man who bought the house. I saw her there two or three times."

"You told him this?"

"I had to."

"Can you think of anything else he said?"

She shook her head. "He said he was going to wait for him. He said something like, he'd use him to get to her." She looked at him. "He is very angry with her. He didn't say why but it was clear."

"OK. I'm going to have the officer take you to the police station and I'll call for someone to bring you back when it is safe."

"Thank you. Thank you so much. You saved my life. I know he would have killed me. I know it." The woman cried against his hand.

"Baker, take her downtown and see that she's comfortable."

Captain Munce grabbed the microphone on his cruiser. "Donald Abington. Come out with your hands up. We know you are in there."

Martin watched as the swat team pulled down their gas masks and fired tear gas into the house. His pulse increased as the seconds ticked by.

*   *   *   *

Donald watched the scene from a shed across the street. He'd been lucky to make it that far. Damn cops were both lousy shots. He'd burst out on them and hit the first in the chest and the second in the head before they knew what was happening. He saw the detective in front of the garage door and bolted through the neighbor's yard and ran straight for the shed.

He was soaked with sweat as he watched the action through the small window in the door. He couldn't leave but he couldn't stay. He should have sliced the bitch's throat and stuffed her in the closet. Donald had smelled the trouble when the cruisers pulled up and stopped a few houses away.

He picked up the old T-shirt off the workbench and wiped the sweat from his face and neck as the cops fired tear gas into the house. His jeep was parked three blocks up the road in the trees by the public beach. He had to figure out how to get there before they widened their search.

Two more cruisers pulled up and one stopped directly in front of the shed. He looked behind him at the riding lawn mower that blocked the other exit. He realized that the door opened out and he climbed over the mower as quietly as he could. His mind raced, searching for a plan. His jeep was north but just three houses south was a marsh area.

Donald knew they were going to fan out. They'd already wasted too much time at the house. He clicked open the handle and eased himself out the back door. He walked to the side of the shed and peered over at the commotion across the street before darting south to the fence. He hopped it and fell onto the sand.

He glanced at the ocean, it would be his last resort. The Atlantic was cold in the summer, in the spring it would be like ice. After scanning the empty yard he ran across to the fence on the other side. Within five minutes he was skirting the edge of the marsh looking for a place to hide.

*   *   *   *

When Helen heard the first shot she grabbed the gun and told Tyler to take the other. China rushed to her side and watched the front door with her.

"You should get in a closet or something." Tyler yelled holding the revolver. "Go hide."

"I'm not going to hide. I'm ready for him but I don't think he knows I'm here." Helen looked at him. "For whatever reason he was focused on your house."

"I'd like to figure out how." Tyler scowled. "What should we do?"

"Stay put. Martin will come back when he can." Helen prayed that he would. She knew Martin had found Abington but she also knew he hadn't caught him. Her eyes were trained on the front door for fifteen long minutes. She wanted to look out the window but didn't dare. Instead she sat at the table, her back to the wall, her hand on the gun.

Twenty minutes went by, then thirty. Her neck was so stiff she thought it would snap if she turned too quickly. She jumped when Tyler finally broke the silence.

"Do you want me to call the police station?"

"No. We know Abington is in the area." Helen said as she looked over at him.

"So we just sit here and wait?"

"That's all we can do." Helen set the gun on the table and lit a cigarette.

"I'll take one of those." Tyler sat beside her.

"You quit years ago."

"This is the perfect time to start." Tyler nodded, holding out his hand.

"I can't argue with that." Helen handed him a cigarette and watched him choke and cough through the first few drags. "They have to nail this bastard. They have to."

"It sounds like they have an army out there."

Helen looked down at China as she rested her big head in Helen's lap. "You feel it don't you. It's going to be okay." Helen patted her head.

Helen thought about all of the lives Abington had destroyed. From the first killings in Kansas to the murdered young woman who was traveling back home to Oregon to be with her family. So many people were hurt. Their lives didn't matter. The only thing Abington had on his mind was his own warped desires.

She'd been plagued by images of the damaged he'd done to innocent people for months. He was like a cancer eating away at human dignity. A black scar on everyone who came in contact with him.

It was ten o'clock before Martin returned. Helen could see by his deep scowl and tight jaw that they hadn't found him.

"You're exhausted." Helen said as he sat at the table. "I'll warm you some dinner."

Thanks."

"It's been all over the news." Tyler raised his martini glass. "Can you have one?"

"I'll pass."

"You aren't going back out there?" Helen turned to him.

"No. I need a shower and a few hours rest. You shouldn't be here without police protection after dark. I should've come back sooner." Martin rubbed his hands over his face.

"Where do you think he went?" Tyler asked as he sat at the table.

"South."

"Why south?"

"It's too open up here. We figure his jeep is in the area. We're just waiting for him to show himself. They've brought in the dogs."

Helen busied herself with the leftovers as the men spoke. She could feel Abington's panic. He was hiding somewhere close.

They watched the news while Martin picked at the late dinner.

"Well, what should I do?"

"Excuse me?" Helen looked over at him.

"I could stay here or go back to my-."

"I'd appreciate it if you'd stay until this is over." Martin said. "I plan to be back out there at dawn."

"Sure. I took tomorrow off to work at my house." Tyler smiled at Helen. "I'll flop in the guest room. Wake me when you leave, Martin."

"Will do."

Helen went to the living room and peeked out the curtain.

"Come here." Martin said as he sat on the couch.

Helen stared down at him. He looked drained like she'd never seen him before. "You need to get some sleep."

"I need to hold you."

Helen sat beside him and smiled as he wrapped his arms around her. She rested her cheek against his chest as he stroked her hair.

"It's almost over." He kissed the top of her head. "Once we've got this bastard we'll talk about my retirement."

Helen sat up. "No."

"No?"

"You said you didn't want to."

"I don't want you in danger. I can't stand it." His jaw twitched as he spoke.

"I used to think these visions started with you...they didn't." Helen kissed his cheek. "They started before we met, with Tim's crash."

Martin scowled. "I don't understand."

Helen explained the vision she'd had when Tim's plane crashed. "I don't know why my gift changed but it wasn't because of you. You're the one who helped me to accept it." She smiled as he touched her cheek. "We both have the ability to help people in our own way."

"Oh, lady, are you sure?"

"Yes. I've struggled for an answer and I understand that I have to use these visions to do good. I can't try to fight them anymore."

"And our future?"

"It's a crazy life. We have to be grateful for the time we do have."

"This sounds familiar." Martin smiled.

"I know you've said the same things but now I understand and believe it."

Martin wrapped his arms around her and kissed her." I love you, Helen."

"I love you, too."

"This will all be over soon."

"I hope so."

"We'll catch him." Martin said as the helicopter flew over head. "There's no way he's getting out of this area."

"Can you stay here until they catch him?"

"Come on lady." Martin smiled. "I have a job to do."

"I know."

"I'll tell you what...my boat is going to be in the water next week. How about we take a week off?"

Helen leaned back as his thoughts came into her mind. "Honeymoon on the boat?"

Martin laughed and squeezed her. "Why not? Will you marry me?"

"Yes."

"Oh, lady." Martin pulled her to her feet and embraced her. "Kids?"

"The whole thing."

"Are you sure?"

"Yes."

"What's going on in here?" Tyler asked as he walked into the living room.

"We're getting married." Martin said as he lifted Helen off her feet and spun her around.

"Married?"

"She said yes." Martin said as he set her down.

"Well, congratulations."

"Thank you."

Tyler scowled. "I hate to break up this party but it's two in the morning."

"No!" Helen looked at the clock. "We'd better get some sleep."

"That would be my point." Tyler smiled. "See you in a couple."

"He's right. We can talk about this once we find Abington."

"That's a deal." Martin took her hand and led her to her room. "You get to bed. I need a shower first."

Helen laid on the bed listening to the water run as the commotion continued outside. She wanted to keep Martin with her until it was over but she knew it was impossible.

CHAPTER 25

▼

China jumped up and rushed to the door. Helen clutched the revolver as Tyler went to answer it.

Martin walked inside. Helen could see in his eyes that they hadn't found Abington.

"I just wanted to check on you." Martin said as he stood by the table.

Martin was rigid as he explained the events of the last two hours. He looked as disturbed as Helen felt. They were doing a sweeping search, checking every bush, every possible hiding spot in every house in the area.

"We aren't going to stop searching until we find him. He's on this point. We have a police boat patrolling the shoreline. Every possible agency is working on this." Martin walked over and kissed Helen on the forehead. "I have to get back out there."

Helen looked up at him. "Put your vest on."

"I will. It's in my trunk." He patted her on the shoulder. "You two are safe here. Just stay away from the windows."

Martin walked outside and Helen watched as he went to his trunk and strapped on his vest. She could see the frustration in his eyes as he slammed the trunk.

Afternoon turned to night. The helicopter flew overhead and the police boat and harbor patrol passed by her house several times. The news had tapped into the story but they had less to report than Helen and Tyler had heard from Martin. Helen's nerves were shot from the waiting and her muscles, taut and aching.

They watched the news interview with the housekeeper who praised Martin for saving her life and cried over the loss of the two officers who'd died.

Tyler shook his head. "I'm going to try that dart board." Tyler said as he waved at her to join him. "Come on."

Helen followed him into the office and explained how to play cricket. She smiled when Tyler's first dart hit the wall.

"Sorry. Damn."

"I'm no better at it." Helen said as she sat at the desk. She looked at the map. She still felt Abington was close and more desperate than ever.

When Martin returned he was soaking wet. He'd been searching the marsh and slipped into the water. Helen and Tyler sat silent as Martin showered and changed.

Martin downed a cup of coffee. "We're doing the house to house again. He could have doubled back."

"It's getting dark. He's going to make his move." Helen said.

"That's what we figure. We've got volunteer officers from four towns out there now. He's not going to slip though." Martin said.

Helen could tell by the look in his eyes that he was losing hope, as much as he was saying just the opposite.

A few minutes after Martin left China was on the alert. She moved to the far end of the house the hair on her back bristling. Helen followed and peered out the window but couldn't see anything.

She followed China to the living room where the dog paced in front of the French doors. Helen could feel the danger closing in. China went into her office and worked her head through the blinds, growling.

"What is it girl? What do you see?"

"What's with the dog?" Tyler asked as he walked through the glass breezeway to the office door. "She's making me nervous."

"She senses the danger." Helen said as she followed the dog back to the breezeway. Helen saw movement near the south stone wall as China let out a low growl. "Shit." She said as she backed into Tyler. "Someone's out there."

"Damn." Tyler grabbed her arm pulling her back into the office. "The guns are on the table."

Helen nodded and wriggled free of his grasp. She bolted past China, still growling ferociously in the breezeway and lunged for the table. She stuffed three speed loaders into her sweater pocket and ran back to the office with a gun in each hand. She handed Tyler the snub nose and crouched by the doorway, her eyes on the stone wall.

"Watch him, China."

The dog growled louder. Helen glanced back at Tyler. "Call Martin." Helen reached up to turn on the backyard lights and as she did Abington jumped the stone wall and froze. "Shut off the office light." Helen called to Tyler. It was too late. Abington spotted her.

They stared at each other for what seemed like an eternity, both frozen in place. Then Abington raised his gun.

"Get down." Helen screamed as the bullet shattered the breezeway glass. She emptied the gun in his direction as he fired off several more shots and quickly reloaded.

"Get in here." Tyler reached for her.

"He can't get away." Helen said as she closed the cylinder. She heard Martin's voice coming from Tyler's open cell phone. "He's in the yard. Get down here."

China jumped through the broken glass and raced toward Abington as Helen screamed for her to come back. A shot rang out as China was in mid air and she crashed to the ground in a tortured howl.

Helen saw red as he ran across the yard shooting at her. She took aim as a bullet whistled by her head and shot him in the side. Abington screamed and stumbled, landing on his knees and then he aimed at something on the side of his house and shot twice as he got to his feet.

∗   ∗   ∗   ∗

Martin rushed around the back of the house. By the time he saw Abington it was too late. He spun to get back to cover and was jolted, mid turn, as a bullet slammed through his side. Martin gasped as he fell to the ground in shock.

He knew as he lay there looking up at the night sky that he was dying. Dying. A ridiculous idea, he thought as he saw a young officer rushing toward him. The man screamed officer down into the microphone mounted on his shoulder and dropped to his knees. He put pressure on Martin's wound as gunfire filled the air.

"Get out your gun."

"I can't. I'll be fine. We both will." The officer pressed on the gaping wound.

"I wore..." Martin struggled for a breath. "My vest."

"Yes, sir...you got hit in the side, between the straps."

"Helen. You...I...I have to see Helen."

"I can't leave you."

"Please."

"The paramedics are here." The young officer kept the pressure on as they rushed to Martin's side. "I'll get her as soon as I can."

"Please." Martin looked at him for a moment before closing his eyes. He had to see her one more time. He had to tell her to be okay.

*   *   *   *

Helen fired as Abington stood and turned to shoot at her again and this time she blew a hole through his wrist. As the gun fell to the ground she shot at his leg.

"Don't move or I'll shoot you again." Helen screamed. He was within a yard of his revolver, his eyes moving between her and the gun. "I mean it. I'll blow your fucking head off if you try it."

The yard was suddenly filled with police and Abington laid on his back, holding his bleeding hand up in the air. "Alright." He yelled as the police rushed toward him and an officer kicked away his gun. "I'm hit. I'm hurt." Abington cried.

Helen dropped the gun and rushed outside as China stood and limped toward her, whimpering. "Lay down girl. Lay down." Helen knelt beside the dog and pressed on the wound in her shoulder. "It's okay girl." Helen looked around at the gathering crowd of police "Martin. China's been shot. Martin." She screamed as she waited for her man.

An officer raced toward her from the north side of the yard. "Detective Hamlin is down." He yelled, waving for her to follow.

"No." Helen screamed as she scrambled to her feet. She ran after the officer around the side of the house to see two paramedics kneeling beside Martin. "No. Martin. No." Helen dropped to his side.

Martin looked up at her, blood trickling from the corner of his mouth. "I love you."

"I love you." Helen saw the wound in his side as the paramedic covered it with a thick bandage. "You're going to be okay. We got him, Martin."

"I love...you." His voice faded and he lapsed into unconsciousness as they lifted him onto the gurney.

Helen ran behind them as they raced to the ambulance. She held onto his hand as the sirens blared and the paramedics continued to work on him. She prayed to God he'd make it even as she felt darkness closing in.

When they arrived at the hospital the paramedics rushed Martin into the trauma center.

"Please wait here." The tall paramedic said as the automatic door began to close behind them. "Someone will come out to get you."

Helen cried and prayed as the minutes ticked by. He was safe. He was in the hospital and they would fix him. They had to.

An hour later a tall doctor walked out through the doors and stopped when he saw her crying against the wall. "Helen Staples?"

"Yes. Is he going-." She froze, as he shook his head no.

"I'm sorry, ma'am..." The doctor looked into her eyes. "He has extensive internal injuries."

"Operate on him." Helen took a step toward him. "Do something."

"He's asking for you. He doesn't have much time." The doctor said as he opened the door to the trauma area.

Helen wiped her eyes and took a deep breath. She felt as though her legs would give out beneath her as she walked to the door.

"Excuse me."

Helen turned toward the voice and saw the chief of police rushing toward them. She continued into the trauma area and saw a glimpse of Martin as the nurse pulled the curtain closed on his cubicle. She braced herself as she walked through the doorway.

"Martin." She said as she rushed to his bedside and grasped his hand.

He opened his eyes and looked up at her. "I love...you." The tears rolled down his face. "I'm sorry."

"Martin, you have to fight." Panic raised the pitch of her voice.

"It's okay. The doctor..." he closed his eyes as the nurse wiped the blood from his lips. "I want you to be...good to...yourself."

"Martin. I can't lose you." Helen cried and kissed his cool hand.

"I'll always...love you." Martin's color when from pale to ashen. His breath was raspy and uneven as he struggled to speak. "You be strong...for us."

"I can't do this. You can't leave me. Please, Martin. Please."

"I want you to think..." he coughed and blood oozed out of the corner of his mouth.

Helen looked at the nurse as she wiped it away.

"Think about...the...good. Think about...our love." He squeezed her hand. "You've made...me...happy." He managed a smile for her.

"I love you." Helen cried and kissed his cheek.

"I'll..." Martin struggled for a breath, his lungs gurgling as they filled with blood. "Always love you." His last words were a whisper.

She stared down at him as the machine behind him flat-lined and the alarm sounded. The nurse flipped off the switch and shook her head.

"He's gone."

Helen laid her head on his chest and sobbed. "No. Martin. No." She squeezed his lifeless body. "Please." She kissed his cheek. "We're getting married. We have-."

"Helen." Tyler said as he walked up behind her.

"Please." Helen cried as Tyler lifted her off of him and turned her around.

"He's gone…I'm sorry." Tyler embraced her, holding her as she wailed out her sorrow. "Let me take you home."

"No." Helen looked up at him, wiping her face. "I, I need to stay with him for a while longer."

Tyler nodded and brought a chair over to the bed. Helen sat down and took Martin's hand and kissed it. She stayed with him for an hour before she was finally ready to leave.

When Tyler escorted her outside the unit there were several police officers in the hallway. The chief walked over to her.

"I'm sorry, Helen. He was a good man and a great cop." The chief patted her arm. "We'll all miss him."

Helen looked up at him as the tears rolled down his red face.

"I'll make the arrangements for him. I'll call you with the details." The chief said.

"Excuse me." The nurse from the trauma center walked over to her holding a small bag. "His personal belongings." She said as she handed the bag to Helen.

"Thank you." Helen clutched the bag to her chest.

The nurse reached into her pocket and pulled out a folded yellow paper. "He asked me to give you this…once he was gone."

Helen sobbed out a thank you as she took the paper and leaned against Tyler for support as he led her down the long hall. Martin was dead. It didn't seem real. She cried all the way home. She was lost. Empty.

When they pulled into the driveway Tyler's cell phone rang. "Yes…Yes…thank you. I'll be there in the morning. Yes." He closed the phone and looked at her. "China is going to be okay." Tyler said as he touched her hair. "She need minor surgery. They're keeping her overnight."

"He was wearing his vest." Helen cried.

"I know."

"Is Abington dead?"

"I don't know. You shot him up pretty bad." Tyler said. "Let's go inside." He got out of the car and helped her into the house.

"Martin was wearing his vest." Helen stood in the kitchen holding the letter in one hand and the bag the nurse had given her in the other. "He shouldn't be dead. He shouldn't be."

"Sit down." Tyler pulled out a chair for her. "I'll fix you a drink."

"I can't believe this is happening. He should be here." Helen said as she set the bag on the table and sat down.

She looked at the folded yellow paper and slowly opened it, staring at the scrawled letters.

My Dear Lady,

I've lived more and loved more in the last few months with you than I had my whole life. I've treasured our time together.

I'll always love you.

Martin

Helen set the letter on the table and looked up at Tyler. "How could this happen?"

"There's something on the other side." Tyler turned over the paper. "His will."

Helen wiped the tears but they continued to fall.

"It says he leaves everything to you. He has no immediate family. He's leaving his boat to you…" Tyler took a deep breath. "He wants you to use it." Tyler put the paper down. "The specifics of his life insurance and such…and it's witnessed by two doctors and a nurse."

"He never had a chance to take me out on the boat. It's in dry dock until next week."

"I wish I had the answer. I'm sorry. As much as I didn't want to like him, I did. He was a good man." Tears flowed from his eyes. "You're going to get through this. You're a strong woman, Helen."

"I don't want to be strong."

"But you are. You took down that murderer." Tyler touched her shoulder. "You saved a lot of people with your bravery."

"I was scared."

"Yes. But you didn't let it stop you. If the bastard makes it he'll spend the rest of his life in jail and that's because of you. I know Martin was proud of you, as I am." He slid the drink closer to her and nodded as she picked it up. "I'll do what I can to help you get through this."

Helen went to her room and laid on the bed feeling lost and empty. She clutched the pillow he'd laid on the night before and cried as she inhaled his scent. Helen cried for hours before joining Tyler in the kitchen.

"I don't know how to deal with this." Helen said as she sat at the table. She lit a cigarette and took a deep drag.

"I'll make the calls for the repairs in a couple of hours. Did you sleep?"

Helen shook her head. "I feel like I did when my father died." The tears flowed from her eyes again. "My father was my rock. My buddy. I felt the sun would never rise again." She looked up at Tyler. "That's how I'm feeling right now."

Tyler sat next to her. "You have a right to feel lost, Helen. You're in shock." Tyler started to cry. "He was a good man. He died doing his job."

A scream welled up inside her and she let it out filling the room with her pain and slamming her fists on the table. Tyler jumped up and wrapped his arms around her.

"Stop." He held her fists still as he cried against her. "You're going to get through it. I promise, you are."

CHAPTER 26

▼

Tyler sat beside her at the cemetery as Helen looked at the three caskets, all draped with flags. The wives and children of the other two officers sobbed as the lone bugler played taps at the close of the service.

Helen was in a daze as she watched the officers fold and present the flags to the widows and then Martin's to her. She smoothed her hands over the fabric as she stared at Martin's bronze casket.

The crowds slowly dispersed but Helen sat there with Tyler beside her and Madeline behind her. An elderly woman walked over to her and touched her hand.

"Miss Staples."

When Helen heard her accent she knew who she was. "Yes?"

"Thank you…the police told me you sent them there to help me." She looked back at the casket. "Detective Hamlin saved my life. He was a brave man. I'm sorry for your loss."

Helen nodded and watched the woman walk away. When they were alone she looked up at Tyler.

"I couldn't see a future with him. Now I know why." Tears streamed down her gaunt cheeks as she spoke. "I was afraid to admit I loved him. I'm glad I let go of the fear long enough to make him happy."

Tyler put his arm around her. "You did make him happy. I could see the love he had for you the first time we met."

"He said we were lucky for the time we had." Helen cried against his chest.

"You were, Helen." Tyler stroked her hair.

Madeline got up and stood in front of her. "He isn't in that box." Madeline said in a soft voice. "You know that. He's with you, in your heart. He's watching over you." She tugged at Helen's arm. "Let's leave here now. The men have work to do." Madeline pointed to the four workers gathered by the road, watching them.

Helen nodded.

"You can stay with me for a few days." Madeline said as they walked toward the cars.

"No, Auntie, thank you. I've been putting off packing his belongings. I have to go to his apartment and take care of that for him."

"I'll go with you." Madeline nodded.

"Thank you."

"Do you want my help?" Tyler asked.

"We'll be fine."

"Call me later?"

"Yes."

Helen got into Madeline's car and leaned back in the seat as they drove to Martin's apartment.

She broke down when she walked into the apartment and saw the dartboard on the closet door.

"Oh, Madeline. How could this be?" Helen picked up his robe off the end of the bed and clutched it against her chest. "He had plans. We had plans."

"I know, dear." Madeline wiped the tears from her eyes as she sat on the sofa. "You don't have to do this today."

"I do." Helen nodded and set the robe down. "I love that man."

"And he loves you. He's in a better place now. His work is done."

Helen knew Madeline was right but found no comfort in her words as she began placing his clothing into the large box.

"Where should I start?"

"There's a small file box over in the corner. Why don't you empty his desk."

"Certainly."

"I was ready to accept what ever the future had in store for us."

"And you must. You shared the gift of love. There's nothing more precious. You also shared the ability to help others. I know Martin would want you to carry on with that work."

Helen nodded and folded the sweater, smoothing her hands over the warm yarn. She looked at the picture on the wall. Martin was smiling on the deck of his boat.

"You're going to be fine."

It was late evening when they finished the job. Tyler came over and they silently loaded the boxes into the cars. It took all of Helen's strength to remain in control as they put the boxes against the wall in her garage.

Madeline held the small box to last. "This should go inside."

"Why?"

"There are things in there that you'll need to read."

"Addressed to me?"

Madeline nodded. Helen walked over and took the box from her. She brought it into her office and set it beneath the dartboard. She'd deal with it's contents another day.

Helen made it through the next few weeks a moment at a time. When Chief Howe called with the news that they'd set a date for Abington's trial Helen felt the end of the ordeal was in sight.

Abington had survived his many injuries though he'd lost a kidney and the use of his right hand. Helen was in the back of the courtroom when the deputies brought in the pale, sickly looking Abington. Chains rattled on his feet and hands as he walked over and sat down at the defense table.

His demeanor struck Helen. He was clearly a defeated man. The realization made her straighten in her seat.

She watched as Abington spoke to his young lawyer. A moment later the attorney was speaking to the prosecutor and they both asked for permission to approach the bench. After a short conversation with the judge they returned to their places.

The judge ordered Abington to stand. "It is my understanding that you are going to plead guilty to each count."

"Yes."

"You've been advised of your rights to a trial."

"Yes."

The courtroom was silent. Helen looked over at Madeline. "I can't believe what I'm hearing." Helen whispered.

"Neither can I."

Helen sat stunned as the judge read each of the crimes and Abington responded with a flat, guilty. After a brief recess the judge returned to impose sentence. Helen was relieved when the judge gave him the maximum penalty for each charge. He slowly read them off beginning with a life sentence for each count of murder.

Helen felt stronger as they walked out of the courthouse.

"He might face other trails out of state." Madeline said.

"As far as I'm concerned it is over."

"Let me take you to dinner." Madeline took her hand. "You've been hiding in that beautiful house of yours and you haven't been taking care of yourself."

"It's been hard, auntie." Helen said as they started down the street.

"Today should help."

"It does. The bastard will spend the rest of his life in prison. I read where they seized all of his accounts pending the civil trials."

"Are you filing suit?"

"No. I'm done. I don't want his blood money. He wouldn't have had a dime if he hadn't killed Gloria Fritz. I still think about that poor woman. She was the closest person to him and he killed her out of greed."

"Sheer evil." Madeline shook her head. "I'm glad you're ready to look forward."

"I am." Helen said as she stopped to open the restaurant door.

Helen returned to the house alone and went into her office with China by her side. She turned on the light and stared at the box beneath the dartboard for several minutes before walking over and picking it up. She carried the box to her desk with tears in her eyes.

China leaned against her as she opened it. There were two envelopes on top. Both with Helen's name neatly printed across them. The first was a life insurance policy. Helen leaned back in the chair when she saw it was dated the day after their camping trip.

Her mind went back to those few relaxed days and the references he'd made to his mortality.

"How could you have known?" Helen asked as she set the letter on the corner of the desk. When she opened the next envelope it was a letter dated the same day as the insurance.

She could hear his voice as she read the letter.

"My Dear Helen. I hope you never read this but my gut tells me otherwise. My hope is that you'll continue to embrace life. Use your gift. Don't let my passing interfere with the good you can do. Sail on the Mystic Winds and think of me. I'll always love you."

Helen took a deep breath and folded the letter before setting it on top of the first. "Thank you, Martin." She said as the tears rolled down her thin face.

She went through the rest of the box setting aside the important documents before putting the box in the garage with the others. When she returned to the living room China rushed past her to the front door.

"Come in Tyler." Helen wiped her eyes as she walked to the door.

"I heard the sentences. How are you holding up?" Tyler asked as he sat at the table.

"I'm better. Glad it's over." Helen nodded.

"You don't look better." Tyler scowled.

"It's going to take time."

"You're done with the police department though, right?"

Helen shrugged. "I told Chief Howe that I'd help him when I could. I'm off the payroll."

"Have you thought about what you're going to do?"

"Yes. I'm going to get back to work. I've been flooded with requests for help. It's time I go through them in earnest."

"Are you up to that?"

"I have the ability to help people. What kind of person would I be if I turned my back on them?" Helen shook her head. "There's a reason for all of this. I have to believe that." She blinked back the tears. "I was thinking about my mother this morning. I think it was fear that kept her from helping people. I can't make that mistake."

"You are one strong lady."

"I don't think so." Helen felt like a weak child but her heart told her she had to follow the visions.

"You know I'm just a few houses away if you need me."

"I appreciate that."

"You look so lost."

"The trial gave me some closure. I'm ready to get on with life." Helen said as she walked to the counter. "I've been marking time waiting to get through it."

"I was surprised when I heard he pled guilty."

"It was a big relief. I hated the idea of sitting through a long trial." Helen turned on the coffeepot. "At least the families were spared that ordeal."

"What are you going to be doing exactly? I mean, well, you aren't going to work on murder cases in the future are you?"

"I'm going to try to focus on helping to find missing persons. It seems to be what I'm best at but at this point I won't rule anything out." Helen took a deep breath. "Tell me what you've been up to?" She managed a smile for him as she got up to pour the coffee.

Tyler told her about his job and some paintings that he'd bought for his house as a storm brewed in the distance. When the rain began pounding at the windows, he took his leave.

Helen turned on the television and sat on the couch. She was thinking about Martin and the fun they'd had painting the house when she was hit by a vision.

She recognized the woman as one from a photo she'd seen days before. Helen could see the woman getting weak from dehydration as she lay whimpering on the ground.

Helen threw off the afghan and ran into her office to find the letter. Flashes of the woman invaded her mind as she frantically rummaged through the open stack of mail.

When she found what she was looking for she held the photo in her hand and dialed the number written on the back of it.

"Hello could I speak to Mary Jones?"

"This is she."

"I'm sorry for the late call." Helen said, staring at the young woman's photo. "This is Helen Staples. I think I might be able to help you find your daughter."

978-0-595-36256-1
0-595-36256-7

Printed in the United States
36257LVS00007B/31